Tough Talk

Tough Talk

How I Fought for Writers, Comics,
Bigots, and the American Way

MARTIN GARBUS

WITH STANLEY COHEN

TIMES ⓣ BOOKS

RANDOM HOUSE

Library of Congress Cataloging-in-Publication Data

Garbus, Martin
Tough talk / Martin Garbus with Stanley Cohen.
p.   cm.
Includes index.
ISBN 0-8129-3017-7 (acid-free paper)
1. Garbus, Martin.   2. Lawyers—United States—Biography.
3. Freedom of speech—United States. I. Cohen, Stanley.   II. Title.
KF373.G29A33   1998
342.73'0853—dc21   97-46346

Random House website address: www.randomhouse.com
Printed in the United States of America on acid-free paper
2   4   6   8   9   7   5   3

First Edition

Book design by Robert C. Olsson

To Sarina

No danger flowing from speech can be deemed clear and present, unless the incidence of the evil apprehended is so imminent that it may befall before there is opportunity for full discussion. If there be time to expose through discussion the falsehood and fallacies, to avert the evil by the processes of education, the remedy to be applied is more speech, not enforced silence.

—*Justice Louis D. Brandeis*

Foreword

Martin Garbus is both my friend and my lawyer, and a much valued peer in both incarnations, so when his editor asked me to write a foreword to this book, I readily accepted. The book, I was told, was about the First Amendment. What could be more worthy? I thought. I readied myself to receive a lengthy and high-minded tome on the value of free speech in a free society. I even had a few no-fault words at the ready: "A book that every American who is concerned with the ever-fragile state of our liberties must read."

Imagine, then, my surprise and delight when I picked up the manuscript and found that it was absolutely irresistible, like eating salted peanuts. Instead of a valuable but heavy treatise on the First Amendment, Garbus has taken us inside some of his most interesting cases. Saints, humanists, rogues, charlatans, and witch-hunters abound in these pages; the good guys—in terms of liberty—are sometimes bad guys in terms of their other human qualities, and the bad guys are sometimes good guys. The result, instead of being a tome, is like coming upon a series of wonderful, connected short stories, full of humanity and irony. The stories are quite seductive and one inevitably leads to another.

There is a phrase from William Faulkner's Nobel Prize acceptance speech about what writers do that I've always loved: Good novelists, he said, depict the human heart in conflict with itself. What Garbus has done here is something comparable: He has given us a portrait of the free society in conflict with itself. He takes us again and again to the cutting edge of that society, where different forces struggle over the right of one faction, usually a minority, to say or do something, often unpleasant, that most people would just as soon not hear or know about. His clients are not always particularly charming. In some cases, their opponents are clearly more likable and would almost surely make better neighbors.

The business of democracy, Garbus is telling us, is often disorderly and on occasion messy and unpleasant. But what he is reminding us of on virtually every page is simple: The ability of unlikable people to do things that most of us don't approve of and to say things most of us would just as soon not hear protects in the long run the rights of all of us, rights that are vital to the continuation of freedom in a large, diverse, pluralistic society.

Marty Garbus has lived a rich and varied life. His clients have ranged from Lenny Bruce and Al Goldstein to Anatoly Sharansky and Andrei Sakharov. Vaclav Havel asked him to draft the new Czech constitution. What he has set down here is a wonderful primer on the importance of freedom, even when it offends majority sensibility. His is a wonderful, engaging book, a tour of grave constitutional issues that remains amazingly accessible—all the more invaluable when you realize that in the end, his true clients are people like you and me.

David Halberstam
March 1998

Contents

Tough Talk

Prologue

The notice from the United States Army read, "You are to appear for Court-Martial Proceedings in Room 114 at Fort Slocum, New York, at 0900 hours on the 17th day of January, 1956."

I was twenty-one years old at the time, a private, first class, and a most unlikely candidate to have taken on the U.S. Army over an issue as randomly elusive as freedom of speech. Nothing in my past suggested a confrontation of this magnitude, for I had never been one to go head-to-head with authority, to raise my voice in protest, no matter how just the cause. One might even say that what finally evolved into my careerlong commitment to freedom of speech grew out of a heritage of fear and silence.

It was a legacy passed on by my father, a Polish immigrant who had fled the anti-Semitic tyrannies of his native land but never quite escaped the specter of persecution and oppression. The memories that plagued him were of no small consequence. When he was a teenager, his back had been broken when a soldier threw him from a hay wagon during a pogrom. His hunchback was a painful, daily reminder to me of the cost of being a helpless outsider. Throughout World War II, he expected a great pogrom to break out in America, and because he did, I did too. We were both spared, I thought, only because Franklin Delano Roosevelt prevented the slaughter of Jews in the United States during the 1940s.

I was a youngster then, a poor Jewish boy growing up in a predominantly gentile neighborhood in the Bronx, and I felt that my safety was always a condition of the moment, a tenuous state whose duration depended on the whims of others. The wisest course, my father made clear to me, was to remain invisible, invisible and silent, and he was the perfect model for such a role. A quiet, withdrawn man, he detested Jews who were too outspoken, who called attention to themselves by their style or manner. If "they" didn't hear you, he felt, if they didn't notice you, then maybe they would leave you alone. He took refuge in his small candy store, where he worked eighteen hours a day, six and a half days a week. Even in those moments when he was out of the store, he seemed to be in hiding. He talked to no one in the neighborhood; he had no friends.

I began helping out at the store when I was eight years old, standing outside and making change at the small newsstand on Sunday mornings. As I grew older, my work week lengthened. We would rise early each morning, often before sunrise, and I would carry the bundles of newspapers in from the sidewalk while my father readied the store for the day's business. The wire that bound the papers would dig into his fingers as he clipped it open, and as I watched, I imagined numbers tattooed on his wrists. His mother and father, his brothers and sisters— eleven members of his family in all—had died in Polish concentration camps, and in 1946, when I was twelve years old, memories of the Holocaust were fresh, and they weighed heavily on both of us.

My mother had died in a fire when I was three, and my father and I had only each other. Yet, though we worked side by side every morning and evening, all day Saturday and half a day on Sunday, we rarely spoke to each other. My father knew little English, and I rejected his Yiddish; we had no need for each other's language. In Poland he had been beaten for speaking the tongue of the Jews, and now, in the Bronx, he still hoarded his fear. Even when he was cheated—when the newspaper delivery was short or a customer claimed to have been shortchanged—my father found it easier to swallow the loss than to speak in his own behalf. He had become accustomed to silence.

Though I was fearful of following too closely in his footsteps, I could not envision a way out. I saw my life defined by the dimensions of this tiny store. It was the smallest candy store I have ever seen, squeezed so tight there was barely space enough for a customer to walk the aisle between the six soda-counter stools and the magazine rack on the wall. It was cramped and dark, and the claustrophobic sense of confinement seemed to be symbolic of the life we led.

Unlike my father, however, I had other cultures to draw upon. I spent what little spare time I had reading, often waiting on customers with a book in hand. The world outside the candy store, I discovered, was replete with heroes who were unafraid, who dared and triumphed, who struggled and conquered. I harbored romantic images of men like George Orwell, who joined the fight against Franco, and Albert Camus and André Malraux, who risked their lives in the French Resistance. I was, for the time, caught in the crosscurrents of two cultures, struggling between a legacy of isolation and fear and the vision of a future that might finally be free of those fears.

At the Bronx High School of Science, where admission was based on a competitive, citywide examination, even brighter worlds unfolded before me. But despite an atmosphere of open inquiry, I remained my father's son, too timid to speak in class, afraid of being wrong, humiliated, or, worse, punished for expressing a difference of opinion. Although I earned good grades, I was the only member of my graduating class with no plans to go to college. I had already received more education than my father ever dreamed of, and he saw no need for further study. He could not run the store without me, he said, and one didn't need a college degree to operate a candy store. So I,

alone among my classmates, received my high school diploma
without having submitted a single college application.

However, during that summer of 1951, circumstance took a
turn in my direction. Hunter College, for many decades a
women's institution of academic distinction, announced that it
would open its Bronx campus to men for the fall semester. The
campus was four blocks west of the candy store. I would be able
to attend classes and continue working in the store. I applied a
month before the semester started and was admitted on the
strength of my high school grades.

Attending Hunter during the McCarthy years, I discovered
a new hero. I found myself mesmerized by Joseph Welch, the
distinguished attorney whose passionate yet humble voice, full
of pain and indignation, spoke to the nation in defense of bat-
tered witnesses who had no voice of their own. I admired all
those who refused to be cowed by the congressional commit-
tees, who took the chance and spoke out, although I never did.
All through college, as in high school, I kept my own counsel,
hesitant to disagree with anyone on anything.

Given my sentiments, however, it was inevitable that sooner
or later I would swallow my fear and break my silence. I chose
to do it in circumstances that least favored open expression, for
I was in the Army at the time. The Korean War had ended by
then, and the McCarthy era was just about over, but the mood
of the country was still brittle. Paranoia had loosened its grip a
bit, but its touch could still be felt. The fifties was not a decade
that welcomed controversy.

Twenty-one years old and a private, first class, I was sophisticated enough to know that the Army was not the best forum
for the airing of ideas, but I was also naïve enough to underesti-
mate the violence of its response. Certainly I had never contem-
plated the possibility of being charged with treason, yet that was
the dim prospect that clouded my future.

After completing basic training, I was assigned to Fort

Slocum on Davids Island off New Rochelle, New York, where I taught current events to enlisted men. Most of the time I commented on news stories in *The New York Times,* but every other week I devoted a full hour to a specific topic, always presenting both sides of the issue but also giving my own point of view. I gave one hour to the reasons why the United States should recognize Red China, another to explaining that those who stood on their Fifth Amendment rights before the House Un-American Activities Committee should not be removed from their jobs or jailed. The commanding officer, a two-star general, acting on complaints from junior officers, called me into his flag-draped office and told me to stay away from controversial subjects. I responded by devoting my next session to the Sacco-Vanzetti case and the prosecution of Eugene Debs during the First World War.

My reaction was entirely out of character, but perhaps I finally sensed that the veil of silence that had muffled first my father and then me must now be lifted, and that if it was finally to be laid to rest, it must be done in the face of an imposing adversary and for a principle worthy of risk. How great the risk was I would soon discover.

One night, after I returned to the base half an hour late—a common enough practice at Slocum—I was charged with being AWOL and with disobeying orders "relating to the performance of my duties." Court-martial proceedings were begun. I faced a military-jail term and a dishonorable discharge.

The court-martial attracted just one spectator, a rugged, fifty-two-year-old master sergeant named James Hatch. Unlike most of the officers at the base, Hatch was a much decorated combat veteran of both World War II and the Korean War, and thus widely respected by the desk soldiers at Fort Slocum who were running the prosecution. I had no idea why he was there. While Hatch often attended my current-events sessions, he had never spoken in class, and so I was unacquainted with his political or social views. As it turned out, though he disagreed with much of what I had said, he was on my side in the court-martial.

One hour into the morning trial, he interrupted the three young officers who sat as my judges and asked for a recess. He met with the officers while I waited alone in the small hearing room. Thirty minutes later Hatch returned and called me aside. He told me the AWOL charge was just a cover, that the officer who instigated the trial believed I should be charged with treason for advocating subversive beliefs.

When the proceeding resumed, Hatch again interrupted. This time he walked past me, right up to the tribunal, and spoke for the record. He told the court that someone who felt the need to express his convictions as strongly as I did should not be punished. The best soldiers, he said, were those with minds of their own, who were ready, on occasion, to violate orders. "Garbus is the kind of person I would pick to lead a patrol," Hatch said, "because he would keep his men safe. He would respect the rules, but he would be willing to break them if he felt he had to." He concluded: "What you are doing is wrong, and if you continue I will take the matter to Washington and make it a public issue."

In the end, a deal was struck. In exchange for the Army's dropping the charges against me, I agreed to leave Fort Slocum, stop teaching troops, give up my security clearance, and be reclassified to complete my service in a radar unit on Long Island. Two days later I left Fort Slocum and finally concluded my two-year Army career without event.

Just prior to my discharge, I had enrolled at Columbia University to do graduate work in economics, my undergraduate major. My father, older now, expected me to return and eventually take over at the store, and I continued to move in that direction. My decision to study economics revealed just how much the shape of my past constricted my view of the future; I believed that a knowledge of economics would be helpful in running the candy store. Even as a college student I could not envision a life that reached beyond the store and my old Bronx neighborhood.

But my Army experience seemed to have cracked a shell of reserve and let loose a rush of new possibilities. For the first time in my life, I had stood up for something I believed in, held my ground, and managed to survive. Hatch and I had tested the Army in its own forum, and we had won. But Hatch had done more than that. Although he had grounded his case firmly on principle, he had made it clear that if his argument were rejected by these three judges, he knew where else to go. The law was implacable, but it needed help. It was only within the forum of the legal process, it appeared to me, that one could find a shield for the timid and fearful. Only the law could offer protection from both physical beatings by police and false accusations of treason by Army officers.

I bid farewell to economics after one semester and set my sights on a legal career. I won a scholarship to Yale Law School, but wishing to stay closer to home and keep my days free for work, I enrolled instead in the evening session of New York University's law school. I was determined that part of my role as an attorney would be to insist, as Sergeant Hatch had done, that conscience deeply felt and reasonably exercised was the backbone of democratic government.

I began trying cases involving freedom of speech not long after being admitted to the bar in 1960. Over the past thirty-eight years, my commitment to the absolute right of free expression has led me into unexplored corners of my own beliefs, taken me to parts of the world I had barely heard of before, and obliged me on occasion to support the rights of advocates whose causes I abhorred. I have defended radical extremists of both left and right, including self-proclaimed Nazis and Professor William Shockley, who espoused the belief that whites were genetically superior to blacks. I have also represented the comic satirist Lenny Bruce, union organizer Cesar Chavez, Russian dissidents Andrei Sakharov and Anatoly Sharansky, the writers Salman Rushdie and Samuel Beckett, and the Czech playwright Vaclav Havel, who, as president of his country's revolutionary government, invited me to help write that nation's constitution.

While the trip has never failed to be gratifying, the road hasn't always been easy. I've defended dissidents in China, India, Pakistan, Nicaragua, and other countries—often finding myself the object of rage, intimidation, and anger. In Rwanda, trigger-happy fourteen-year-olds sprayed bullets at my car when I was moving through Kigali after hours. In Russia I was detained and nearly arrested when I smuggled out Andrei Sakharov's and Anatoly Sharansky's letters to Jimmy Carter. In South Africa, dogs were let loose on me and other demonstrators at an ANC trial. I have been thrown in jail, expelled from countries, even shot at. Disbarment proceedings were brought against me after I wrote critically of South Africa's legal system. I have been ushered to and from court by a police guard, my family has been threatened, I have been roused by hate calls in the middle of the night. It has, in all, been a long, often lonely journey from the cloister of my father's candy store.

The defense of freedom of speech, our country's First Freedom, has grown more complex even as its constraints have been gradually lifted. In the first one hundred years after the passage of the Bill of Rights, the Supreme Court heard only twelve First Amendment cases. Now it is likely to hear several times that number every year. Each step forward invariably opens the way to fresh concerns, introducing questions that previously were not even considered. The emerging imperatives of politically correct speech, the advent of electronic communication, the obsession of both liberals and conservatives with the effects of pornography, the expanded boundaries of the laws governing obscenity have all subjected the First Amendment to new interpretations. They have also brought to the surface cadres of would-be censors ready to limit freedom of speech in the interest of what they deem to be a higher cause. The left of the political spectrum is now often allied uneasily with the right in the conviction that the legislation of permissible speech will somehow serve to modify the way people think and act.

Yet, history testifies to the contrary. It suggests that stifling any form of speech always puts freedom at peril. It is a lesson easily embraced but one that can be sustained only at the price of suffering its consequences. For there will always be instances of speech that fall heavy on the ear, that offend one's sensibilities, that transgress the bounds of decency, that violate the truth. Censorship often begins at the threshold of good intentions. It is perhaps for that reason that I've found its grip so tenacious, that while it assumes new forms and shapes, it never quite disappears.

PART I

Talking Dirty

Chapter 1

I had flown cross-country to California the previous night, but the time difference might have been measured in years rather than hours. It was as if I had gotten trapped in a time warp, for here in Los Angeles, on a winter morning in 1994, I was reading from testimony I had elicited thirty years earlier in the heart of a New York summer. The cases were vastly different in legal context, but they shared a common thread, which was this nation's obsessive preoccupation with the concept of obscenity.

My client of three decades past was the legendary Lenny Bruce, who was tried for giving an obscene performance in a Greenwich Village nightclub and sentenced to four months in jail. Now I had come to California to represent Martin Lawrence, a popular young, black comedian, at a hearing before the Rating Appeals Board of the Motion Picture Association of America. The MPAA, which assigns ratings to movies, had saddled Lawrence's concert film, *You So Crazy,* with an NC-17, a euphemistic updating of the old X rating.

It was hard to believe that all these years later I would again be covering ground that had been virgin soil at the onset of the sixties. The country, after all, had been largely transformed since then. A succession of Supreme Court decisions had defused most state and local laws that restricted the use of language. The concept of obscenity, never easily defined, had

15

become so vague that the courts were reluctant to touch it. But Martin Lawrence was not entangled in the legal machinery. He faced, in fact, no charges at all. He was confronted with a more insidious form of censorship.

The significance of an NC-17 rating is not merely cosmetic. While technically it does nothing more than limit theater admission to those over the age of seventeen, its consequences cut far deeper. Many newspapers and television stations will not carry advertisements for films labeled NC-17; theaters in malls and residential neighborhoods are often prevented by lease from showing them; and some of the nation's largest video retailers refuse to stock the tapes. David Dinerstein, vice president of marketing at Miramax, the film's distributor, estimated that such a rating could cut box-office receipts by as much as half. In Martin Lawrence's case, the damage would likely be even greater, for his style and material appealed chiefly to the youthful and the hip.

As a performer, Martin was a composite of anger-driven street talk and soft, socially acceptable fluff. He was mainstream enough to have his own prime-time sitcom and to appear in a number of first-run movies. At the same time, his stand-up routines were laced with a slashing, brutally frank humor including explicit descriptions of sex and body parts that left little to the imagination. Framed largely as social satire, they were delivered in a vernacular common to the streets, their dialect and themes most accessible to a black audience in the same way that Bruce's routines were often sprinkled with Yiddish phrases and references.

Lawrence had built a following with a weekly HBO show, *Def Comedy Jam,* and a sold-out concert tour, which included five record-breaking nights at New York City's Radio City Music Hall. The concert film, which was shot at the Brooklyn Academy of Music's Majestic Theatre in 1993, drew heavily upon his previous work. It was for that reason that Lawrence,

Miramax, and HBO Independent Productions, which produced it, were stunned by the NC-17 label. It was unusual, if not unprecedented, for such a rating to be affixed to a film based on language alone.

"Think about it," Lawrence told me when we met. "A sixteen-year-old can turn on the television and see my act. He can see me live on the stage of Radio City Music Hall. But if the same act is shown on the screen at the same theater, he can't get in even if he's with his parents."

I agreed to handle his appeal after viewing a videotape of the film at my office. I watched it several times. At first I missed much of the humor, and the satirical thrust eluded me. Martin was using a language that was largely unfamiliar to me, dealing with issues that belonged to another culture. But as I watched the film a third time, then a fourth, I gradually became adjusted to his cadence, and the points he was making no longer seemed alien. Then, for the first time, I began to understand why the wit and satire of Lenny Bruce, so close to the marrow of my own perceptions, eluded the grasp of many otherwise sophisticated listeners. Bruce and I, in large measure, shared the same roots, our sensibilities tuned by background to a common pitch. But how could he be easily understood by the sons of another time and place? Who would have been bold enough to try to explain to the choirmaster of a Southern Baptist church that when Lenny depicted a black protester telling Barry Goldwater, "Don't lay that jacket on us, motherfucker," he was not commenting on style of dress or expressing an attitude toward incest?

It would be no easier, I suspected, to explain the work of Martin Lawrence to the members of the MPAA's Rating Appeals Board. I had appeared before the board before, and I knew that the climate in the hearing room would be less than agreeable. The proceedings, held in a small auditorium, began with a showing of the film, and I could see from the start that the members of the panel were totally offended. I had, of course, expected as much. These fifteen people were an unlikely audience for this type of movie. The average age in the room was about fifty, and only one person was not white. There was clearly an unfathomable gap that separated the members of the board from a constituency for the knife-sharp humor of a young black comic. I based my case on that distinction.

The substance of my argument was that it was inequitable to allow a handful of volunteers, with no particular credentials, to assume the role of surrogate parents through an arbitrary rating system. Lawrence, I contended, uses a language and explores a social structure with which the members of the board were unacquainted, and therefore they were not equipped to determine its worth. While the MPAA represents itself as serving merely in an advisory capacity, when it comes to the NC-17 rating, its members are offering more than guidance. They are, in effect, telling me that they are more qualified than I am to judge whether my sixteen-year-old son or daughter is mature enough to see a particular film.

Arguing the case for the MPAA was Richard Heffner, who for the past twenty or twenty-five years had served as the organization's general counsel and did double duty as president of the Rating Appeals Board. Heffner, who was a professor at Rutgers University in New Jersey and for many years chaired a quasi-intellectual talk show on PBS called *The Open Mind,* presented himself as something of a populist with liberal leanings. But he was well on in years and clearly out of touch with the subculture that spoke Lawrence's language or had a feel for the issues he addressed—the percentage of blacks in prison, their sexual habits, the hostility of blacks toward whites. It was indeed as if Barry Goldwater were trying to comprehend the speech and dialectic of the protest movement in the sixties.

Heffner, who has a bit of the actor in him, enjoyed playing the part of the homespun country lawyer who was wading in waters that might be over his head, when actually he was a well-educated, sophisticated academic who was quite at ease riding the currents of big-city life. On his television show, he had no difficulty exchanging ideas with some of the leading intellectual figures of our time. But now he seemed to have cast himself in the Jimmy Stewart role in *Mr. Smith Goes to Washington.*

He addressed the board, of which he was a representative, as if it were a panel of jurors chosen for their objectivity. His strategy was to turn the hearing into a kind of class war in which he spoke for the interests of mainstream America while I championed the cause of a small underclass that was looking to turn conventional values upside down. When I introduced the question of censorship and First Amendment rights, he responded in a tone suggesting that a simple, unpretentious college teacher like himself could hardly be expected to debate such matters. He explained that he was not a high-priced attorney, that he did not wear fancy, hand-painted neckties, that he was, at heart, just an ordinary guy who understood what American parents wanted and needed.

Heffner, of course, was preaching to the choir. He was in the enviable position of an attorney who has a jury made up of his clients. When the lunch break came, I went across the street to a diner while he remained in the hearing room having sandwiches and no doubt discussing the case with members of the Appeals Board. The constraints of the courtroom, needless to say, do not apply to hearings before an independent body such as the MPAA. Such proceedings run according to their own peculiar dynamics—one side sets the terms, makes the rules, and picks the jury. If you happen to be the party taking the appeal, you know the deck has been stacked.

I had prepared for this hearing by gathering material that contained language similar to that used by Lawrence. I picked up CD's and tapes of 2 Live Crew and other rap groups, which carry cautionary wording like "Parental Advisory—Explicit

Lyrics." My intent was to show that opposition to the use of such language would be a form of de facto censorship, for it would strip the culture that used it of its most potent form of expression. Toward the same end, I had taken with me a copy of an earlier book of mine, *Ready for the Defense,* which contained verbatim testimony from the trial of Lenny Bruce.

The format of the hearing called for each of us to give a thirty-minute opening presentation followed by fifteen-minute rebuttals and finally ten-minute summations. By the time I got to my closing remarks, it was clear to me that I had done little to tilt the board in my direction. It was then that I decided to introduce some of the testimony taken at the Bruce trial. Among the most persuasive arguments made in Bruce's behalf were those offered by Dorothy Kilgallen, a widely respected newspaper columnist and television personality of that era and as unlikely an advocate of public profanity as one might hope to find. Ever prim and proper in her demeanor, Kilgallen, long associated with the Catholic church and Cardinal Spellman, projected the image of a woman with drawing-room manners who would be more at home sipping tea than watching Lenny Bruce deliver his hard-edged social commentary in a Greenwich Village café. Yet there she was, as stiff and stately as she appeared on *What's My Line?,* a popular Sunday-night TV show on which all the participants wore formal evening clothes, testifying in behalf of a nightclub comic who spoke words never before uttered on a public stage.

Kilgallen's testimony seemed particularly appropriate when Heffner represented my position as being totally permissive. If it were left to me, he suggested, nothing that Lawrence might say or do would be considered unacceptable for public consumption. That, of course, missed the point entirely. My argument was that context was critical and that Lawrence was addressing issues and using language that were consistent with his culture. At the Bruce trial, Kilgallen had made the same distinction in direct response to a question from one of the judges.

"Well, Your Honor," she had said, "to me words are just words, and if the intent and the effect is not offensive, the words in themselves are not offensive. . . . I have seen entertainers, and I have criticized them, who didn't use these words but were offensive, nevertheless." A bit later, in response to a follow-up question, she noted, "If you said 'ass' and you meant a donkey, you could say it and you wouldn't blush."

Unfortunately, Kilgallen's testimony, as perceptive and precise as it was, served Lawrence no better than it had Bruce. The vote went against him, 12 to 3. The producer chose to release the film without an MPAA rating, which meant that its distribution was severely limited. It was shown in selected theaters and did reasonably well. Martin continued to thrive on network television and in MPAA-rated feature films. He went on delivering his stand-up routines unencumbered by legal restrictions or threats of arrest. Lenny Bruce had not fared nearly as well.

I was not quite thirty years old and just five years out of law school when I became involved in the Bruce case. I had recently begun working with Ephraim London, one of the country's preeminent civil-liberties attorneys. London, who handled a great many First Amendment and censorship cases, had come to public notice with a two-volume set of books called *The World of Law,* which was published in 1960 and sold very well. I was familiar with London's work, particularly his handling of the appeals of Alger Hiss and Jack Sobel in two cold war espionage cases. He had precisely the kind of practice I wanted, and I was ready at the time for a career change.

I had cut my teeth as a young attorney working for Emile Zola Berman, who was then perhaps the greatest trial lawyer in America. My affiliation with Berman began in 1959 when I was still in law school. I attended classes at night and worked as an apprentice during the day. I was paid about thirty dollars a week and served mainly as a gofer who carried the great man's briefcase to court and then as an investigator and trial-preparation assistant. But it was an education that went far beyond law school. Berman was a brilliant criminal lawyer whose notable cases included the defense of Robert Kennedy's slayer, Sirhan Sirhan, but he tried mainly negligence cases, which were more lucrative, and he was in court every day from September to June. By the time I received my law degree I had logged hundreds of court days, prepared witnesses for every conceivable kind of case, and investigated crimes and accidents in half a dozen states. I started trying cases the day I was admitted to the bar. And from then on I, too, was in court every day.

Working with Berman was an extraordinary experience. In the courtroom he was spellbinding; you couldn't take your eyes off him. Small, slender, with a beaked nose protruding from an otherwise flat face, he evoked a Giacometti sculpture. But his physical appearance was offset by his voice and manner. He spoke in meticulously modulated tones that could be either coarse or soothing, at times accusatory and at other times reassuring. Always elegantly attired, he moved about the courtroom with a stately grace, his every movement transmitting to the jury a conviction of the truth of his case, and you could see the members of the panel, in something resembling a hypnotic trance, drawing closer to him as he proceeded.

Because of his reputation, Berman's caseload was enormous, and those cases in which he had little interest were passed along to me. That was how I got my first obscenity case. I represented a filmmaker by the name of Jack Smith who had run into trouble with an experimental movie called *Flaming Creatures,* a homosexual drag film. It was a welcome break from negligence work, and I realized, probably for the first time, that it was possible to combine trial work with issues that interested me. Nevertheless, the grind of trying cases every day, of seeing one trial stretch into the next and clients merging into one another, had begun to wear me down. The life of a trial lawyer was compelling, but the pressure was fierce. Every day you walked into court and your day came at you with a rush. You might find yourself trying a criminal case, an antitrust case, or a negligence case. A top trial lawyer is like a natural hitter. It was said of Ted Williams that you could wake him in the middle of the night, put a bat in hands, and he would hit the ball somewhere, hard. Trial lawyers are called upon to do that every day.

On some mornings, when you're still new at your trade, you walk into court for a trial that is to start at ten, and at quarter to ten you don't know what the case is about. In boilerplate criminal and negligence work, you barely know who your client is. Someone hands you a file, and you realize that you probably know less about the substantive law in the case than anyone in the courtroom. So you soak up as much as you can in the time remaining and tell the judge your case is ready, because given the circumstances, you are as ready as you'll ever be.

You learn to familiarize yourself with the facts of the case as you proceed, questioning witnesses and reading documents for the first time. The trial lawyer is at a marked advantage in the courtroom because he asks the questions and sets the framework for the trial. At the outset, the judge knows nothing of the facts of the case but knows the law; the jury knows neither; but the attorney knows both, and this allows him to control the proceedings, if he knows how. For example, cross-examining a witness while looking at a document containing his previous testimony makes it possible, often easy, to get a witness to contradict what he said earlier. People rarely mean exactly what they say, and a skilled cross-examiner can add complexity and texture to a statement that at first seemed unambiguous. The ability to get exactly the response you want from a witness is one of the first mechanical techniques a trial lawyer must learn.

Thanks in large part to Berman, I had it down pat in my twenties, and once you learn it, it stays with you.

What cannot be acquired so quickly, however, is the ability to be flexible, an essential trait in a good trial lawyer. Every trial has its surprises, and you must be able to adapt to the emergence of new facts and testimony that you haven't prepared for. An unexpected answer to a question can shift the focus of the proceedings in an instant, making it necessary to restructure your case around the new evidence, and it takes years of experience to be able to do that. Every good trial lawyer, to some degree, has the instincts of a sleight-of-hand artist. He understands that, at trial, illusion is truer than reality. The trick is to impose your own version of the facts on the members of the jury so that their view of reality is the same as yours. This is why the legal system is often seen as a contest in which truth plays only a part. For trials are less about truth than about the perception of truth.

Once a trial starts, for the next six or seven hours a day you are totally absorbed in the process; nothing seems to exist outside the courtroom. The days stretch into weeks, sometimes months, and it becomes its own self-enclosed world. Trial work is really high-wire stuff. You learn quickly under those circumstances, but the tension can become unbearable. It came as no surprise to find that drinking was an occupational hazard among trial lawyers. I knew many who spent their days in court and their nights in a bar, and their personal lives were often as chaotic and unpredictable as their worst days at trial. While working with Berman, I decided that I didn't want that kind of life and it would be best to get out while it was still early.

During the previous few years, I had crossed paths with Ephraim London on a number of occasions. While doing trial work for Berman, I had started my own practice, reflecting a different set of values, handling a number of censorship cases for Greenwich Village artists, poets, and principally filmmakers. Foreign films were just coming into vogue during the late fifties and early sixties, and many of them stretched the boundaries of what was considered acceptable in the United States. This was the era of underground moviemaking, of experimentation on film. There were no ratings in those days, but you needed a license to show a film in a public theater, and the censors were busy denying them. I took as many of those cases as I could handle, often for little or no money. London was doing the same kind of work on a far grander scale, and I kept running across his name. He represented Grove Press and Janus Films, distributors of many of the foreign films that were having censorship problems. Eventually, we got to know each other. We acted as cocounsel on a few cases and found that we complemented each other rather nicely.

London was basically an appellate attorney. He did very little trial work. I, on the other hand, had been doing nothing but trial work for the past three years. I had virtually been baptized in the free-for-all climate of the courtroom and had grown secure in the feeling that if eyes locked hard, I would not be the first to blink. But I had never argued an appeal and was unaccustomed to the more scholarly demands it entailed. The appellate attorney begins with nothing more than a trial record, and if his side has lost, he must develop new, imaginative arguments that competent lawyers before him failed to make. It means spending many hours in libraries, reading scholarly law journals and advance sheets of the thousands of decisions that come down each week throughout the United States. It requires a different disposition from that of a trial lawyer; a style for which London could have been the prototype.

London possessed the manner of a patrician. He was a man whose stately elegance suggested that he deemed himself above the fray. I, by contrast, was a streetwise kid who grew up in

Bronx tenements alert to the possibility of danger around every corner. These were qualities that often proved useful in the rough-and-tumble of the courtroom. They would be particularly welcome in the pyrotechnic atmosphere that surrounded the obscenity trial of Lenny Bruce.

Chapter 2

The trial of Lenny Bruce was not simply a legal proceeding; it was a cultural event. It took place on the near side of the divide that separated America's past from its future. At the time of his arrest, in the spring of 1964, the stirrings of change could already be felt. The civil rights movement was growing in intensity, and as the war in Vietnam began to escalate, the first sounds of protest were being heard in the streets of the cities. The world of the arts—on film, on stage, in print, even on television—was inching toward the horizon of a new era. Courts high and low had begun to loosen the restraints that bound performers, writers, and artists to an uneven, often bizarre patchwork of obscenity laws. The fabric of society was being rewoven in the midsixties, and Lenny Bruce found himself caught in the warp that joined the old to the new.

I was living in the Village at the time, and I had seen Bruce perform several times during the previous four or five years, usually at the Village Vanguard. He had undergone a gradual transformation since the early fifties—from an impersonator who won a Talent Scouts competition on national television to a stand-up comic who sometimes used off-color language to a biting social satirist who, with perfect pitch, employed the street vernacular of the characters he portrayed in his sketches. But what truly defined Bruce was that he aimed for the heart and chose no easy targets. While other comics who viewed them-

selves as social commentators drew the line at caricaturing political leaders and public figures with barbs of good-fellow
cheer, it was Bruce's disposition to probe deeper. He struck
where the meat was most tender, seeking to expose the fine
strain of hypocrisy by which even the best of us lived. His
brightest success was to make one laugh and squirm at the same
time, to draw attention to the wart on even the prettiest face.

With the tempest that would become the sixties still simmering beneath the surface, America was not yet ready for
Lenny Bruce. The arrests for speaking obscene words in public
began in 1962, first on the West Coast—in Beverly Hills and
San Francisco—then in Chicago. Shortly after he was booked to
perform at the Cafe Au Go Go in March 1964, word began to
circulate that New York would be next. Each night Lenny
would survey the room with an eye peeled for the improbable
witness who might be taking a note or two. He had already
begun lacing his fifty-minute act with observations about his arrests and litigation.

"I'm doing my act and a guy comes in. I know he's a cop—
I've had plenty of experience with them. He starts taking down
as much of my act as he can. He doesn't miss a dirty word; he
doesn't get too much of the rest. He arrests me. We go to court.
Me and my lawyers have to defend the act he says I gave. All he
says are the dirty words. *His* act *is* obscene. I'm convicted and
have to hire lawyers, maybe go to jail—because of *his* act.
There's something screwy about the whole thing."

On April 1—ironically enough, April Fools' Day—the cop
came in. He took some notes. Not only did he not miss a dirty
word, he added a few. Two days later Lenny was arrested. He
had to hire a lawyer, and the lawyer he hired was Ephraim London. Ephraim wasted little time bringing me in on the case. He
sensed right from the start, I think, that he and Lenny would
not mix well. London—meticulous and refined, Lincolnesque
in appearance and formal in manner—and Lenny—by now

looking frayed and harried, strung out on drugs and drained dry by almost two years of legal harassment—would indeed have made an odd couple.

The two men, after all, inhabited altogether different worlds. London's was the world of aristocratic German Jews who were very successful, very affluent, very well connected. He was married to the daughter of Max Schuster, of the Simon & Schuster publishing house, one of his clients. His uncle was Meyer London, the first Socialist elected to office in the state of New York. Ephraim was a partner of Graham, London & Buttenweisser, a distinguished old law firm with roots sunk deep in the richest soil of the profession. His all-white office was furnished with two highly polished partner desks where, in the 1920s, his father and his uncle—both attorneys—had sat across from each other. It was an Old World office, as tastefully elegant as his fashionable, nineteenth-century home in the Washington Mews, and a setting in which Lenny Bruce, bearded and shirtless in his denim suit, looked quite out of place when they met.

Of course, when it came to obscenity proceedings, London was on familiar ground. He had handled about 250 such cases, including those involving *Lady Chatterley's Lover, Tropic of Cancer,* and the films *The Miracle* and *The Lovers,* many of which he argued before the U.S. Supreme Court. For added measure, his connections were as good as his credentials. He had no trouble enlisting the aid of big-name expert witnesses, and he was known and respected by every court in the jurisdiction. Yet the Bruce case had its troubling aspects for even the most battle-scarred veteran of the obscenity wars.

For one, the creator of a work was rarely the defendant in an obscenity trial. D. H. Lawrence and Henry Miller had never faced charges or stood trial although it was their works that had been judged obscene. The defendants in those and similar cases were either booksellers, distributors, or the operators of movie theaters. What's more, the works in question—usually books or films—left little doubt as to the points of contention. The book said what it said, the film showed what it showed; there was no argument as to content. The Bruce case, however, centered on an oral, often impromptu performance, for Lenny's act was never exactly the same. At issue, therefore, was whether the defendant actually said or did what the prosecution had charged him with—how accurate, in effect, was the testimony of the state's witnesses. And of course, the wild card in this case was the defendant himself.

Lenny had, by this time, logged a good bit of firsthand court experience. He was well practiced in the give-and-take of courtroom procedure, and there was no ear better tuned to its rhythms. He had also taken the time to acquaint himself with both the statutory and case law in the field and now deemed himself something of an authority on the subject of obscenity. There are few clients more difficult to deal with than those who are familiar with some of the substance of the law but entirely innocent of its nuance. They are unaware that the law rarely can be tracked across a straight path; it is a labyrinth whose twists and turns must be navigated with care and precision.

New York's crusading district attorney, Frank Hogan, not only knew his way through the labyrinth, he knew how to cut some corners along the route. He had been at it for many years, was well acquainted with the political climate in his jurisdiction, and had a killer's feel for the heart of the matter. He understood, surely, that New York was the toughest place in the country to prosecute an obscenity case. Not long after Lenny's arrest, the city's intellectual community rallied to his defense. A petition was circulated and signed by one hundred prominent artists and writers including Lionel Trilling, Norman Mailer, Theodor Reik, James Baldwin, and William Styron. What were the chances, Hogan might have wondered, of finding a New York jury that would turn in a conviction? It was here that the prosecution exercised its first bit of strategy. Since the charge against Bruce was a misdemeanor, a trial by jury was not mandatory. Hogan opted instead to have the case tried by a panel of three judges, headed by Judge John M. Murtagh, a seasoned, impeccably groomed jurist who presided over his courtroom with a stony air of dignity and decorum.

Finding an attorney to prosecute the case was a more difficult matter. Gerald Harris, an assistant D.A. who normally tried such cases, told Hogan he could not in good conscience take it because he did not think Lenny's act was obscene. A number of others on Hogan's staff also declined, insisting that a conviction would not stand up on appeal. Nonetheless, Hogan pressed on; it was as if he had embarked on a holy mission and could not turn back. In fact, that might not have been far from the truth. Hogan was an esteemed member of New York's archdiocese, and I suspected that he and his close friend Cardinal Spellman were more deeply offended by Bruce's frequent references to the church and religious hypocrisy than by the words he used. So Hogan was determined to choose a prosecutor who was ready to use every resource available in an effort to ensure a conviction.

Finally, he found his man. He was Richard Kuh, a young, relentlessly aggressive assistant D.A. with an eye cast toward higher office. Kuh, who had the hard, square build of a middleweight boxer and the attack instincts of a German shepherd, was the best trial lawyer in Hogan's office. Equally important, he was a zealot when it came to prosecuting obscenity cases and had the blessings of the Catholic church. Kuh was hungry for the assignment; here, he believed, was a case upon which a man could build a reputation. What's more, he expected it to be a speedy, uneventful proceeding.

"It's a standard obscenity case," Kuh said at the arraignment. "The entire trial shouldn't take more than two days." I, in turn, explained that the defense intended to call a number of expert witnesses who would testify that Bruce was a serious political and social satirist and that the words he used were necessary for his performance. I estimated that the trial would require at least two weeks. We had both miscalculated. What ensued in the next six weeks was the longest, costliest, most fiercely contested and widely publicized obscenity trial in American history. Perhaps most notable was the fact that, though it made no new law, it would be the last of its kind ever held in the United States.

At the time of Lenny's arrest, the legal test for obscenity was derived from a 1957 Supreme Court decision in a case called *Roth* v. *United States.* The majority opinion, written by Justice William Brennan, said that a work could be judged obscene if, "to the average person, applying contemporary community standards, the dominant theme of the material taken as a whole appeals to prurient interest and is without redeeming social importance." It was a doctrine vague enough to beg interpretation by a cadre of classically trained Talmudic scholars, for it raised more questions than it answered. Who was the average person? Which boundaries framed a community, and who would determine its standards? Whose prurient interest would provide the basis of measure? Who would be the judge of what is socially important? It was around considerations just so elusive that we structured our defense.

Most of the elements in the *Roth* decision had first been applied in 1934 when James Joyce's *Ulysses* found its way to the U.S. District Court of New York. The U.S. Customs Service had refused to allow copies of the book into the country under a law prohibiting the importation of obscene material. The publisher appealed the action, and Judge John Woolsey transformed obscenity law when he ruled that the book was not legally obscene. In his decision, Judge Woolsey introduced two new criteria, initiating a gradual erosion in the reach of a law that had remained essentially unchanged for nearly a century. He said that a work must be considered in its entirety rather than on the basis of isolated passages and that the material must be judged by its effect on an average person, not one who was most sensitive to its content. In its essence, *Roth* affirmed those standards while adding for the first time that for a work to be held obscene it must be "without redeeming social importance."

Brennan's closing phrase had pried the lid open an increment wider. We decided it would be far easier to demonstrate that Lenny's act had some redeeming social value than to attempt to define community standards or determine the sensitivities of the average person. We began assembling a list of prominent artists, writers, educators, and clergymen who might testify as expert witnesses.

The trial began on June 16 in one of the largest courtrooms of the vast, fortresslike Criminal Courts Building in downtown Manhattan. The courtroom was crowded with district attorneys and legal-aid lawyers working in the building who wanted to see a good show as well as with members of New York's literary, intellectual, and journalistic community, there to show their support for Lenny.

The prosecution opened its case with its chief witness, Herbert S. Ruhe, an inspector for the city's licensing division. Ruhe, a former CIA agent, had monitored Bruce's act at the Au Go Go. In his own words, "I was there to witness a performance of the performer Lenny Bruce, to note vulgar, objectionable, and lewd materials which he might produce." Ruhe did that part of his job exceptionally well. Reading from notes he had made during the show, he recited, reluctantly at first, a litany of "dirty words" interrupted by fractured references to Las Vegas, Jackie Kennedy, or Barry Goldwater. Gradually, Ruhe's initial reticence seemed to dissolve. He began performing Lenny's act, as best he understood it, sounding, someone said, like a Lenny Bruce impersonator auditioning for a variety show. Soon he was pronouncing the words in question louder, more distinctly, rolling them around his tongue. Judge Murtagh, who claimed to be entirely innocent of such language, asked on occasion for the witness to repeat a word. Ruhe would enunciate it with the awkward gusto of a student playing Hamlet in a high school play; Murtagh, in turn, would repeat it for emphasis.

Lenny, outraged by the performance, typically touched his finger to the nerve. He leaned over to me and whispered, "Look at their faces when they say those words. They're enjoying it. They love saying *cocksucker.* They've never been able to say words like that before, and here they are in public yelling them out loud. It's too much."

Before he left the stand, Ruhe offered a piece of testimony that hurt us badly. He said he saw Bruce slide his hands up and down the microphone as part of a "masturbatory gesture." He also said he saw Bruce touch his crotch. Lenny reacted immediately. He knew enough obscenity law to understand that he could be convicted more easily for what he did than what he said. "That's it," he said to me. "That's the trick! That's how they're going to get me. Martin, I would never do anything like that—I know better. It's one thing to talk about tits and asses. But to show how to jerk off—they'd put me away for life."

The next witness, Patrolman Robert Lane, also testified that Bruce made gestures originating in the area of his crotch. When Kuh asked him to demonstrate, he got up from his chair, held his arms way out in front of him, and slid his hands back and forth. He and Ruhe were, to all appearances, the only ones in the audience who had seen these gestures.

The prosecution rested its case after three days of testimony. All their witnesses concurred that dirty words had been spoken, but no expert contended that Bruce had "exceeded contemporary community standards." No one claimed that his work had aroused prurient interest. The issue of redeeming social importance had not even been raised. By no legal measure had the state proved its case. We filed a written motion that the charge against Bruce be dismissed on the grounds that the prosecution had not made a prima facie case for obscenity. More than a week would pass before we had the opportunity to make our plea. Lenny had fallen ill with pleurisy and was hospitalized. The trial was adjourned for ten days. During that time the United States Supreme Court handed down two decisions that dramatically changed the substance of obscenity law.

Both cases were decided on June 22, and both had direct bearing on the Bruce trial. The first concerned Henry Miller's *Tropic of Cancer,* which had been banned in Florida on the basis of its "vulgar and indecent" language. The verdict was appealed, and the Court ruled that "dirty" language alone was insufficient grounds to sustain a conviction. This was a critical decision because in its prosecution of Bruce, the state had directed its attack primarily on his use of taboo words, since it could not easily prove that his act was erotic or appealing to prurient interest.

Later that day, the Court issued an even more compelling decision in a case called *Jacobellis* v. *Ohio.* Nico Jacobellis, the manager of a movie theater in Cleveland Heights, had been convicted on two counts of possessing and exhibiting an obscene film. The film in question was *The Lovers,* a serious, mainstream French movie featuring Jeanne Moreau. Ephraim London and I had taken that case on appeal, lost in Ohio, and then carried it to the Supreme Court. Interestingly enough, the case was argued on April 1, the very day Lenny was giving the performance for which he was cited. We were well aware that the legal principles in *Jacobellis* were key issues in the Bruce case, and as that trial proceeded we kept looking over our shoulders, awaiting the Court's decision. When it came, it could not have served us better.

Although five separate opinions were written, the Supreme Court decided each of the issues we presented in our favor. Again writing for the majority, Justice Brennan rejected the argument that "contemporary community standards" referred to local norms. The standard must be a national one, he said, as "it is, after all, a national constitution we are expounding." Even more significant was Brennan's rejection of what was known as the "balancing test"—weighing social relevance against prurient appeal. "A work cannot be proscribed," he wrote, "unless it is 'utterly' without social value." Henceforward, any degree of social relevance would be enough to salvage a work from a charge of obscenity.

The *Jacobellis* decision indicated to Bruce's judges that the Supreme Court would examine every obscenity verdict to see whether the material violated a national standard and whether it had any social value. The *Tropic of Cancer* ruling informed them that the Court would almost certainly reverse any conviction based solely on the use of objectionable language. The trial, in recess at the time, should never have resumed. But our motion to dismiss was rejected.

In arguing against the motion, Kuh drove home a number of legal points that, while questionable, were damaging to our case. First, he insisted that Bruce's performances were obscene in substance, not just in language; they were prurient even if they were not erotic, because prurience as a legal term meant not only erotically stimulating but "filthy and disgusting." Then, what would prove to be even more crippling, he drew a narrow distinction aimed at cutting the legs out from under the *Tropic of Cancer* decision. He argued that Lenny's work "can be judged *only* by its words as it has no 'whole.' Unlike literature, such as *Tropic of Cancer . . .* ," he said, "there is no unity of purpose, no cohesion, no cumulative point or statement to be made. He meanders, wanders, deals with a hundred unrelated things; an incoherent anthology with no common theme but filth." Under the law, he concluded, the presence in an anthology of some items that were not filthy was no defense against the judgment that others were in fact obscene. It was a clever bit of legal gymnastics, mostly "lawyers' talk," but the judges accepted it and imposed a new burden on the defense. Now we would be obliged to offer evidence that Bruce's act was indeed a unified piece of work that must be judged as an artistic entity.

On June 30 we began presenting our case for the defense. While Lenny was hospitalized we had begun interviewing and preparing witnesses. We spoke with more than thirty people who had seen Bruce's act, and all were ready to testify that he had not made a masturbatory gesture. We decided to call the twelve who, by disposition and background, we thought would make the most effective witnesses. Then we turned to the more arduous task of screening experts who could testify on every fragment of the Supreme Court definition of obscenity. Trying to touch all the bases, we selected a literary critic, two newspaper columnists, a cartoonist and playwright, a professor of comparative literature, a nationally known sociologist, and a Congregational minister.

We were hoping to add to our list another nightclub comic who would be able to testify about the nature of humor and satire and how a performance in an after-hours club might differ from one on television. I spent more than an hour with Mort Sahl, a popular stand-up humorist who had built his reputation in the fifties by munching on the meat of the Eisenhower administration. I thought he would make an ideal witness because he was culturally acceptable in a way Lenny was not, but he refused to testify. Sahl, who saw himself as an avant-garde political satirist, was openly resentful of the adulation and respect accorded Bruce by the liberal intellectual community, an audience he felt did not take him seriously enough. But what brought Lenny his devoted following was his inclination to get people to "dig the lie," to burst the bubble, while Sahl was content to poke around the edges. Dressed as an overage college student, Sahl seemed always to be wearing an invisible sign across the front of his V-neck sweater that read EDITED FOR

TELEVISION. He craved both respectability and intellectual approval, but there were times when the two did not mix well. "Respectability," Lenny once said, "means under the covers; the crime I committed was pulling the covers off."

Lacking a nightclub performer, we relied chiefly on members of New York's academic and literary elite. We chose as our leadoff witness Richard Gilman, the literary and drama critic for *Newsweek* magazine, and almost immediately the proceedings began to resemble the Theater of the Absurd. It is a commonplace among attorneys that bad facts can make bad law. It is no less true that bad laws make for odd trials.

At one point Gilman was asked by Judge J. Randall Creel, clearly the most sympathetic of the three judges, "Are you saying that, as Bruce uses these words, there is no sexual connotation at all?"

"No more than when one individual calls another a motherfucker," Gilman replied. "It's common parlance and does not mean that the individual is being accused of having had intercourse with his mother."

"But what about a word like *goy?*" Creel asked.

"I believe that is just a Yiddish term for one who is not a Jew," Gilman said.

"It doesn't refer to a sex act?" Creel asked.

An even more stunning exchange, revealing the distance that separated the trial judges from Lenny's world, took place between Gilman and Kuh. Gilman had testified that Bruce's use of words that were ordinarily taboo was intended to "liberate them from the weight of shame that society has laid upon them." Kuh, who seemed to enjoy hearing such words spoken in open court, asked Gilman to "give us some more words that you and Mr. Bruce would like to liberate from shame."

"At the risk of being facetious," Gilman said, "I would like to liberate the word *truth* from shame."

Kuh shot back: "Would you give us more words and answer the question instead of volunteering your own poppycock."

Here London interjected, "Would Your Honor direct Mr. Kuh not to characterize the witness's testimony?"

"I ask that he answer the question," Kuh insisted, "and when he comes up with a word like *truth* in a courtroom, I say it's poppycock."

"And what's more," Lenny said to me, "if I ever hear the word *justice* in here, it's the chair."

Now, with a clearer idea of what we might expect, we continued with our parade of expert witnesses: Dorothy Kilgallen, the Hearst newspaper columnist; Nat Hentoff, author and critic; Alan Morrison, an editor with *Ebony* magazine; Daniel Dodson, professor of comparative literature at Columbia University; Jules Feiffer, playwright and *Village Voice* cartoonist; Herbert Gans, sociologist and city planner; Forrest Johnson, minister of a Bronx Congregational church. They testified to the social relevance of Bruce's work, that it was well within current community standards, that the words he used would arouse no prurient interest in the average person. It fell to Kilgallen to refute Kuh's contention that Bruce's act did not constitute an artistic whole. In her poised, almost aloof manner, she said, "His unity, I believe, is social commentary. He goes from one subject to another, but there is always the thread of the world around us and what is happening today and what might happen tomorrow, whether he's talking about war or peace or religion or Russia or New York—there is always a thread of unity."

On July 7, two days before we rested our case, we learned that the Supreme Court of Illinois had ordered Bruce's Cook County case reargued to bring it in line with the *Jacobellis* decision. Lenny had been convicted in Chicago earlier in the year, and it was reasonable to infer that the Illinois court now intended to reverse the conviction and retry the case. A week later, the New York Court of Appeals, also reacting to *Jacobellis,* held that John Cleland's eighteenth-century novel, *Fanny Hill,* could not be suppressed as obscene. If it had not been clear before, it was now a virtual certainty that a conviction of Bruce would be overturned, for an appeal would be heard by the same court that had ruled in favor of *Fanny Hill.* All the same, the trial pushed on toward the end of July.

After a two-week adjournment to allow Judge Murtagh to take his summer vacation, court was back in session, and the prosecution surprised everyone by calling its own cadre of five expert witnesses. Each was chosen, by occupation, to offset a witness who had been summoned in Bruce's defense. They testified briefly and disapprovingly of Lenny's performance, and two days later, six weeks after it began, the trial ended.

It would be several months before the judges rendered their verdict. Lenny, who had increasingly shown signs of wear during the court proceedings, now appeared ready to unravel. He was running out of funds borrowed from his friends and unable to find work. Even the most sympathetic club owners were aware that a new obscenity arrest would implicate them as well as the performer, and few were prepared to take the risk.

My relationship with Lenny had grown beyond that of lawyer and client in recent months, and I visited him often at his quarters in the Hotel Marlton, a sullen, uninviting hospice on Eighth Street in Greenwich Village. His room, never free of clutter, now resembled a storage space that had been ransacked by vandals. The bed, the top of the bureau, and the floor were strewn with a cascade of legal documents—thousands of pages of court decisions, case books, briefs, trial transcripts, judicial opinions. He had schooled himself well and believed he had become expert in the laws of obscenity and criminal proceedings. He was ready, he thought, to act as his own attorney.

From the very beginning, Lenny had insisted that London

and I were not communicating with the trial judges and were interested only in making a case that could be won on appeal. He believed that if he could speak to the court he would be able to persuade the judges of the rightness of his cause. He was desperate to testify and enraged that we would not allow him to take the stand. It was his naïve conviction that the law was a perfect and independent organism that would produce a magical justice if only it were left to operate unencumbered by those who practiced it. He would have been summarily acquitted, he believed, if we had let him perform his act for the court. He was unmoved by the fact that he had been convicted after doing his act in a Chicago courtroom, testifying voluntarily, as it were, against himself. He still harbored visions of performing for the court—if not this one, the court of appeals, perhaps even the Supreme Court. Yes, he might yet be the first stand-up comic to play the U.S. Supreme Court.

On October 5 he fired us and was recognized by the court as his own counsel. November 4 was decision day, and I sat beside Lenny to offer help if it was needed. He made an impassioned, heartbreaking plea to have the case reopened. "Please, Your Honor," he said, "I so desperately want your respect. . . . The court hasn't heard the show, they haven't heard me testify . . ." The words, the emotions, bottled up for so long, now came with a rush. As I listened, I could not suppress the feeling that perhaps his more human approach would have been more effective than ours. But it came to nothing. Murtagh, impassive as ever, ordered him to be seated and pronounced the verdict. The court, Judge Creel dissenting, found the defendant guilty as charged.

On November 24 the Illinois Supreme Court reversed its previous conviction of Bruce, relying on precedents that had come down during his trial. Murtagh appeared not to notice. On December 21, despite Lenny's plea that he not be sent to jail, Murtagh sentenced him to four months in the workhouse on Rikers Island. Over Kuh's objection, a stay was granted, pending appeal. Kuh had asked that Bruce be jailed immediately because he showed "a notable lack of remorse." Lenny, "to set the record straight," told the court he was not remorseful. "I come to the court," he said, "not for mercy but for justice." He got neither.

Ever trustful in the law, Bruce filed suit in the federal courts, seeking to enjoin the police from interfering with his performance unless they obtained a prior court ruling that the act was obscene. When the injunction was denied in the lower court, he appealed to the circuit court of appeals. He lost there too.

Barred from working in New York, he tried his luck in California but fared no better there. A year after his conviction, he was declared a legally bankrupt pauper by the district court in San Francisco.

On August 3, 1966, Lenny Bruce died of a drug overdose.

Eighteen months later the appellate term in New York reversed his conviction.

In the final reckoning, Lenny was vindicated. His quaintly persistent faith that justice will somehow find its way was confirmed. But what he never quite understood was that even when it works well, the law often works slowly. Justice has a rhythm of its own; it is, finally, a lethargic process that moves to the ticking of its own clock. There are casualties along the way. Lenny just ran out of time.

Chapter 3

By the latter part of the sixties, the prosecution of obscenity cases had become a dying industry. Local jurisdictions were finding that the cases were too costly to try, there were an increasing number of reversals on appeal, and the public seemed to be losing interest. Most important, the *Jacobellis* decision had given state and district courts reason to pause. Prosecutors were aware that to bring in a conviction they were obliged to prove each element cited in the ruling, and the concepts of community standards, the average person, and redeeming social value were elusive enough to make the outcome uncertain. Obscenity was one of those legal doctrines that defied precision; the more closely it was defined, the less comprehensible it became.

Justice Potter Stewart addressed that difficulty in his dissenting opinion in *Jacobellis*. "I shall not . . . attempt . . . to define it . . . ," he said, "but I know it when I see it." But he did not know it when he saw it; nor did anyone else. Justice William O. Douglas, who was light-years ahead of his Supreme Court brethren on the subject of obscenity, was far closer to the truth when he said, "There are as many different definitions of obscenity as there are human beings," and "they are as unique to the individual as his dreams. . . . Whatever obscenity is, it is immeasurable as a crime. . . . It is entirely too subjective for legal sanction."

I handled only one other criminal prosecution of obscenity after the Bruce trial, the appeal of a conviction that had been returned on November 18, 1964, exactly two weeks after Lenny's conviction was handed down. It was an obscure but unusual case involving a turn-of-the-century French poet, Pierre Louÿs, and a mail-order distributor, Joe Davis, who was charged with selling phonograph records of Louÿs's "obscene" poetry through the mail. Davis had been found guilty in the Southern District of New York after a trial by jury in which neither side presented any testimony. Both parties stipulated to every aspect of the crime except that the recordings and their wrappings were obscene. The jury, then, was left to consider on its own the literary merit of the poet's work.

Dead forty years at the time of the trial, Pierre Louÿs was a poet and novelist whose literary credentials passed muster in the highest quarters. The *Columbia Dictionary of Modern European Literature* said that his poems, "by their pure and flexible harmony of style may well become immortal; indeed few poets have ever had a more fervent worship of beauty and a more profound respect for form. The works of Louÿs have inspired several musicians, among whom the most notable is Claude Debussy."

The recordings in question contained excerpts from his most celebrated work, a long prose poem called *Songs of Bilitis,* which tells of the coming of age of a young Greek girl on the island of Lesbos and is a celebration of homosexual love. The poem was published in 1894, and an English translation had been circulated widely and with little notice in the United States since 1904. It was not regarded as underground material. The poem was included in anthologies published by Random House and Little, Brown and was part of Avon's Classic series. Its content, which could hardly be called graphic, was not very different from passages in the work of Walt Whitman. But Louÿs was an easy target: he was foreign, he was dead, he was a homosexual, few people had heard of him, and the work now deemed obscene was published seventy years earlier. He was not a man likely to attract the attention or sympathy of the public.

As for Davis, he ran a small mail-order house and probably had little knowledge of the value, literary or otherwise, of Louÿs's poetry. He advertised the recordings as "party records" and mailed them with garish yellow labels trumpeting the "sexational" material that awaited the listener, but there was no indication that Davis believed he was selling forbidden items. Such knowledge, called the doctrine of scienter, was essential to the prosecution's case, for a person cannot be held responsible for distributing obscene material unless he is aware that the nature of the material is obscene. The law recognizes that it is unreasonable to presume that a person who sells books or records would be familiar with the content of each item. And even if he is, how can he be expected to judge whether the material is obscene when the courts themselves rarely agree on that issue? In Davis's case, the most immediate evidence favored his innocence, since the sale price of the Louÿs records was no higher than those of poetry readings by Dylan Thomas or T. S. Eliot.

The case against Davis was woefully weak. Had a proper defense been mounted at the trial level, there would have been no conviction to appeal. But the defense presented no case at all. Indeed, after the prosecution placed into evidence its exhibits—consisting of the phonograph records, the record jackets, the labels, and the advertisements—and played the records for the jury, the defense offered no evidence of its own and moved to dismiss. The motion was denied, and the case went to the jury, which took just thirty-five minutes to return a verdict of guilty. A defense motion to set aside the verdict also was dismissed. Davis was fined one thousand dollars and given a six-month suspended sentence.

I was retained to appeal the decision, first to the U.S. Court of Appeals, then to the U.S. Supreme Court, but as is often the case, the appeals had effectively been lost at the trial level. An appeals court does not retry a case; it hears no new evidence, takes no new testimony. It simply reviews the record of the trial for judicial error and hears arguments regarding interpretation of the law as it affected the decision. For that reason every trial embraces two often contradictory goals: to win the case at the trial level while at the same time building a record that leaves room for reversal if the verdict goes the other way. In the Bruce case, we introduced a wealth of evidence that would allow the appeals court to reconsider such issues as social relevance and contemporary national standards. No such record was made at the Davis trial, so it was not surprising that the court of appeals voted 2 to 1 to affirm the decision against Davis, with each side, directly or indirectly, alluding to the dearth of evidence it was left to consider.

We fared no better in the Supreme Court. Our request for a writ of certiorari, which would have compelled the lower court to review the record of the case, was denied by a vote of 5 to 3. The Court's decision, narrow as it was, had no effect on the evolution of obscenity law. By the midsixties the very notion of obscenity as a legal issue had begun to seem archaic. America had arrived at the threshold of a cultural revolution that would soon reshape the contours of its mood and turn it in a new direction.

My own life was changing direction as well. For the past ten years I had been living in Greenwich Village and was very much a part of that culture, the world of the Beats. I knew Allen Ginsberg and Gregory Corso and represented them and their friends on various matters including, on occasion, drug busts; I represented Andy Warhol's films against obscenity charges and some of his people on drug charges. At one time or another I shared living quarters with Corso, and with Albert Finney and Yoko Ono. I was immersed in what was typical of Village life in the fifties, a unique blending of time and place that has been enshrined in the memory banks of nostalgia—poets like Ginsberg and Corso reading their work in coffeehouses, artists exploring their skills in gaping sunlit lofts, jazzmen such as Charlie Mingus and Thelonious Monk sending their riffs drifting into the early-morning hours in pinched, smoke-filled clubs. It was a lifestyle that had a seductive appeal to a young man who had come of age in a modest Bronx neighborhood, nurtured on a middle-class morality as compelling and sound as it was uninventive, instructing its sons in the virtues of hard work, fair play, and an inclination to risk as little as possible.

Like many another heir to the wisdom of our immigrant fathers, I cherished the bedrock values on which I was raised but could not easily deny the allure of another, somewhat reckless call to a wider range of experience. America, after all, was not Poland. We had the right, perhaps even the obligation, to ask for more than mere survival. Unwilling to relinquish what was mine by birth but eager to explore courses not fully charted, I straddled the two worlds for a time, drawn in a different way to each and trying to be true to the values of both.

During the day I was a trial lawyer, wearing pinstripe suits, working in a tightly controlled, often hostile courtroom environment, trying to bend precise rules and regulations to my advantage. At night I slipped easily into a life with looser constraints, living among people who made their way a step at a time, walking a tightrope at the fringes of a society they observed closely with a mixture of indifference and disdain. The contrast between lifestyles was equally striking when I was working with Ephraim London, for his was a practice several cuts beyond the rip-and-tear courtroom dramas that occupied Emile Zola Berman. I had taken a sharp pay cut when I went to work for London, but I was introduced to an aspect of life I had not previously imagined. All at once, I entered upon an intellectual climate of high culture, sophistication, class, and status. I would go to dinner at Ephraim's house and find myself seated beside Alger Hiss, W. H. Auden, or Igor Stravinsky, dining at a table set with fine china and glassware. Just a few years earlier I had been drawing sodas and dishing out ice cream in my father's candy store, and now I would look around me and wonder at how quickly that distance could appear to be bridged and, in the end, how little I comprehended its meaning.

I was working and mixing with people whose political and social views were compatible with mine, but our roots, and therefore our orientation, were different, and my place in that world was uncertain. Although I was in that milieu, I was never really of it. I had come to a point where some of the pro bono work I was doing seemed to have more value and presented a greater challenge than the work I was being paid for. Lyndon Johnson's War on Poverty was in full sway, and I was doing a good deal of legal work for a fledgling organization called Mobilization for Youth. MFY, as it was known, was an early product of the Great Society years, growing out of that rich sense of social consciousness that marked the Kennedy era and was a prelude to the emotional eruption of both the civil rights movement and the protests over our involvement in Vietnam. It was an organization that aggressively championed the rights of the poor, the young, the oppressed, and it developed some of the most innovative youth and legal programs in the country. In a short time, it became effective enough to attract the type of political attention it would have preferred to avoid.

During the 1965 mayoralty campaign in New York, Republican candidate John Marchi, a state senator, made MFY a major political issue. He said he would prove it was being run by people with Communist affiliations who were causing unrest among New York's poor. Marchi focused his attention on the founder of the organization, Edward B. Sparer. Sparer was a lawyer who had been involved in a number of left-wing causes in the late forties when red-baiting and Communist witch hunts were at their peak. Marchi claimed that funds for the poor were being misused, that it was really revolution that was on the minds of MFY's leaders. He began feeding stories regarding Sparer's past activities to the press and local television stations in an effort to discredit the organization. At Sparer's request, I agreed to represent him and other members of MFY who had come under investigation. After weeks of public hearings, we succeeded in rebutting the charges and shutting down the investigation, but the damage had already been done. The reputations of many involved were seriously harmed, and while MFY continued to exist, it never again was the force it had been before Marchi launched his attack.

In the end, Sparer shared the fate of many others of that era who had tried to give voice to those who could not speak for themselves. He was hounded and besieged at every turn and finally felt compelled to resign. He had fallen victim to a form of censorship even more pernicious than the laws governing obscenity, for it was not so much the message that was the target as the person delivering it. Obscenity laws, though difficult to define, could at least be identified, tested, refined, and, if a state court saw fit, even expunged.

While hearing fewer and fewer cases, the Supreme Court continued to fine-tune the legal definition of obscenity. In *Miller* v. *California,* the Court decided that a work can be judged to have value "regardless of whether the government or a majority of the people approve of the ideas the work represents," effectively limiting the reach of "community standards." In *Pope* v. *Illinois,* it stretched the value test yet further, ruling that a *reasonable* rather than an *average* person must be used as the standard of measure. Justice Brennan, for fifteen years a moderate voice on such matters, concluded, in a dissenting opinion in a 1973 case called *Paris Adult Theater* v. *Slaton,* that obscenity laws could not be enforced without intruding on speech protected by the First Amendment. He proposed finally that obscenity be deregulated in matters regarding consenting adults.

In 1987 the Oregon Supreme Court carried Brennan's proposal to its logical conclusion, ruling unanimously that no form of expression can be prohibited on the ground that it is obscene. In the Constitution's bicentennial year, Oregon in effect rewrote the language of the First Amendment, spelling it out clearly: "No law shall be passed restraining the free expression of opinion, or restricting the right to speak, write or print freely on any subject whatever." In Oregon at least, the crime of obscenity had ceased to exist. The concept, however, was alive and well throughout most of the country, and nowhere were the legions of propriety more vigilant than in the motion-picture industry.

Although by this time films that might be judged patently offensive by even the most forgiving standard were being shown in big cities and small towns, the MPAA was still playing censor, using its rating system to banish serious films from mainstream movie houses. In 1989 it affixed an X rating to a film called *Scandal,* which dealt with a political sex scandal that toppled a British government in the early sixties. The Profumo affair, as it was known, was a watershed in British social and political history. It resulted in the resignation of Secretary of War John Profumo and the collapse of the Conservative government of Harold Macmillan, and helped usher into power a new Labor prime minister, Harold Wilson.

The film, which contained few explicitly sexual images, was a detailed and accurate rendering of the incident, which concerned class, power, and money as well as sex. It featured prominent British actors such as John Hurt, Ian McKellen, and Joanne Whalley-Kilmer, and employed news clips to give the movie the feel of a documentary. The film quickly broke all box-office records in the United Kingdom, but the X rating threatened to severely restrict its circulation in the United States.

The MPAA members who voted to give the film the X rating were unaware that it was basically nonfiction and closer to the truth than documentaries dealing with the same events. I appealed the rating to the Classification and Rating Administration (CARA) of the MPAA, pointing out the historic significance of the film and noting how absurd it seemed that British adults could see it on an unrestricted basis while Americans could not. The vote was close, 8 to 7, but we lost. The point of contention was a one-minute, fifty-second "orgy" scene that showed no graphic sex and that one reviewer described as an "oddly orderly orgy." The scene was central to the story because it illustrated the role sex can play in the quest for power and political advancement. In the end, the scene was cut and the movie was released with an R rating.

The practice of appealing restrictive ratings to the same body that issued them was clearly a futile proposition. If the judicial system were run on similar mechanics, there would be no need for a court of appeals. Thus, when the MPAA board denied our request to reclassify the Martin Lawrence movie in 1994, I had decided it was time to challenge the system. That opportunity came a year later when *Kika,* an art film by the Spanish director Pedro Almodovar, was saddled with an NC-17 rating.

Almodovar was an award-winning director of international renown, and *Kika* had already been released to rave reviews in Spain, France, Belgium, and Germany. But the MPAA rated it NC-17, citing two comedic scenes, one of rape and one of consensual lovemaking. When the date of the appeal was set, I formally requested that members of the media be permitted to attend the hearing, but we were told that all MPAA sessions would remain off-limits to the media. Then, to substantiate our case, October Films, the distributor of the movie, prepared a thirty-four-minute videocassette depicting rape scenes from six major American movies that had received R ratings. At the end of the tape was the scene from *Kika,* which clearly was no more graphic than the others. However, the appeals board refused to view the tape, saying it was its policy "to exclude any filmed comparisons including videotapes, because they are not germane to the Rating Appeals process."

At this point I decided to bring suit in New York County Supreme Court, charging that the entire rating system violated the free-speech clause of the First Amendment and was therefore unconstitutional. The case raised several interesting questions and produced enough interpretive gymnastics to engage even the most speculative legal mind.

The MPAA was represented by a prominent First Amendment lawyer whose public posture would lead you to place him on the other side of the issue. In behalf of the MPAA, he contended that our attempt to nullify the rating system would violate the association's right of free speech and be tantamount to "a new form of state-sponsored censorship." Our petition, he said, would place the court in the role of state censor and interfere with "MPAA's constitutional freedom to determine for itself what to say—and what not to say."

Clever as it was, the argument seemed to me a classic case of begging the question, assuming as true what was yet to be proved—that an independent organization, operating solely on its own sanction, had the right to determine who might be permitted to see or hear a particular film. In effect his case rested on the circular argument that one was guilty of censorship if he interfered with a censor's right to censor.

We based our own case on a novel proposition that was equally tenuous but was grounded, we thought, in firmer terrain. It was a position not without precedent. In a recent decision, the Supreme Court had ruled that Amtrak, a privately owned railroad, could not prevent a political billboard from being displayed in Grand Central Station. The Court thus had removed Amtrak from private status on the ground that it performed a public function and was therefore bound to offer the same free-speech protection as a governmental agency. We contended that the MPAA had no less a public charge than Amtrak and should be subject to the same constraints. Since the First Amendment's guarantee of free expression applies only to infringement by government, we argued that government involvement with the MPAA and the motion-picture industry was sufficient to apply First Amendment standards. But the court denied our appeal, ruling that our First Amendment argument could prevail only if the MPAA was a purely governmental agency rather than a private organization. As our client did not wish to incur the cost of further appeals, the rating system remained intact, and has not been challenged since.

As a consequence, the MPAA continues to wield extraordinary power. It has managed to preserve an outdated view of obscenity while imposing its will in more enlightened times. The urge to censor, it seems, shadows every effort to liberate speech from moralistic restraint. Obscenity is not its only target. Speech that challenges governmental policy or authority has troubled the national conscience since the birth of the republic. It is one of many small ironies that the government that conferred the right of free speech as its First Freedom has, all too often, been the agent that strived most militantly to limit its range.

PART II

"Congress Shall Make No Law . . ."

Chapter 4

The sixties was no time for neutrality. It was as if the first half of the decade was spent choosing sides and the latter half in a collision that seemed at times to be on the brink of revolution. I had always known which side I was on, but by the middle of the decade I felt the need to make a firmer commitment. While working with London, I had the time to take on significant issues and cases where fees were not the primary concern. I became chairman of the Committee to Abolish Capital Punishment, tried a dozen murder cases, and wrote extensively about criminal justice. Still, my activities were limited by my daily practice, and I was looking to shed those constraints. Many of the people I knew and respected—some of them lawyers—were deeply involved in the civil rights and antiwar movements. They were out in the streets, organizing the poor, creating and defending new political movements, developing innovative legal concepts, trying to effect change, and while I sometimes represented them, I was eager for the chance to play a more active role in those struggles.

The opportunity presented itself in 1966 when Ed Sparer, after resigning from Mobilization for Youth, asked me to join him in creating a legal wing for a national organization to aid the poor. Based at Columbia University, it was to be called the Columbia Center on Social Welfare Policy and Law. We would choose our own cases and litigate them in any state in the country. The first year's funding was already assured: one third of the costs would be paid by Columbia University; another third would come from private foundations, including the Ford Foundation; and the federal government would contribute the remaining third. We hoped to be able to eliminate the government's participation entirely in future years.

Ed was a man of total dedication who knew more about laws affecting the poor than anyone in the country and was hooked into poor people's movements nationwide. An academic with virtually no experience at litigation, he was in need of a trial lawyer who understood practice and constitutional law, someone who could determine which cases to bring to court, who was prepared to try them anywhere in the country, who could protect people when they banded together to demand their rights.

It was an inviting prospect but one that would require a good deal of sacrifice and not a little risk. I had gotten married a few years earlier and had a one-year-old daughter. Ephraim London had promised me a partnership in his firm. To join Sparer at this juncture was to mortgage my future and plunge headlong into the unknown. My income would be about half what I was earning with London and one third of what I was making with Berman. It meant that in my first seven years out of law school each move I made took me in the wrong direction on the financial scale. It would also involve a precipitous change in lifestyle. I would be leaving a world that was safe and predictable, a climate of intellectual aspiration and achievement, polished offices in the high-rent district, the promise of a lifetime of security, in exchange for a toss-and-tumble existence that would take me to unfriendly outposts like Alabama and Mississippi, to pockets of poverty deeper than I had ever imagined. But I would be answering a call to the future from a voice that echoed from my not-too-distant past. I accepted Sparer's offer and, with great difficulty, parted company with Ephraim London.

Ed and I were given positions as adjuncts on the faculties of Columbia Law School and the School of Social Work. This assured us free student help as well as library resources and the opportunity, should the heat be turned on by Southern states, to proclaim our status as professors, rather than radicals. Our headquarters was a seven-room apartment on Riverside Drive and 116th Street that was reserved for faculty. When we moved in, there were no lights, no gas, no furniture; the place was in a state of total disrepair. Over a weekend, we painted it ourselves, had phone lines installed, and gave it the look of respectable law offices.

With the first $250,000 we received, we added twelve young attorneys to our staff, but the rudder for our operation was provided by three veterans of the poverty wars. George Wiley, head of the National Welfare Rights Organization, was the spearhead who was most critical to the project. Wiley had the grassroots connections that Sparer and I lacked. He was involved with people whose welfare rights were being taken away or who were being evicted from public housing because they protested or complained about conditions. His client base could provide the appropriate test cases needed to attack specific laws in the Southern states.

The two others instrumental to the project's success were Richard Cloward and Frances Fox Piven, both professors of sociology at the Columbia School of Social Work, who had worked with Sparer to create MFY. Cloward and Piven had coauthored a seminal book called *Regulating the Poor,* in which they identified legislative techniques that state governments used to turn welfare or housing law against the people it was intended to help. It was an area of law totally outside my experience. I knew the legal system of the courts, but before you got to the courts you had to work your way through this maze of regulations, different in each state, and they had the compass. So Wiley gave us the clients; Cloward and Piven pointed out the inequities in the system; Sparer interpreted the welfare law and wrote handbooks explaining it to welfare recipients; I was the lawyer who would carry the mandate to the courts throughout the country.

The government's share of the seed money came from the Office of Economic Opportunity, a federal program designed to give legal aid to those in need. We knew, however, that once we hit full stride as an advocacy agent for the poor, promised OEO funds were likely to dry up, and we immediately began seeking financial aid from additional private foundations to get us through the first two years. Sparer had learned at MFY how to apply for grants. I used some of the contacts I made while working for London to solicit donations from individuals with money and liberal leanings. So, reasonably if modestly funded, and staffed by a few veterans and a small cadre of young, committed attorneys, we set forth on a course that, it turned out, was mined with more hazards than any of us suspected.

Whatever success we were to have depended in large measure on how wisely we chose our cases. We needed cases that would test the validity of a law, that would establish a precedent that state governments would have to follow. Initially, much of the civil rights struggle was based on free-speech concepts. Under Chief Justice Earl Warren, the Supreme Court had recognized that speech involved more than oral expression; it embraced the right to act—to demonstrate, to sit in, to boycott, to picket. If a woman was evicted from public housing because she took part in a demonstration protesting the conditions in the housing project, we wanted a court decision that said the eviction violated her First Amendment rights.

But state agencies were aware of the pitfalls of allowing cases to go to court. If a particular case appeared to be solid, they would, after endless delays, simply concede the issue and yield to our demands before their action could be legally tested. If a woman had been evicted, she was allowed to move back into her apartment; if her welfare payments had been taken away, they were restored. It would be a victory for her and for us, but one without future ramifications. We would have spent many hours and gone to great expense to achieve justice for one person, but we would have accomplished nothing for the hundreds of thousands of others who suffered the same inequities. Winning at the lower level did not effect substantive change. The test-case approach was a long-range strategy. We often culled as many as fifty cases before we could get one into court, and we tried to file that case in a place where it could serve as the foundation for a local movement.

We set up educational and political programs throughout the South and in big northern cities like New York, Chicago, and Detroit. While I went to court and attacked the laws, rules, and regulations, Sparer wrote welfare manuals on "poor law," advising people of their rights so they could derive full benefit from laws passed in their behalf. Ed's job was more difficult than mine. I operated in an area where there were rules, where you knew who your adversaries were and could call them to account. Sparer's terrain was a quagmire. The laws he was trying to interpret varied from state to state; they were difficult to comprehend in the best of jurisdictions and nearly impossible in the South, where the interests of the state were often better served by obscuring rather than clarifying the issues. As a consequence, few poor whites or blacks had any understanding of what their rights were and fewer still were bold enough to walk into a welfare office and demand them. It was no surprise, then, that when we sifted our list of plaintiffs for potential test cases, most of them were in small backwater towns in the Deep South, which at the time was caught in the crosscurrents of change and seething with a venom that had been on its breath for more than a century.

For the next year and a half I lived out of a suitcase. My colleagues and I spent a good part of our time in southern courtrooms, and we lost far more often than we won. The work we were involved in lacked the high visibility of much of the civil rights movement. There were no sit-ins or boycotts, no freedom rides or dramatic marches led by nationally recognized leaders. Working with people whose names nobody knew, addressing legalistic issues that held little appeal for the media, we did not enjoy the thin measure of protection that the light of publicity often provides. I was jailed twice, beaten up, shot at, and through it all I understood that the hardships I faced were but a shadow of what the people I worked with endured every day of their lives.

At one point I lived for a month near a town called Mound Bayou in northern Mississippi. It was the oldest black community in the United States and possibly the most impoverished. Families lived in one-room wooden shacks, often without heat or running water, with little in the way of sanitary facilities. They had virtually no medical care. With nothing in the town to attract the white population, the blacks were left to their own devices. It was not long, however, before the civil rights movement took notice. For here in the heart of redneck country was a self-contained black community, apparently untroubled by the world around it, that seemed to accept abject poverty as the price of peace. Liberal agencies and foundations started sending in money for health care and other services that the community had been lacking. Civil rights workers encouraged the people of Mound Bayou to organize and become politically active. When I arrived there, in the spring of 1966, the backlash had already begun. Those who dared to speak out were being arrested on trumped-up charges intended to buy their silence.

I was in court or preparing for court almost every day and often succeeded in getting the charges dropped or the sentence suspended. But my chief goal was to help the people organize themselves, to make them aware of their rights and get them to understand that ultimately, when the white civil rights workers left, they would have only one another to rely on. It was a simple message but one not easily communicated. My appearance on the scene was greeted, naturally enough, with a degree of suspicion. A carpetbag lawyer from the North was not likely to be their first choice when it came to investing their trust. These were people, after all, who were not new to a sense of betrayal. They had seen civil rights people come into their community for a day or two, stir things up, and then leave town without so much as a backward glance. So right from the start a visitor from the North had to assure them he would not promise more than he could deliver. If you took a hotel room, they were convinced you would be gone on the first bus out. You had to live with the people you were representing, share their meager quarters, and at times subsist, as they did, on a diet of collard greens. Thirty years later, I can still smell the acrid aroma of the boiling collards mixed with the scent of propane gas.

I eventually earned a certain level of trust, but it never was total and I knew it never could be. I was who I was, I came from an entirely different culture, and the gap between us could never be bridged. I would set up a meeting and fifty or sixty people would attend; we would agree to stage a demonstration the next day at the welfare office. Everyone would be cheering and eager to take part, but the following day I would wait for hours and only two or three people would show up. It was frustrating, but I soon learned to tailor my expectations to fit the temperament of the people I was working with. I was also becoming aware that all real change must come from the bottom and that working at that level was difficult and, at times, even hazardous.

Near the end of my stay in Mound Bayou, I was in court with a client when the local police came in and arrested me. I was charged with practicing law without a Mississippi license, a technicality rarely introduced in such proceedings. I was summarily hauled from the courthouse and ushered to a white jail cell where I spent the night before some local attorneys, acting at Sparer's behest, arranged for my release.

When I returned to New York I continued to organize meetings in small towns in Alabama, Georgia, Mississippi, and Florida. I would spend about ten days at each location, and invariably it was an agonizing experience. I tried to set up the meetings a week in advance, I'd talk to a dozen or more people who said they would make the arrangements, and when I got down there I would find that nothing had been done. These were people who had difficulty enough attending to the bare details of their lives. Some were afraid to attend the meetings; others were simply unable to get to the location. They had no cars, no phones, and they were often separated by large distances. I spent days going from town to town, house to house, trying to assemble an audience. The meetings were always scheduled for late at night, usually around ten o'clock, because most of these people worked during the day and needed time to feed their children and travel to the meeting site. I found myself in remote, unlit areas of a town where the streets were empty and no one knew who I was. It was a high-risk venture, and you never knew what the outcome might be.

In the end, the Columbia Center succeeded in bringing a number of cases to the Supreme Court, and some of them made new law. I argued *Smith* v. *King,* the first welfare case ever heard by the U.S. Supreme Court, which struck down a regulation that denied benefits to hundreds of thousands of poor Americans. But it was not long before the center lost its federal funding, and I came to understand that no real social change will ever be brought about by programs paid for by the government. Government programs, whether at the federal or state level, are designed to allow just enough change to preserve the status quo; they are never intended to tilt the balance of power.

If I needed any further instruction in this regard, it was not long in coming. On one of my visits to Florida I represented some migrant workers in Homestead, a town of about ten thousand people at the southern tip of the state. It was there that I met Cesar Chavez and began to appreciate the true meaning of poverty and despair.

Chavez at the time was trying to broaden his California-based United Farm Workers union by establishing a base in southern Florida. He was engaged in a struggle that predated the Great Depression and whose prospects had improved little since the days of *The Grapes of Wrath*. Yet he sustained a vision that seemed immune to circumstance, that remained undimmed despite thirty years of loss and failure. The sheer force of his presence gave the promise of hope in the face of utter desperation. From the moment I met him I was deeply moved by him and his cause.

I spent the next two weeks with Chavez in Homestead, beginning an association that would last until his death. He was a brilliant organizer, but he needed legal help. Farmworkers were being jailed for demonstrating, for giving speeches, for walking picket lines. The primary issue was always freedom of speech, and I was particularly well suited to offer my services. In many respects, the work I was doing was similar to the welfare cases I handled for the Columbia Center in Mississippi, Alabama, and Georgia. But there were significant differences. What we lacked in our efforts at the Columbia Center was a core of independent local leadership that remained constant. We would establish ties in a community, and they would unravel as soon as we left; the only permanent change we created resulted from test cases that made new state law. But Chavez had a fixed base of operation, the gut issues around which a movement could be built, and a nucleus of workers who were ready to follow his lead. If he said, "I'm setting up a meeting and there will be two hundred people there," the meeting would be held as scheduled

and you could count on at least two hundred people showing up.

Chavez was a union organizer in the classic tradition. He
began with a clearly defined issue, established a solid base in a
small area, expanded to a statewide level, and then endeavored
to enlarge his cause and make it national in scope. After our two
weeks together in Florida, Chavez was ready to return to Southern California. I felt I had done all I could at the Columbia Center and decided to go with him. Before leaving for Florida I had
accepted an offer from the American Civil Liberties Union to
serve as its associate director and director of its newly formed
Roger Baldwin Foundation. But before heading home, I would
spend two months with Chavez in Bakersfield, Delano, and
Riverside, three California whistle-stops that made Homestead,
Florida, seem like a modern metropolis.

My getting involved in the cause of migrant farmworkers
meant taking yet another step down the social and economic
ladder. No matter how desperate and barren the lives of the
welfare recipients in Mound Bayou, they at least had some
rights. They could walk into a government office and say something; they had a place to live, an address where mail could be
sent. The migrant workers had nothing. What I had read about,
what Chavez had told me, even what I had seen in Florida was
little preparation for what confronted me in California. It was
ghastly there, desolate; the towns in which the union was organizing were miles from anywhere and totally lawless. In the
South there was a kind of lurking menace, the expectation that
something might happen at any time. But out West it was all in
the open, an unbridled violence without disguise or pretense.
The farm owners had their own private goon squads, and the
police were basically company cops who took orders from the
growers. They knew who I was and why I was there, and they
did not welcome my presence. I was pushed around during a
demonstration in Riverside, charged with resisting arrest, and

again held in jail overnight. In Delano I was shot at. I was sitting in a room, talking with some of the workers, when suddenly the door was kicked open, I heard someone shout, "Kill that fucking New York Jew," and then a shot was fired into the room. I don't know whether the gunman intended to kill me or just issue a warning, but the incident left an indelible impression.

Chavez had become accustomed to such occurrences, and he was every bit as tough as his adversaries. He had, from the very beginning, wrapped his movement around the cross, around a homespun Christianity that appealed to his predominantly Hispanic Catholic constituency. In passionate terms, he preached nonviolence and turning the other cheek. He spoke of a Christian revolution that would show people the way and change them for the better. But if he felt he or his people were threatened, and he often did, he was capable of cracking your skull with a hammer when your head was turned.

Grim as it was, the plight of the farmworkers had failed to capture the imagination of the public. It remained an isolated movement buried amidst the clamor of antiwar demonstrations, riots in the cities, and sit-ins on college campuses. Chavez understood that if he was to truly go national, he needed an issue of some urgency, one that could be taken to heart in major cities throughout the country. He found it when he discovered that grape growers in Southern California were spraying their crops with pesticides that could be harmful to consumers. He championed a nationwide boycott of grapes, which took root first in California and then spread east. When the boycotts hit Chicago, New York, and Washington, Chavez knew he had the issue that would draw the spotlight to his cause. Picket lines formed in front of stores and supermarkets that sold California grapes, and where there were picket lines there were newspaper reporters and television cameras. In this instance, there were also arrests.

Since the stores selling the grapes had nothing to do with

the use of pesticides, protesters were charged with conducting a secondary boycott, which was prohibited by the Taft-Hartley Act. We responded by filing lawsuits all over the country, contending that this aspect of the Taft-Hartley Act infringed upon speech protected by the First Amendment. I prepared a set of boilerplate complaints, motions for restraining orders, and legal briefs that could be filed by nearly any attorney anywhere. These enabled a lawyer who was less than expert in First Amendment law to walk into court and, more often than not, secure the release of picketers who had been arrested and nullify an injunction against the boycott. It was not our aim to get the Taft-Hartley Act rewritten; we knew that wasn't possible. We were looking to buy time, to tie the cases up in court, get people back on the picket line, and keep the boycott alive. To that extent, we succeeded.

I worked with Chavez long after I returned to New York, first with the ACLU and later when I was in private practice. At the ACLU, I raised $25,000 in foundation grants to set up a legal operation in California and hired a few lawyers to work with him out there. That allowed me to retain a degree of control, while Chavez had the benefit of having experienced attorneys at his elbow. Efforts such as this broke relatively new ground for the ACLU. It had until then been concerned almost exclusively with traditional free-speech issues, steering clear of involvement in political and social causes. But the role of the Roger Baldwin Foundation, as I saw it, was to make the organization a voice for the politically oppressed, the poor, and ethnic minorities.

My colleagues and I stretched the boundaries of the ACLU as far as we could, sometimes reaching into areas that had little to do with free speech. One of the brightest stars on the ACLU staff and then with the Baldwin Foundation was Charles Morgan, a University of Alabama law school alumnus who first gained notice in the South when he condemned the bombing of a Birmingham church in which four black children were killed. Morgan's activism drew him out of the South and landed him in Washington, D.C., where he achieved a measure of national prominence. Now, working through the Baldwin Foundation, he and I, along with a small group of others, mounted something of a social crusade. We instituted a program called Operation Southern Justice, which was at least a partially successful attempt to integrate juries in the South. At Chuck's instigation, the Baldwin Foundation agreed to handle the defense of Howard Levy, an army doctor who refused to train Green Berets, insisting that teaching people to kill was a violation of the Hippocratic oath. We also came to the defense of Muhammad Ali when he was prosecuted as a draft-dodger during the Vietnam War.

One of the last cases I dealt with at the ACLU was also one of the most significant. It involved a New York City welfare recipient, John Kelly, whose payments were terminated without notice after he took part in several political demonstrations. Curiously, I had initiated the case, and won it, several years earlier when I was at the Columbia Center. Now I served as one of the counsels on the appeal before the U.S. Supreme Court, which, by a 7-to-2 margin, upheld the lower court's ruling. The decision, one of the most important of Justice William Brennan's opinions, affirmed that a person eligible for government benefits received them as a *right* rather than a *privilege* and therefore could not be denied such benefits without a "fair hearing" or due process of law.

By the time the Supreme Court handed down its decision, in March 1970, the Baldwin Foundation had about a dozen lawyers on its staff and a budget of more than two million dollars. Among the advantages of working for a not-for-profit organization in those years was that it was relatively easy to raise funds, there was never a shortage of people working for you, and there was an abundance of important cases to litigate. There were, however, disadvantages as well.

The larger the organization, the more intricate was its bureaucratic network. The Baldwin Foundation had been growing
at an alarming rate, and the ACLU was concerned that the tax-
free foundation might soon overshadow the parent organization; the tail would be wagging the dog. ACLU founder Roger
Baldwin, who had been jailed during World War I as a conscientious objector, was now in his eighties, and he did not care to
see a foundation bearing his name engaged in activities he believed were best left to other institutions. He viewed the ACLU
as basically a First Amendment organization and was insistent
on keeping it that way, and I was unable to move him from that
position. I thus became enmeshed in the bureaucratic paradox
that the larger and more effective the Baldwin Foundation became, the more difficult it was to get things done.

I realized after a while that I was not by disposition suited to
that type of operation. I was becoming increasingly deskbound,
sitting at contentious board meetings, playing the uncomfortable role of fund-raiser, working on budgets that would enable
others to try cases. I wanted once again to be able to choose my
own cases, to run at my own tempo, to be responsible to no one
but myself and my clients. I had been practicing law for ten
years now, and I decided it was time to try to build my own
practice around social and constitutional issues. I formed a
loose affiliation with two other lawyers in a firm called Romer,
Klein & Garbus. It was really less a law firm than an agreement
under which we shared office space and facilities while I received a fee for trying some of their clients' cases. I spent a good
deal of my time writing my first book, *Ready for the Defense.* As
for my practice, I was ready now to pursue the issues that interested me and decide, case by case, when and how I should earn
my fees.

Chapter 5

Late in the fall of 1969, I was in Washington for what turned out to be the biggest peace demonstration of the Vietnam era. Having just returned to private practice, I was looking forward to a period of unwinding after three or four tumultuous, often frustrating years. By the time I returned to New York, however, I had taken the first steps along a perilous route that would place me at the fringes of one of the most celebrated First Amendment cases in decades.

While in Washington, I visited with a friend of mine, Patricia Marx, and the man she was planning to marry. I had met him several times before and was somewhat puzzled by the liaison because while Patricia's political views were close to my own, he took a hawkish position with regard to the war. He had worked as a policy analyst for the Rand Corporation, a think tank whose principal client was the federal government, which I suppose helped account for his convictions. Yet, on subsequent visits, I had begun to detect a softening in his position; an edge of uncertainty had crept into his tone. As it developed, he had good reason to reexamine his stance. For the man was Daniel Ellsberg, and he had in his possession a sheaf of papers that troubled his sleep.

Ellsberg, who had recently left the Rand Corporation, told me about these documents, which later became known as the Pentagon Papers. They had altered his judgment of America's involvement in Vietnam, and he thought the public had a right to see them. But he was apprehensive about leaking them and not without cause. He asked me, as a friend and a confidant, to read the papers and assess the political effect of their being made public as well as the legal consequences that might await anyone involved in their release. The files were voluminous, filling four large cartons, and they contained hundreds of pages of highly classified documents.

Only five copies of the Pentagon Papers had ever been made. One went to President Johnson; two others to Secretary of Defense Robert McNamara and Secretary of State Dean Rusk; one was sent to Congress, where it was held under lock and key; and the fifth was at the Rand Corporation, the source of Ellsberg's copy. I was sitting on documents that members of Congress could read only if they got special clearance, went to a designated room, and signed in. I read the papers before most government officials knew they existed, then stored them under the eaves of the garage adjoining my house in Woodstock, New York.

I came to three conclusions. The first was that the papers should be released. I also thought that, given the climate of the times, there was a good chance that if Ellsberg was identified as their source, he would be prosecuted. And finally, if he was prosecuted, I believed he was at risk of being convicted of espionage. I advised Dan of the risks involved, and he said he was prepared to take his chances. He was certain that release of the documents, which plainly showed that the government had been systematically lying to the American people, would lead to the war's end.

I was less certain, and I was aware that, as Ellsberg's accomplice, I too was placing myself at considerable risk. I was just then entering private practice, was married, and had two young children. I knew that if I was caught with the papers, I faced criminal prosecution and the likelihood of disbarment. Dan was convinced that the government knew he had the papers and that he was being watched closely. His suspicions were not unfounded, for I too appeared to be under the watchful eye of federal agents. I noticed a black car parked outside my house from time to time. The driver wore a crew cut and was dressed in a fashion that was totally out of place in Woodstock. I suspected I was under FBI surveillance, and I knew that my phones were tapped. Still, despite my doubts about the effect publication of the papers might have on ending the war, I thought they should be made public. I decided to help Ellsberg press for their release.

Selected sections of the documents began flowing in and out of my garage as we offered them first to Senator William J. Fulbright of Arkansas, then to Melvin Laird, Nixon's secretary of defense, then to New York's Republican senator Charles Goodell and Democratic senator Mike Gravel of Alaska. The senators we approached had all expressed misgivings about the conduct of the war, and we were hoping that if they introduced the papers on the floor of the Senate, the congressional immunity extended to the congressmen might provide something of a shield for us as well. But none of them would touch it.

Finally, Dan took the papers to a friend of his, Neil Sheehan, a Washington correspondent for *The New York Times.* Sheehan was interested, but the *Times's* attorneys, Herbert Brownell and Louis Loeb, advised the paper not to publish. Brownell, who as attorney general of the United States had persuaded President Eisenhower not to pardon the Rosenbergs, warned that publication could result in the Justice Department's prosecuting the paper under the Espionage Act. The *Times,* however, rejected his advice and chose to proceed with publication.

The first installment appeared in the Sunday edition on June 12, 1971, nearly two years after the papers had come to Ellsberg's attention. Dan, who had not learned of the *Times's* decision to publish the papers until the day before, was at once gratified and shaken by the news. We were both concerned about what the government's reaction might be and fearful at the prospect of criminal prosecution. I drove up to a motel in Boston, where Dan had checked in under an assumed name, and we discussed the full range of possibilities. The government's initial reaction was immediate and predictable enough: It would seek a court order prohibiting further publication. There was no mention of criminal action. Dan and I were certain that the government knew the source of the leak but thought it might not feel compelled to act so long as the source remained secret. The *Times,* of course, could be trusted to shield Dan's identity. Others, we soon discovered, could not. Just four days later, Dan learned that his cover had been blown.

Sidney Zion, a former *New York Times* reporter, announced on Barry Gray's radio show that it was Ellsberg who had leaked the papers. Zion proffered the explanation that it was his duty as a newsman to make public what he knew about the case. He noted too that other reporters knew of Ellsberg's involvement and were certain to break the story if he didn't. Nevertheless, the effect was disastrous, for it forced the government's hand. With the source of the papers now public, it had little alternative but to initiate criminal proceedings against Ellsberg.

Leonard Boudin, a renowned civil-liberties attorney, was retained to represent Ellsberg, and for a brief time he also represented me. I had been subpoenaed to appear before the grand jury investigating the theft and was told I would be charged as an unindicted coconspirator. The FBI, as we suspected, knew about the set of papers hidden in Woodstock and was aware that they had been shown to members of Congress. Boudin, who later became a close friend of mine, contended that I had been acting as Ellsberg's lawyer and therefore what passed between us was protected by client-attorney privilege. The subpoena against me was ultimately dropped, but I was uncomfortably conscious of the fact that I could still be indicted and that a complete set of papers remained in my garage. I decided to move them, and one night I loaded them into my car and drove to my sister-in-law's apartment in Boston. She was a student at a college up there, and despite her fears, she crammed them into the back of a closet and kept them hidden there for the duration of the legal proceedings, which lasted more than two years.

The case against the *Times* moved through the courts quickly. District court judge Murray I. Gurfein, applying the First Amendment as it was written, ruled that the courts lacked all authority to prevent a newspaper from publishing information in its possession. The government appealed, first to the appellate court in New York and finally to the U.S. Supreme Court. In a 6-to-3 decision, the Supreme Court ruled that, despite a national-security exception to the First Amendment's ban on prior restraint, the government could not stop further publication of the Pentagon Papers.

It was a substantial though not a total victory. The majority opinion held that since publication of parts of the papers had already disclosed information sensitive to national security, an injunction at this point would be meaningless. The substance of the decision did not say that the government couldn't make a case for prior restraint, but that in this case it had failed to provide sufficient evidence of imminent harm. Justice Byron R. White's dissenting opinion, calling for treason indictments against all who were involved in the publication, remains a dangerous dictum.

Undeterred by the court's ruling, the Nixon administration continued to press criminal charges that could have sent Ellsberg to jail for the rest of his life. It pursued the case vigorously and with little regard for legal constraints. The authorities, it was later discovered, destroyed logs, tapes, records, and documents that a judge had ordered turned over to the defense. In a prelude to tactics that later would attract national attention, the office of Ellsberg's psychiatrist was burglarized and his confidential files stolen.

The case finally was dismissed after it was learned that President Nixon twice invited William Matthew Byrne, Jr., the federal judge presiding in the case against Ellsberg, to his summer house at San Clemente. There Nixon purportedly suggested that Byrne might be appointed director of the FBI if Ellsberg was convicted. When the meetings came to light, Judge Byrne, acting on his own motion, dismissed the case because of the government's misconduct in its prosecution of Ellsberg.

Government misconduct was more the norm than the exception in the early seventies. The revelations that would soon lead to the Watergate debacle had just begun bubbling to the surface in 1973 when it was learned that the federal government had embarked on an even more brutal transgression of its legal authority. In defiance of constitutional law, military equipment and personnel were being used to subdue a civilian disturbance at Wounded Knee, South Dakota.

The site of a bloody massacre in 1890, Wounded Knee had become something of a shrine to American Indians, a symbolic reminder of their oppression by the United States government. It was there that they chose to hold a demonstration protesting their mistreatment by the Bureau of Indian Affairs (BIA) and other government agencies. Several hundred Indians made the journey and occupied the town. They held a few whites hostage for two days, then allowed them to depart unharmed. On March 4, five days after the protest had begun, an Army intelligence report noted, "The Indians do not appear intent upon inflicting harm upon the legitimate residents of Wounded Knee, nor upon the federal law enforcement agents operating in the area." It concluded that "the seizure and holding of Wounded

Knee poses no threat to the Nation, to the State of South Dakota or the Pine Ridge Reservation itself."

Nevertheless, a massive, quasi-military operation was mounted. Declaring the demonstration "part of a long-range plan of the Communist Party," the government launched an attack on the tiny hamlet. For seventy-one days, agents of the FBI, BIA police, U.S. marshals, and United States Army troops disguised as civilians rained bullets upon the ninety-six Indians who had defied the order to evacuate the area. Roger Ironclad, a Vietnam veteran who took part in the protest, said, "We took more bullets in seventy-one days than I took in two years in Vietnam." When the shooting stopped, two Indians had been killed, while eighteen others and three whites were wounded.

The leaders of the American Indian Movement, Dennis Banks and Russell Means, and many of their supporters were prosecuted on charges ranging from assault on federal officers to attempted rebellion against the government. The defendants contended that the government, in violation of the Constitution, had approved the "further and continued and unceased" use of military forces to quell a "civilian disorder" that could "threaten the country." Army personnel, they said, were dressed in mufti, and armaments were camouflaged to prevent the offensive from being identified as a military operation.

I flew to Wounded Knee, and for the next month I handled as many cases as I could, most of them preliminary hearings in which charges were dropped because of improper legal procedures. The cases that were held over for trial were moved out of the state. Banks and Means, who were represented by the flamboyant defense attorney William Kunstler, were tried in St. Paul, Minnesota. I went to Lincoln, Nebraska, to try the cases of six defendants who were in the second line of leadership.

The two federal judges—Alfred J. Nichol in St. Paul and Warren Urbom in Lincoln—each made independent findings of a similar nature. They determined that the Army at Wounded

Knee had attacked a civilian population with military equipment, including sixteen armored personnel carriers, 400,000 rounds of ammunition, 100 protective vests, a Phantom jet, three helicopters, 120 sniper rifles, twenty grenade launchers, and an arsenal of other equipment. Under cross-examination, Lieutenant Colonel Volney Warner admitted having put two hundred men of the Eighty-second Airborne Division on twenty-four-hour alert and ordering in chemical-warfare officers to teach civil law-enforcement officers how to use military grenade launchers; he acknowledged that the gas grenades used were military equipment. All that manpower and matériel were arrayed against ninety-six Indians armed with no more than twenty-four rifles, most of which were incapable of reaching the Army bunkers that surrounded Wounded Knee.

Of my six cases, five were thrown out either because of technical errors in the indictments or for lack of conclusive identification. The sixth defendant was acquitted after a jury trial. The cases against Banks and Means were dismissed by an angry Judge Nichol, who said: "The fact that incidents of misconduct formed a pattern throughout the course of the trial leads me to believe that this case was not prosecuted in good faith or in the spirit of justice. The waters of justice have been polluted and dismissal, I believe, is the appropriate cure for the pollution in this case." In all, 562 men were arrested at Wounded Knee, 185 indicted, and only 16 convicted.

The siege at Wounded Knee and the trials that ensued are evidence of how tenuous First Amendment rights can be when confronted by the awesome power of governmental authority. Civil laws can have a chilling effect on the freedom of expression, but criminal sanctions, most notably those involving perceived threats to national security, are the ultimate weapons.

For that reason, a First Amendment practice is incomplete if it divorces itself entirely from the criminal-justice system.

In fact, I was doing a good deal of criminal work during the early seventies, not all of it related to First Amendment issues. I had become a partner in a law firm called Emil, Kobrin, Klein & Garbus and was building a private practice. As the firm grew, we began to diversify, in particular trying to anticipate changes in the entertainment and communications industries. I continued to be involved in political and social issues and had begun to muse upon the possibility of running for public office, specifically the office of Manhattan district attorney.

An investigation of police corruption was being conducted at that time by the Knapp Commission, and its findings indicated that it was rampant. In the past, I had represented a number of people in drug cases where the arresting officer testified that the defendant had dropped a bag of drugs on the street while being pursued. Had the cops been telling the truth each time such testimony was offered, New York would have been shrouded in a white cloud of dust from the confiscated drugs. I reviewed the transcripts from about ten cases and found that the arresting officers testified in precisely the same way, using the same terms and references, as if they were reading from a script. It was basically perjured testimony. The cops had planted the evidence and then lied about it in court. Such occurrences, I was learning, were not unusual. Police perjury was endemic; it was part of the system. Those within the system knew about it but looked the other way.

I became absorbed by the issue of police corruption and began to consider running for district attorney more seriously. I wrote a cover story for *New York* magazine entitled "The Case Against D.A. Hogan," arguing that he was not doing enough to rout out police corruption. Still, the thought of entering the political arena remained an inviting but remote prospect until

January 1974 when Frank Hogan, critically ill, resigned as Manhattan D.A. Governor Malcolm Wilson promptly named Richard Kuh, the implacable prosecutor of Lenny Bruce, to fill Hogan's term until the November elections. Given his record of convictions, his designation as Hogan's heir apparent, his extensive experience with the criminal-justice system, and his rightwing orientation, it seemed possible that Kuh could receive the Republican endorsement while at the same time holding the Democratic line as Hogan's anointed successor. Rather than risk seeing Kuh handed the office, I decided to run against him in the Democratic primary.

For a while I was the only opposition candidate. Then, as it became clear that Kuh would receive little support in Manhattan's liberal Democratic strongholds, other candidates jumped in. In no time at all the field was crammed with Democratic hopefuls. Had I known there would be so many willing contenders, I might not have entered the race, but once in I decided to make a run for it. I began making the rounds of political clubs all over Manhattan, meeting some rivals on the way in and others on the way out. It was not an altogether gratifying experience. I heard candidates take one position in a Harlem clubhouse and another before a predominantly Jewish audience in Washington Heights. I was becoming increasingly ambivalent as the campaign progressed. Finally, a late entrant in the race tilted the balance. Robert Morgenthau, a former U.S. attorney, onetime Democratic candidate for governor, and heir to the Morgenthau political legacy, announced his candidacy, and the field quickly began to shrink. Kuh, of course, remained steadfast. The race began to take shape as a three-way struggle, with Morgenthau the clear favorite.

After about three months of campaigning I met with Morgenthau, and he asked if I would consider withdrawing from the race. "You can't win the election," he told me. "You don't have the time, the staff, or the finances that Kuh and I have at our disposal, and the campaign still has four months to run. All you can accomplish by staying in is to siphon enough votes from me to get Kuh elected, and I know you don't want that."

He was right, but I had some personal reservations about the man. As a U.S. attorney, Morgenthau had relentlessly prosecuted antiwar demonstrators, particularly conscientious objectors and those who burned their draft cards. We also had our differences regarding how the D.A.'s office should be run and what measures needed to be taken to ferret out police corruption. A quiet, shy man, Morgenthau did not seem a likely choice to attack all the entrenched judicial and prosecutorial fiefdoms that had grown up under Hogan. He was basically a cautious, conservative Democrat, but I felt our differences were negotiable, while Kuh and I were ideologically at opposite poles.

I withdrew my candidacy, but I did not make my decision immediately. I recalled a line written years ago by the sage political columnist Murray Kempton. "Politics is property," he said. If Morgenthau wanted me out of the race, it followed that I had some chips to barter. We met again, and I agreed to drop out in return for Morgenthau's support of basic changes in the criminal-justice system, most notably the establishment of a civilian police-review board on which I would be a member. Morgenthau now had a clear road ahead. He defeated Kuh handily and won the general election in a landslide, but my program for reform somehow got lost in the shuffle. After the election, Morgenthau never returned any of my phone calls; the postelection meeting that had been promised never took place.

Jack Newfield, a friend and a reporter who had covered New York politics for many years, had suggested that I get any agreement in writing before making a commitment. I didn't think it was necessary, but I was dead wrong. It was the last lesson in my political education. The most enduring lesson was that I wanted no part of electoral politics or the district attorney's office. Ideologically, emotionally, by temperament and background, I was best suited for private practice.

In the years ahead, I tried many criminal cases, always at the table for the defense, most often in the interest of First Amendment rights. I soon learned firsthand what I had already known, that criminal trials growing out of social protest often add an incendiary quality to the proceedings, for more is at issue than the trial itself. The perception of a wider threat hovers in the background and raises the stakes. Such trials are often shadowed by the possibility of further violence, and rarely was that prospect closer to the surface than in 1982 when Kathy Boudin was tried for homicide.

A veteran of the sixties underground movement, Kathy Boudin was arrested on October 20, 1981, while fleeing the scene of an armed robbery of a Brink's truck at a shopping mall in Nanuet, a Rockland County suburb of New York City. During the robbery and attempted escape, a Brink's guard and two policemen were shot to death. Four of the five suspects arrested with her said they were members of the Black Liberation Army and that the $1.6 million stolen from the truck was to be used to finance their movement. Boudin, the driver of the getaway car, was unarmed and never fired a shot. Ordinarily, she would have been charged as an accomplice and faced with a brief jail term. Instead she was indicted on three counts of second-degree murder and six counts of first-degree robbery, and she confronted the possibility of spending the rest of her life in prison. But, then, Kathy Boudin was a woman with a past.

In the sixties she had been a member of the Weather Underground, an activist arm of Students for a Democratic Society. In 1969 she had jumped bail after being arrested during the "Days of Rage" demonstrations that surrounded the conspiracy trial of the Chicago Seven, who had led a street protest at the Democratic National Convention. A year later she was seen running from the rubble of a Greenwich Village townhouse in which three Weathermen were found dead following an explosion in a bomb factory in its basement. Since that time she had been living underground, her notoriety heightened by the fact that she was the daughter of Leonard Boudin, who had represented me during the Pentagon Papers incident.

Upon her arrest, Kathy, now thirty-eight years old and the mother of an infant, was taken to the Rockland County Jail. However, Rockland County district attorney Kenneth Gribetz, concerned about a lack of adequate security, had her transferred to the Metropolitan Correctional Center, a federal prison in Manhattan. There she was placed in administrative detention, a euphemism for what is more commonly known as solitary confinement. The conditions under which she was held were unusual even for a convicted killer; for a pretrial detainee who had never been convicted of a crime, they were utterly unique. Segregated from the other inmates, she was held in a lighted cell around the clock except for one hour of solitary recreation in the hall adjoining her cell. No contact visits were permitted, not even with her infant son; when visits were made, the one-year-old baby was strip-searched while the mother watched. During the first visit, she and the baby were placed at opposite ends of a table and were not permitted to come closer. Once, when the baby crawled toward her, the visit was summarily terminated. All of Kathy's meals were served in her cell. Except for brief visits with her immediate family, she was permitted to speak with no one except her attorneys. In effect, Kathy Boudin was treated as a political prisoner whose presence, even in maximum security, was seen as a threat to the community.

Not long after her arrest I received a call from Leonard Boudin asking me to take the case. Leonard was a superb constitutional lawyer but had little experience trying criminal cases.

My first priority was to get Kathy released from administrative detention. I filed an action in the U.S. District Court and, at a hearing before Judge Kevin T. Duffy, called as witnesses prison administrators who testified that Kathy's political affiliations made her a security risk and warranted her being held in solitary confinement. They raised the ludicrous though intimidating prospect that her colleagues in the Black Liberation Army might free her in a jailbreak if she were held in the general prison population. I argued that there was no evidence that Kathy posed a threat to the prison staff or other inmates or to the security of the institution; she was being punished, I contended, for expressing her views, a clear violation of her First Amendment rights. Judge Duffy agreed.

In a decision edged with rancor, he declared the defendant's constitutional rights to be at stake. "Liberty for all Americans," he said, "no matter to what philosophy they may adhere, is . . . to be enforced in a totally nondiscriminatory manner. Adherence to these principles both by individuals and by government officials cannot be avoided because of mass hysteria over the alleged revolutionary ideas of an individual nor from the craven fear of criticism from the mass media." He noted that Boudin, as a pretrial detainee, was not to be punished. "To date," he said, "she has never been convicted of any crimes. . . . The severity of this confinement has not been shown to be at all related to any institutional security need." He concluded that prison officials "have exaggerated their response to the genuine security considerations" and ordered Boudin released immediately from administrative detention.

The "mass hysteria" to which the judge alluded was in evidence from the very first day of preliminary hearings in the homicide trial. The scene outside the courthouse in New City, Rockland's county seat, resembled an armed camp. Barricades had been set up for blocks around the building. There were thirty to forty helmeted police in the streets and marksmen positioned on rooftops. Helicopters circled overhead. Pylons were placed outside the courthouse to prevent tanks or trucks from coming through in what some believed would be the inevitable attempt by the Black Liberation Army to spring Kathy from custody.

We were obliged to park three blocks from the courthouse and were ushered through the barricades each day by a police escort. It was the most terrifying experience of my life, worse than being jailed or shot at in the South, because with the number and variety of weapons at hand you knew that the slightest spark could trigger an explosion. Leonard Weinglass, who was working with me as cocounsel, had represented the Chicago Seven in a trial famous for its pyrotechnics both inside and outside the courtroom, but he felt the atmosphere in Chicago to be tame compared with what we were up against in New City.

It was clear to us that we couldn't get a fair trial in Rockland County. The cops who were killed were local residents, and we didn't want their neighbors serving on the jury. In addition, Rockland is home to many New York City police officers and firefighters, and they would make the worst possible jurors for the defense. We asked for a change of venue. I would have preferred to have the case moved to New York City, where we might get a more sophisticated jury pool to choose from, but we finally had to settle for White Plains, a Westchester suburb, which constituted something of a compromise.

Jury selection proceeded for about three months in a charged, hostile environment. The media were having a field day with the story; there were hundreds of newspaper articles, television interviews, magazine commentaries. Our basic defense was that Boudin was unarmed and was not involved in the shooting, but there was no denying her complicity in the crime; she had driven the getaway car. If convicted on all charges, she was likely to serve a life sentence, and Gribetz was prosecuting the case as if a piece of his future were staked on the outcome.

Weinglass and I decided that our most expedient course was to negotiate a plea with the D.A.'s office. We agreed to a guilty plea of second-degree murder and first-degree robbery in the shooting of the Brink's guard if the charges of killing the two police officers were dropped. The sentence we settled upon was twenty years to life, which meant that Boudin would be eligible for parole on October 20, 2001, at the age of fifty-eight. There remained, of course, the possibility that, parole being denied, she might yet spend the rest of her life in jail.

In December 1994, the last month of his term in office, we submitted a petition for clemency to Governor Mario Cuomo. He had been defeated in his bid for reelection by George Pataki, and we reasoned that whatever slim chance a plea for clemency had was best taken before Cuomo left office. He and I spoke, and while he made no commitment, the governor told me to submit the petition. But the petition was never granted.

Today Kathy Boudin remains in Bedford Hills Correctional Facility, where, described as a model prisoner, she teaches adult basic education and English as a Second Language to the other inmates. Her article "Learning in Prison" drew professional acclaim when it appeared in the *Harvard Educational Review,* and a book she coauthored with another inmate, *Breaking the Walls of Silence,* which described how prisoners can avoid contracting AIDS, was favorably reviewed when it was published in 1997.

Chapter 6

The doctrine of "national security" has long served the government well as a veiled instrument of censorship. It is an all-purpose concept that can chill free expression even when it is not invoked, for it has within it the power to intimidate. Charges of violating national security can introduce the threat of criminal sanctions and serve notice that one proceeds at no small risk.

Jeffrey Toobin received such notice in 1990 when the government tried to prevent publication of his book *Opening Arguments: A Young Lawyer's First Case—United States v. Oliver North*. Toobin, a former associate counsel on the staff of Lawrence Walsh, then independent prosecutor in the Iran-Contra investigation, had told Walsh when he resigned from his position in May 1989 that he intended to write a book giving a behind-the-scenes account of the trial of Oliver North. Walsh, formerly a federal judge, voiced no objections. Toobin signed a contract with Penguin USA, which was to publish the book under its Viking imprint. Under the terms of his nondisclosure agreement, Toobin submitted drafts of the book, chapter by chapter, to the Office of Independent Counsel and deleted passages that the OIC said contained classified material about the roles North and President Reagan played in supporting the Contras. The final, edited draft of the manuscript was delivered on March 3, 1990.

After reading it, Walsh concluded that Toobin had exceeded his mandate and that publication of the book could jeopardize the entire investigation. He also expressed indignation that a former member of his staff was ready to disclose what he deemed to be privileged information. Walsh said he objected to large but unspecified portions of the book on the grounds that they made public internal office discussions among attorneys on the case, material that should not be made available to future Iran-Contra defendants, and that they violated the secrecy of grand-jury proceedings. In addition to endangering subsequent inquiries, he said, the revelations could taint criminal convictions that had already been procured. Once again, the claim of national security was invoked.

Toobin, an aggressive young lawyer and a talented writer, was unsettled by the prospect of criminal prosecution and the possibility of losing his license to practice law. But with Penguin's support, he chose to move forward. As Penguin's attorney, I tried to get Walsh and the OIC to identify specific passages in the book that they considered objectionable, but I received no response. Instead, they embarked upon an extrajudicial campaign of threats and intimidation.

Walsh referred the manuscript to the U.S. Department of Justice for initiation of a criminal proceeding, but the Justice Department declined to take any action. The CIA, too, found no security objections and granted prompt clearance for publication. Walsh, claiming with some degree of merit that the government chose to take no action because it wanted to derail his investigation, threatened to prosecute Toobin and Penguin on his own. He warned Penguin that if it published the book, it would be acting as Toobin's "agent in the publication of illegal materials." Toobin was told that he would lose the job he then held as assistant U.S. attorney for the Eastern District of New York. The OIC sent his employer a proposed disciplinary complaint against him, charging violations of the Code of Professional Responsibility and suggesting that he be either fired or placed on administrative leave.

In response to the threats from the government, I requested clarification of the charges and contended that under the First Amendment, the government did not have the right to interfere with the book's publication. After nine months of correspondence, it seemed clear to me that it was the OIC's intent to thwart publication without seeking judicial approval of its action. It was trying to use the threat of legal action to keep the case out of the courts, no doubt hoping at the same time to force editorial changes that would make the book acceptable. Actually, Walsh's evaluation of the case was not without basis. Penguin USA was owned by Pearson, a corporation based in Great Britain, whose publishing culture was far more restrictive than ours. With no First Amendment to offer protection, British publishers traditionally deferred more readily to the government's desires for secrecy. It seemed reasonable to presume, therefore, that Pearson might balk at becoming involved in a process that could lead to the prosecution of its officers.

Given such considerations, I decided to employ a somewhat unorthodox legal strategy: We would make the first strike. On November 28, 1992, Penguin USA and Toobin filed a suit in U.S. District Court in Manhattan charging prior restraint under the First Amendment. We asked for a permanent injunction preventing Walsh and the OIC from hindering publication and a declaratory judgment that publication would not violate Toobin's confidentiality agreement.

The trial, before Judge John F. Keenan, placed me at loggerheads with Judge Walsh, a man I respected and admired and whose basic political sympathies I shared. Walsh and I were on the same side of the Iran-Contra issue. He was pressing his investigation against powerful government forces, and I had no desire to see his efforts jeopardized. It was one of those instances, not uncommon, in which I found my own beliefs to be at odds with a free-speech principle. Still, I did not believe there was anything in Toobin's book that could derail the investigation or impede the prospect of criminal prosecutions. Judge Keenan, a former Manhattan district attorney, agreed. He granted the declaratory judgment, noting that Walsh had not persuaded him that national security was involved and that the book contained no information that had not already been revealed in public congressional hearings and reports, judicial opinions, and speeches by Walsh.

"Not only has the government placed this information into the public domain," the judge said, "but the public is more informed about this particular investigation than about any in the history of our government other than, perhaps, Watergate." The judge also rejected Walsh's contention that his office had not threatened Toobin but merely refused to tell him what they would do if the book were published. He held that Toobin "ha[d] been threatened, albeit subtly." In fact, he said, the vagueness of Walsh's stance made it "more threatening for the absence of particularity."

The judge's verdict was issued on January 31. Walsh immediately filed an appeal with the U.S. Court of Appeals for the Second Circuit and requested an expedited review of Judge Keenan's decision. Penguin and I decided to inform Walsh that we were going to rush publication of the book. Walsh asked me to wait until the appellate process was complete. I declined and suggested that if he wished to delay publication, he should seek a stay of the proceedings from the lower court. Walsh knew that if he moved quickly, he could stop publication, but he was reluctant to take a chance on having a request for a stay denied. Instead, he advised me that it was my duty as a responsible American citizen to await the outcome of the appeals process. I told him my duty was to First Amendment principles and to my client. I told Penguin to proceed with its publication schedule.

The first thirty thousand copies were shipped within two weeks of the lower court's decision.

There was good reason for our moving quickly. For while the judge granted a declaratory judgment, he had denied our request for a permanent injunction. The distinction between the two is more than cosmetic. The declaratory judgment simply said that Toobin had not violated his confidentiality agreement and preventing him from publishing his book would constitute prior restraint, an infringement of his First Amendment rights. The permanent injunction would have barred future government interference with Toobin, Penguin, or publication of the book. As it stood, Walsh was left free to pursue his case and seek legal remedies through criminal or civil action against Toobin and the officers of Penguin and Pearson.

Our decision to move forward with publication before the appeal was heard did not sit well with appeals court judge Irving Kaufman. Judge Kaufman, a distinguished jurist who nearly forty years earlier had presided at the espionage trial of Julius and Ethel Rosenberg, was openly contemptuous of our action. He treated the government's claim of national security with great deference and abruptly dismissed my counterarguments on the issue. Ultimately, his decision, though it favored our side, took the form of a judicial reprimand. "When parties invoke the judicial process and secure favorable declaratory relief," he said, ". . . it is not unreasonable to expect them to postpone further their conduct until their opponent has been afforded the safeguard of appellate review." Yet, he noted, *Opening Arguments* had been published and widely circulated before this Court had an opportunity to hear arguments or pass on the merits of the appeal from the district court judgment."

He dismissed the appeal on the ground that publication of the book had rendered the issue moot. At the same time, he noted, it had denied the defense its fundamental right to appeal.

In what amounted to an indirect but firm rebuke of our tactics, Judge Kaufman added: "In deciding that this case must be dismissed for mootness, we do not express any view on the merits or the propriety of the district court's conclusions." He then vacated the judgment of the district court, chastising us in the only way he could, by expunging our lower-court decision from the record.

Nonetheless, we had achieved the victory I cared about most; the book had been published. I knew from the start that our decision to publish was likely to be viewed with disfavor by the court, but I felt our action was justified by First Amendment principles. There are few moral victories in the judicial system, and no points are awarded for close decisions. Given the opportunity to disarm the opposition before going to court, I had little choice but to seize it.

Of course Walsh was still not without recourse. If he believed that *Opening Arguments* gave away state secrets or violated the confidentiality of grand-jury proceedings, nothing prevented the OIC from taking legal action after the book was published. But I knew he wouldn't. If we were prosecuted, I would have claimed, quite correctly, that we had proceeded with publication on the basis of Judge Keenan's decision. As a practical matter, I felt certain that Walsh was reluctant to get involved in a sideshow that would have deflected attention from his investigation and been looked upon with disfavor by many of his supporters. Walsh's intent, I had thought from the start, was to suppress publication by brandishing the prospect of criminal sanctions without ever invoking them. The threat of government action by itself can be an intimidating force, and it was precisely to blunt its edge that the First Amendment was adopted.

Just a few years earlier we had all learned how extreme the consequences of free speech can be in nations that do not afford writers similar protection. In 1989 the Iranian government placed Salman Rushdie under a sentence of death, or *fatwa,* for what Muslim leaders saw as an unfavorable portrayal of Islam in his novel *The Satanic Verses,* which had been published by Penguin in Great Britain. Rushdie, an Indian-born Muslim who was living in London at the time, had won the Booker Prize, Britain's most prestigious literary award, for an earlier novel and was a Fellow of the Royal Society of Literature. *The Satanic Verses,* a rich and complex novel, had been trouble for Rushdie from the time of its first publication in London in the fall of 1988. It was banned in India following violent demonstrations by Muslims who said it offended their religion and defamed Muhammad, the founder of the Islamic faith. There were equally bloody riots in Pakistan and Bangladesh. The protests came to a boil in February when the Iranian leader, Ayatollah Khomeini, issued his death decree, ordering Muslims to kill Rushdie and the publishers of the book for having blasphemed the Islamic religion.

In the United States, Penguin was preparing to publish the book under its Viking imprint on February 22, with an initial printing of fifty thousand copies. The bomb threats had begun more than a month earlier when shipments of the book started making their way to bookstores. The first target was Viking's New York offices, which received a series of threatening calls, causing the entire building to be evacuated. Viking's employees were rushed into the January cold, many of them coatless, and left standing on Twenty-third Street for two hours while a police bomb squad searched the building. Not long after, a similar scene unfolded at 666 Fifth Avenue, where the skyscraper housing a B. Dalton bookstore was emptied onto Fifty-second Street.

With publication day less than a week away, the country's major bookselling chains—Barnes & Noble, Waldenbooks, and B. Dalton—announced they would halt sales and removed the books from their shelves. The prudence of their decision was reinforced two weeks later when two Berkeley, California, bookstores that featured the book in window displays were fire-bombed. On the same day, the offices of *The Riverdale Press,* an award-winning weekly newspaper in the Bronx, were blown up after it carried an editorial denouncing the threats and support-ing the sale of the book. In England, a Penguin bookstore was bombed and an employee's legs were blown off.

I was in Viking's offices in February, March, and April, when further bomb threats came, and hundreds of people were sent out into the streets waiting for the building to be cleared and searched. Peter Mayer, the chairman of Penguin USA, was right behind Rushdie on the ayatollah's hit list. He changed the name on the door of his apartment and issued statements anonymously, saying that Viking would continue to publish. Mayer knew he was at great risk. While Rushdie lived under-ground under heavy guard, Mayer refused any security. Each day he arrived at his office and acted as cheerleader for his em-ployees, who could little have suspected that book publishing would be so perilous an occupation.

As Viking's attorney, I met with Iranian groups here and in London, trying to get them to take the pressure off. I also met with members of the American Booksellers Association and drafted a full-page ad in *The New York Times* urging the book chains to show courage and restock the book. But their fears could not be taken lightly. It's hard to tell a bookstore employee earning five dollars an hour that he has a moral obligation to put his body on the line for the Constitution or Thomas Paine, let alone for Salman Rushdie. It may have been easy to criticize the chains that pulled the book from their shelves, but their concerns were substantial. Having already been threatened, they bore both a moral and legal responsibility to their employ-ees and to those who shopped in their stores. Eventually, they agreed to put the book back on their shelves, but the campaign of terror continued.

Penguin offices in New York and London were cordoned off and under police guard for months. Employees had to pass through a sophisticated security apparatus, exquisite in every detail, which made going to work a traumatic experience. The return trip was no easier. Workers feared being attacked on the way home and worried that bombs might be planted in their cars. Rushdie's adamant stand on the issue did not make matters easier for others, less intimately involved, who were obliged to share his risk. He believed that publishers and booksellers had a professional and moral duty to proceed as if no threats had been made, as if no bombs had been detonated, no people injured or maimed. Of course Rushdie himself was in hiding, his whereabouts unknown, his every movement overseen and guarded by British police. Meeting with him was no simple matter. I was blindfolded, forced to change cars a number of times, and permitted to see him only when it was clear that neither I nor my colleagues had any idea where he was staying.

It owed something to my naïveté regarding Iran's internal politics and the fervor of religious zealots that I continued to meet with Iranian groups hoping to solicit their aid in reaching an accommodation. One man in particular claimed to have connections in all the right places. He said he thought he could get the *fatwa* lifted if I got a statement from Viking Penguin or Rushdie that in some way would appease those who were offended. I met with him about thirty times. We traveled to London and other British cities together, and he set up meetings with people who identified themselves as government officials. He told me we were making progress and that eventually we might be able to meet with people in Iran. But as the meetings drifted to more remote locations, often in run-down hotels, I began to feel personally vulnerable and I suspected that we

were headed nowhere. Finally, I concluded that he had little or
no authority and knew no one who had real leverage in the deci-
sion-making process.

I did not fully grasp the hopelessness of my efforts until
some time later when I spent a few days with a Harvard-
educated Muslim who was a professor at Princeton University.
He was an extremely intelligent, well-spoken man and was
steeped in Western culture. We had read and appreciated the
same books and held similar views on most of the issues of the
day. I felt a closer kinship with him than with most people with
whom I shared a common background. He was concerned
about the backlash against Muslims living in the United States
and was eager to seek a resolution of the Rushdie situation with
"powerful people in Iran." He agreed that *The Satanic Verses*
must be judged as a work of literature, that characters in a novel
should not be identified too closely with the author. Then, at
the end of our conversation, in a soft, scholarly voice, he said: "I
will try to make sure that the book can be sold in the West and
that no one at Penguin will be injured." Then he added, "But of
course Rushdie must die."

I was stunned. Until that moment I had never properly
gauged the depth of the distinction between reason and belief.
A trial lawyer, by the very nature of his work, invests heavily in
the notion that thought is a process that runs on straight tracks.
If one agrees to the premises, the conclusion will follow. But belief, true belief, is a prism that scrambles the signals. The conclusion comes first; the premises are allowed to fall where they
may. As a consequence, now, nearly ten years later, the *fatwa*
still stands and Rushdie, though somewhat freer than he was, is
still often surrounded by guards when he makes a public appearance. Almost a decade after the fact, Peter Mayer does not
yet have his own name on his apartment door.

.   .   .

Over the years, the fear of imminent, random violence on the part of Iranian Muslims intensified, receiving fresh impetus in 1993 when six people were killed and scores of others injured after a bomb exploded in the underground garage of the World Trade Center. Ironically, I soon found myself representing Rushdie's enemies and supporters of the *fatwa*.

The bombing was the first strike in a conspiracy that listed among its targets New York's tunnels, bridges, and the United Nations building. It was a devastating incident that ignited our deepest fears of the unexpected and the unknown, of death and destruction that comes without warning, of foreign terrorists whose motives and tactics defy comprehension.

Just how deep resentment against the Iranians ran became apparent when I entered the World Trade Center case at its farthest margins. I was never involved in the criminal aspects of the trial, but for a brief time I represented two of the defense attorneys and their clients in an effort to lift a gag order that barred attorneys on both sides from discussing the case with the media. Though it was strictly a First Amendment issue, I was roundly condemned for interceding in behalf of the defendants. I received a number of threatening phone calls, and a few of my clients questioned our continued relationship. Nor, I discovered, was I very popular with the defendants. When they learned I had been involved in the defense of Rushdie, they refused to speak with me, and all communication between us was carried out through their lawyers.

The gag order had been issued by U.S. District Court judge Kevin Duffy, the same Judge Duffy whose ruling ten years earlier freed Kathy Boudin from solitary confinement. Angered by leaks to the press, Duffy embellished the order with a graduated series of prospective fines that were as unprecedented as the order itself. Violators would be fined two hundred dollars for a first offense, and that sum would be squared for subsequent infractions—forty thousand dollars for a second violation and sixteen million dollars for a third. "If you keep on going," Judge Duffy said, "you will pay off the national debt." Those unable to pay the fine, he added, could "work it off in the prison system at seventy cents a day." The judge said the order was designed "to insure the fairness of the trial and the ability to obtain a jury that will be fair and impartial." He indicated that the decision was equitable since it applied both to the defense and the prosecution.

The difficulty with the judge's argument was that while it is always easy to silence the defense, which at most consists of a handful of lawyers, it is impossible to muzzle the government. For it is not just the prosecutors who are involved, but the entire law-enforcement network—the police, the FBI, the hundreds of state and federal officials involved in the investigation, not to mention the state's witnesses. A gag order, therefore, favors the prosecution no matter how evenhandedly one seeks to apply it.

I had had great respect for Judge Duffy since the Boudin case, and I felt he regarded me warmly as well. I dropped in on him one day in his chambers in the federal courthouse and, as casually as I could, suggested that since the gag order was certain to be reversed, he might consider lifting it himself. He responded angrily and told me to leave his chambers. This case from its very inception was brimming with acrimony, gave every promise of growing even more heated, and had already begun to take its toll on the judge.

On behalf of two of the defense attorneys, Leonard Weinglass and Jesse Berman, and the defendants they represented, I filed what is known as a writ of mandamus with the U.S. Court of Appeals asking that the gag order be lifted. I argued that a gag order is a prior restraint, which the U.S. Supreme Court has held to be "the least tolerable and most severe restriction on free speech." The appeals court wasted no time in vacating the order, saying it was overly broad and insufficiently justified. The three-judge panel scolded Judge Duffy for invoking it without examining other, less restrictive methods of ensuring a fair trial. "There is no indication that the court explored any alternatives or considered imposing any less broad proscription," the appeals court said in a brief, six-page decision. "Indeed, the court discouraged counsel from even proffering possible alternatives."

Judge Duffy's order had been an unusual and impulsive response to a rash of leaks to newspapers from both sides in the case. His action, admirable in its purpose, was intended to stem the flow of information and opinions that he felt might prejudice a jury and interfere with the defendants' Sixth Amendment right to a fair trial. As a rule, however, gag orders are as impractical as they are unconstitutional, for there is no way to effectively enforce them. The World Trade Center case had already elicited comments from the governor of New York, the president of Egypt, and more than a few members of Congress, none of whom are bound by a gag order, not to mention the freewheeling speculation in the press.

The concern that the premature release of information might poison the well of prospective jurors, like the claim of national security, tends to be overwrought and exaggerated in proportion to the degree of public interest in a case. It is my experience that jurors who sit in criminal cases make a serious attempt to blot out their biases and decide a case only on the evidence presented in the courtroom. Perhaps more significant is the fact that potential jurors are remarkably uninformed. Even if they are acquainted with the basic elements of a highly publicized case, they rarely recall the critical details, particularly when the case is tried many months after the crime.

There are, of course, instances when jurors make up their minds how they will vote even before the evidence is heard. Attorneys try to ferret out such prospective jurors during the process of voir dire and remove those they think might be hos-

tile to their side. It is at best an inexact technique. Sometimes
we miscalculate; on many occasions we might even profit from
our failure to assess a juror's bias.

A number of years ago I was trying a criminal case in which
the defendant was a black man, and given the facts of the case, I
knew the selection of the jury would be critical. One of the
members of the jury pool was a distinguished-looking Polish
gentleman who came to court each day with a book about Polish history or a history of the Poles and Jews, which he would
read assiduously. When I questioned him under voir dire, I
learned that he was a professor of Slavic languages at Columbia
University, but there was something in his bearing that made me
uneasy. I sensed a certain detachment, perhaps even a cool disdain that might be directed at my defendant, a black man, or
me, a Jew. I felt certain that he would become a commanding
presence in the jury room. He was intelligent, he spoke with assurance, and he was likely to be far more persuasive than the
other panelists I had interviewed. I tried to disqualify him, but I
had already exercised all my peremptory challenges and could
not establish cause for his dismissal.

The trial lasted two weeks, and throughout its course I continued to sense his utter indifference to anything I said. I try to
establish a relationship with a jury, to get the members of the
panel to trust me, but each time I looked in his direction I could
sense him studying me, defiantly I thought, as if to let me know
that he was not one to be easily swayed. When the case went to
the jury, I felt that he would come down very hard against me
and my client.

The jury remained out for several days, and the rumors that
filtered from the jury room were not encouraging. I heard that
the vote was 10 to 2, and I assumed that the majority, led by the
Polish professor, needed to convert only two jurors to return a
conviction. But I was totally wrong. After four days of sometimes stormy debate, the jury returned a verdict of not guilty. I

cornered one of the jurors on the way out of the courtroom and asked him what had happened. I told him I suspected that the professor was set on conviction and had to be turned around. Quite the contrary, he told me. At one point it was 11 to 1 for conviction. The professor was the lone holdout. One by one, over four days, he converted the entire jury.

I felt compelled to dig deeper. I got the professor's phone number and called him at home. I told him I had heard what happened in the jury room and that I was astonished. "I make decisions about jurors all the time," I said, "and I had a completely different sense of your attitude toward me."

"Let's have lunch," he said.

Our discussion at lunch seemed to come straight from the Twilight Zone.

"Your name is Garbus," he said to me. "Do you know how you got your last name?"

I knew that Garbus had not been my father's real name, that it bore no relation to the original, but I knew nothing else about it.

"Your father was Polish, wasn't he?" he asked me.

"Yes," I said.

"Did he come to America through Ellis Island?" he asked.

Again I said yes.

"Do you know if he first tried to come in through Boston or some other port but was unsuccessful?"

I told him I thought that was true.

"Did he come through legally?"

I told him I didn't know.

Finally, he asked me, "Was your father a hunchback?"

"How could you know that?" I asked.

"Let me tell you what I think happened," he said. "Your father came into this country, either legally or illegally, at a time when not many Jews were being admitted. He failed once, then tried again at Ellis Island, and he was terrified. They asked him his name. It was a Polish name that they were unable to pronounce or spell. They became impatient, and somebody referred to him as *'harboos.'* In Polish *harboos* means watermelon, but it is often used as a pejorative term for a hunchback. Someone wrote it down on his admission card, and that's how your father got his name. That's how you got your name, Garbus."

"What does that have to do with what happened in the jury room?" I asked.

"Your father was a Polish immigrant," he said. "I am a Polish immigrant. From the moment the case was called and I heard your name I made up my mind that I was not going to let you lose."

PART III

In Defense of
the Offensive

Chapter 7

A First Amendment attorney makes few enemies in liberal or intellectual circles when he defends a victim of government censorship. It was, after all, precisely to tether the government's lust for control that the amendment was written. There are, however, other, subtler forms of censorship that often draw support from these very groups. Speech that offends a person or a particular group has fallen under increased scrutiny in recent years and has become perhaps the most endangered species of free expression. The popular adage that freedom of speech obliges us to defend even those whose ideas are most repugnant to us is a sentiment more easily proclaimed than followed.

When members of the American Nazi party announced their intention to march through the streets of Skokie, Illinois, in the spring of 1977, the loudest roars of protest came from some of the most liberal voices. Of course, Skokie, a suburb of Chicago, was not your average Midwest community. Its population of 70,000 included some 45,000 Jews, about 7,000 of them survivors of the Holocaust. It came as no surprise, then, that they were horrified at the specter of hundreds of jackbooted Nazis in storm-trooper uniforms marching down their quiet streets, swastikas flying, in a demonstration scheduled for the Fourth of July. The Village of Skokie, fearful that a planned counterdemonstration might ignite a riot, obtained a court in-

105

junction banning the march. What was to become a long and tedious battle, in and out of the courts, was joined when the
American Civil Liberties Union offered to represent the Nazis
on appeal.

The reaction to the ACLU's decision was more volatile than
one might have imagined. The Jewish liberal community, long
the backbone of the organization, voiced its outrage in every
available forum, from pulpit to airwaves. "Freedom of expression," said one critic, "has no meaning when it defends those
who would end those rights for others." A distinguished attorney known for his vigilant support of First Amendment rights
denounced the ACLU and said that allowing Nazis to march in
Skokie would lead to Jews being fed into American ovens.
Thousands of ACLU members resigned from the organization,
and many times that number failed to renew their membership.

In the midst of the turbulence, I received calls from the
ACLU and Chuck Morgan, now an eminent civil rights lawyer,
with whom I had worked closely on Operation Southern Justice
some years earlier. They asked me to lend my support, to meet
with Jewish and liberal groups and try to explain why the protection of all speech was in their own interest, that if the law can
be bent to silence Nazis today, it can be turned tomorrow to
keep Jews from speaking out. I spoke at synagogues and
schools, took part in television and radio debates, and soon discovered that reasoned argument was a feeble weapon in an
arena fueled by the heat of emotion. Instead of persuading or at
least soothing the opposition, my talks seemed to provoke it, in-
flaming the passions of those who saw our defense of the free-
speech rights of Nazis as an act of treason. Just how deep the
resentment ran soon became apparent.

The first call came late one night after I had spoken at a
meeting in a Long Island school. "It's people like you," the
voice said, "who were responsible for the Holocaust. People
like you allowed the concentration camps to be built and six

million Jews to be exterminated. You are the worst kind of anti-Semite, a traitor to your own people." It was just the beginning. After that the calls came more frequently, often at two or three in the morning, and they grew more vicious as the debate intensified. My life was threatened, my family was threatened. It reached the point where I told my two young daughters not to answer the telephone, for the callers were not above telling them that their father was a traitor and must be killed. After a week or two and a dozen or more such calls I changed to an unlisted phone number. The calls stopped for a while, then started again. I don't know how they got my number, but it was truly terrifying, for I realized there was no way to hide. If they wanted to, they could find me. We lived in fear for two or three months while the case played itself out, and it was a brutal awakening for me.

I had never experienced hatred that intense before, not in the South, not in California with Cesar Chavez. I was more prepared for the blind hostility of Southern racists and Wild West militiamen, even the simmering rage of a band of burned-out Nazis than for the unthinking animosity of people whose background I shared and whose convictions I thought were similar to my own.

Despite the furor, the case spun to a conclusion with less of a First Amendment bang than a constitutional whimper. The Illinois Appellate Court granted the ACLU's appeal of the injunction that would have prevented the march but split the difference and ruled that the marchers were forbidden to wear or display swastikas. Still not satisfied, the Skokie legislature passed a set of ordinances imposing criminal sanctions on certain forms of speech and assembly. Among other strictures, it prohibited any demonstration that would "incite violence, hatred, abuse, or hostility toward a person or group of persons by reason or reference to racial, ethnic, national, or religious affiliation." It was an ill-conceived law that had little chance of withstanding judicial scrutiny, no different in its essence from the short-lived statutes aimed at stopping civil rights demonstrations in the South during the sixties. The Illinois Supreme Court, the state's highest tribunal, settled the issue by ruling that the Nazis had a constitutional right to demonstrate, swastikas and all. It had little effect on the outcome. In the end, the Nazis chose to bypass Skokie while staging an orderly demonstration in a nearby town. By all accounts, it attracted more protesters than Nazis.

I was, needless to say, relieved when it was over and pleased with the result. The First Amendment, ever resilient, had escaped unscathed. The American Nazi party was exposed as an impotent cluster of timeworn fanatics. The ACLU, which lost nearly 20 percent of its membership, began a slow process of recovery. As for myself, I was at that time becoming more involved in representing authors and publishers and building a successful private practice.

I had recently entered into a new law partnership, Frankfurt, Garbus, Klein & Selz, which has grown in the past twenty years to a firm of twenty-five partners and about one hundred employees. By 1977, when the firm was founded, I had evolved a clear perception of where I wanted to concentrate my efforts and how to go about it. I understood that it can be difficult to do the things you want to do and still maintain a diverse and meaningful private practice. If you represent unpopular clients, you alienate those with more traditional views. If you become identified as a left-wing attorney, you run the risk of driving off those who lean to the right as well as those who perceive your practice as strictly political. It seemed to make sense to structure a partnership whose members ranged far enough across the spectrum to allow me to pursue the kind of issues that appealed to me while the others played to their own strengths.

Since I had chosen to invest most of my time in First Amendment work, defending clients charged with libel or invasion of privacy, I would for the most part be representing publishing, television, and movie companies, which tended to be of a liberal persuasion. Arthur Klein, who had been a partner in my previous firm, was an entertainment-contracts lawyer who wanted to represent movie studios and those in the performing arts. He enjoyed the social side of legal practice—entertaining clients, attending film openings, evenings at Elaine's—activities for which I had little taste, and so we complemented each other nicely in that regard.

Mike Frankfurt and Tom Selz were both involved in the new media, which include film and the electronic world of videos and computers. Mike had several prominent clients in the entertainment field, Robert Redford among them, and Tom was a fine technical corporation lawyer, so our respective skills and interests blended well. We succeeded in crafting a multifaceted firm capable of handling assignments as varied as estates, litigation, and corporate work. While my partners did not always share my political views, they were broad-minded enough not to be too troubled by some of the causes I represented and the unfavorable publicity I sometimes attracted.

The Skokie incident, coming as it did in our first year of practice, tested, perhaps even strained, their allegiance. They questioned the wisdom of my defending the Nazis, concerned that it might damage the reputation of the firm before it had quite gotten off the ground. It did not help, of course, that we received no fee for this activity, which dragged on for months, occupied a good bit of my time, and seemed to offer little but the promise of angry clients and a future spent in defense of dubious causes. Like many of my other friends and associates, they agreed with the principle at issue but could not comprehend the fervor I mustered in defense of a group I despised. They knew that members of my family were victims of the Holocaust and could not fathom how I could rush to defend a group of Nazis who would like nothing better than to resurrect the concentration camps and rebuild the gas chambers. But while I felt nothing but the most intense hatred for the neo-Nazis, I was able to sit in the same room with them and not lose my composure. It was as if I were dealing with aliens from another planet. There was no juncture at which our thoughts met, no common ground we shared. The distance between us was so vast that all efforts to communicate were like trying to come to terms with a phenomenon beyond all reason and understanding.

Some years before the Skokie incident, in 1973, I had tried reasoning with a distinguished Stanford University professor who preached that blacks had smaller brains than whites and were therefore intellectually inferior. The professor, William B. Shockley, had gained international prominence in 1956 when he was awarded the Nobel Prize in physics for his part in inventing the junction transmitter, more commonly known as the transistor. He was hailed at the time as this century's greatest electronics pioneer. Unfortunately, it was not that distinction for which he would best be remembered.

In the late sixties, with little warning and no apparent qualifications, Professor Shockley insinuated himself into the field of genetics. With the same tenacity that drove him past the threshold of discovery in electronics, he pursued the theory that the poor, especially blacks, inherit a genetic inferiority that cannot be overcome. He insisted that the intelligence of blacks rises with the proportion of white blood in their ancestry and advocated that those with subpar I.Q.'s be paid to accept sterilization. Enamored of his theory and eager to spread the gospel, Shockley took to the lecture circuit at college campuses around the country. Of course, his message always preceded him, and most of those who attended the lectures came not to hear him but to shout him down.

When Shockley was invited to speak at Staten Island Community College in 1973, cries of protest resounded through the corridors of academe. A conference on racism was held at New

York University, an institution long celebrated as a bastion of liberalism. Attended by some seven hundred professors and students from around the country, the conference produced the Resolution Against Racism, urging "professional organizations and societies, academic departments, and editors of scholarly journals to condemn and refuse to disseminate racist research," declaring that the ideology of racism cannot be "legitimately called 'controversial' and open to debate."

A group of faculty members and students from Staten Island Community College issued a rejoinder that stated the case for an open forum as convincingly as one could have it. It concluded: "We believe that any community that silences one person for what he thinks is not a safe community for any of us. The real danger of Shockley is not that he will persuade an audience to act but that some bureaucrat somewhere will encounter his ideas and assume that they must be correct because they have not been refuted. Hence we cannot afford to be silent, nor can we afford to silence Shockley. The First Amendment is so essential that its protection must be given to all—even to William Shockley."

Nevertheless, the college's first impulse was to withdraw its invitation. I interceded in Shockley's behalf and welcomed the opportunity to meet with the professor and discuss his views. He was a tall, lean, soft-spoken man, articulate and nimble of thought, with a penetrating intelligence and ease of manner that made even the most absurd of his views sound coherent as he expressed them. He wasn't ranting or frothing at the mouth, he wasn't shouting slogans or echoing the incantations of a madman. He was a scientist, a Nobel laureate no less, and he laid out his argument with a thoughtful precision, carefully documenting the results of his studies. And it was precisely his unbending assurance that I found most disturbing. He had this extraordinary faith in a truth that he felt was grounded in logic. Not only was he certain of the correctness of his position, he was equally certain that he could convert to his cause anyone sufficiently intelligent and open-minded enough to listen. As I spoke to Shockley, I recalled the words of the writer Ford Madox Ford, who said he was prepared to believe most anything but not a word of science.

I believed that people like Shockley were far more dangerous to a free society than a claque of uniformed, flag-waving Nazis who bore the stigma of the past and whose transparent rhetoric could appeal only to those already in the fold. Shockley, after all, came with credentials. He taught at one of the most prestigious universities in the country; he was a recipient of the world's most coveted prize. If people like him were not to be taken seriously, whose lead would we follow? By the same token, if Shockley could be deprived of a platform at a public college, where would we finally draw the line?

In the end, he was granted his platform but was not allowed to deliver his message. He was shouted down by a group of predominantly white students and faculty members who made it impossible for him to be heard. Similar receptions awaited him as he made his way from campus to campus across the country. In a curious fashion, Shockley had been packaged as a balm for the liberal conscience. One could display, at the same time, a tolerant goodwill by inviting him to speak and a righteous indignation by drowning out his message. Professor William B. Shockley, electronics genius and academic racist, had become perhaps the first victim of political correctness.

Like many another stultifying movement, political correctness emerged from a well of good intentions. Its aim was to protect sensitive feelings by cleansing the language of terms likely to offend on the basis of such characteristics as race, ethnic background, or gender. Devising a mechanism to afford such protection, however, is always a dangerous business. Every twist that tightens the constraints on what is permissible invariably leads to another, and it is often the most zealous advocates who get to define the limits. The point of crisis is reached when efforts are made to chisel into law what was intended only as a guide to good taste. Such attempts end, more often than not, in an assault on the First Amendment.

The most vigorous campaign to entwine offensive speech in the trappings of the law has been waged by the far right of the feminist movement. That is not surprising, since its chief advocate, Catharine MacKinnon, is a professor of law at the University of Michigan. I first met MacKinnon about ten years ago at a meeting in my office with the porn-movie star Linda Lovelace and Lyle Stuart, a book publisher. Lovelace, known best for her featured role in the film *Deep Throat,* had written a book published by Stuart describing the manner in which she had been exploited and fitted for her role as the movie queen of pornography. Now a wife and mother, she was eager to shed her film reputation and, with MacKinnon as mentor, was looking to sue the men who had abused her before, during, and after the film. For nearly two hours I listened to her tale of woe, and while some of her story was convincing, I found it difficult to believe that she was not an eager and willing participant in the events that shaped her career.

It was, however, the intervention of MacKinnon that led me to turn the case down. Lovelace couldn't complete a sentence without MacKinnon jumping in to orchestrate her narrative. She was not clarifying so much as lecturing, packaging Lovelace's story in a litany of feminist jargon. Worse yet, I thought her legal analysis of the issue was utterly preposterous for a law professor at a distinguished university.

The heart of her argument, advanced with great passion by her coadvocate, the feminist writer Andrea Dworkin, was that pornography, in its essence, not only exploits and demeans women but causes real injury and thus violates their human rights. No novice when it came to the application of the law, MacKinnon was careful not to call for criminal sanctions against the distribution of pornographic material, which inevitably would bring charges of prior restraint and censorship. Instead, she and Dworkin tried to skirt the First Amendment entirely. Taking their cue from the civil rights movement, they argued that pornography was a violation of women's civil rights, since, based on sex alone, it denied them equal opportunities in such areas as employment, education, and use of public accommodations. Therefore, the argument went, women, whether directly abused or not, should be permitted to sue pornographers for damages in civil court.

It was a clever bit of legal maneuvering but entirely without substance. For while few would deny that women often were discriminated against in a male-dominated culture, there was no reason to believe that pornography was the cause, rather than a result, of such attitudes. In fact, no independent study—including one by President Reagan's attorney general, Edwin Meese, and another by his surgeon general, C. Everett Koop—ever found conclusive evidence that exposure to pornographic material led to actions that abused or oppressed women.

Even if a causal relationship had been established, the MacKinnonites had no case, for the "civil rights" they sought were based on the legally specious concept of group libel. The U.S. Supreme Court has ruled consistently that an individual member of a group cannot claim damages on the basis of remarks made about the group as a whole. That is, if a disparaging statement is made about blacks as a race, an individual black cannot file suit unless he was specifically named in the statement.

The MacKinnonites were not unaware of the free-speech implications raised by their campaign. MacKinnon lightly dismissed those who opposed her initiatives as "First Amendment wimps." A spokesman for the National Organization for

Women addressed the subject more directly, suggesting the use of a balancing test: "It is a civil rights issue," she said, "when a group of citizens are being degraded. This is an issue where civil rights should supersede First Amendment rights." The remark was a candid admission that the advocates of the MacKinnon/Dworkin doctrine were ready to sacrifice a slice of the First Amendment at the altar of a higher good.

All the same, MacKinnon succeeded in carving her theory into law in several cities in the United States and in Canada. The first such statute was passed in Indianapolis in 1984. In passing the law, the Indianapolis City Council maintained that pornography "discriminates against women by exploiting and degrading them, thereby restricting their full exercise of citizenship and participation in public life." Pornography was defined as "the graphic sexually explicit subordination of women, whether in pictures or words." What the ordinance meant was that if a woman was sexually assaulted and claimed that her attacker had been incited by reading "sexually explicit" material, she could sue the author of the book, the publisher, and even the bookstore owners who sold it.

Fortunately, the MacKinnon doctrine proved both short-lived and ineffective wherever it was adopted or proposed. In Indianapolis the courts declared it unconstitutional; in Minneapolis the mayor vetoed it; in Cambridge, Massachusetts, it was rejected by voters in a referendum. In Canada, which does not have a First Amendment, the law was interpreted so narrowly that it didn't apply to much of the material it was intended to suppress. Despite their repeated failures, MacKinnon and Dworkin persisted in their efforts to enact laws that would invoke civil sanctions against pornography. They thus alienated their segment of the feminist movement from its natural base of support on the left and created an improbable alliance with right-wing moralists whose only sympathy with the cause of women's rights was its appetite for censorship.

It is one of the ironies of political correctness and its assault on open speech that elements of the left and right appear to have switched positions on the issue. The traditionally liberal supporters of First Amendment rights have adopted what some have called a left-wing fundamentalism, zealous in their efforts to purge the language of terms that might offend. By contrast, the hard-line moralists of the right, never squeamish in their impulse to trim the First Amendment to the temper of the times, have taken a laissez-faire attitude toward the use of emotionally charged speech. Nowhere has the switch been more apparent than on college campuses, where restrictive speech codes have been adopted, most often at institutions of liberal persuasion. Among the first to put them into practice were the University of Michigan, Stanford, and a number of Ivy League schools, including Brown University, where my daughter Elizabeth was a student.

Brown's code attracted public attention in 1992 when more than 250 students were arrested in a campus demonstration protesting the university's decision to cut back its program of financial aid to minority students. The students took over the administration building, held it for a day, and then were ushered out by Providence police amidst a crescendo of cheers from hundreds of supporters. The student body, however, was not of one mind on the matter. A sizable contingent expressed their disfavor by jeering at the demonstrators; some hurled epithets; a few made their feelings known late that night by shouting "nigger lovers" outside the dorms of protesters. The students in custody faced a variety of misdemeanor charges. Their opponents, those who shouted "nigger lovers," were threatened with disciplinary action by the university.

The following day, my daughter, who had taken part in the occupation of the administration building but was not one of those arrested, called and asked if I could intervene in the students' behalf. I flew up to Providence, into an atmosphere reminiscent of the turbulence on college campuses during the civil rights and antiwar movements of the sixties. I wound up in the paradoxical position of representing the students who shouted "nigger lovers" while at the same time defending the position of those who opposed them. I met successively with leaders of both student groups; Vartan Gregorian, president of Brown; the university's attorneys; and the prosecuting attorneys in Providence. The student activists were indignant. They felt they had responded to a moral imperative and were reluctant to back down; at the same time, they were frightened at what might lie ahead. These youngsters were, for the most part, children of privilege who now saw themselves faced with the prospects of criminal proceedings and immediate expulsion. Their parents, products of the sixties, were divided on the issue. Some defended their offspring's action as an expression of free speech; others threatened to withdraw their financial support if their children did not act in a more compliant manner.

Gregorian, who was new at Brown, was outraged. He believed that a private university should be allowed to employ whatever disciplinary sanctions it deemed necessary, including taking criminal action. I spent a good part of the next three weeks shuttling back and forth to Providence, acting as both arbitrator and defense attorney. I told the students that while I supported their right to protest and the need for minority funding, I also appreciated the practicality of the matter. Brown was indeed strapped for funds, and Gregorian felt that much needed capital improvements and the addition of new courses would have to be sacrificed if too many minority students were given scholarships.

The students appeared ready to compromise in the face of financial reality, but Gregorian remained adamant in his position. Insisting he was a confirmed supporter of aid to minority students, he was offended by the students' action. "I have said time and again that I do not require throngs of people to convince me," he said. "The issue is not whether need-blind [financial aid] is good; the issue is how do we do it." I told Gregorian that he had acted too quickly, that if he had not called the police, the students would have been out of the building by nightfall. But the attention of the media made it difficult for him to step back. We agreed to adjourn the court proceedings until the issue faded from public view.

Finally, as the heat subsided and the debate grew less strident, he became more conciliatory. Most of the criminal charges that had been filed against the students were dropped, and a settlement was reached. The students signed a statement acknowledging guilt, expressing remorse, and requesting that they be placed on probation for two semesters. As for the students who shouted "nigger lovers," only one was positively identified, and although he was disciplined, his school life went on uninterrupted. However, his case, though less dramatic than that of the demonstrators, raised issues that in many ways were more elusive and divided opinion along harder lines. Most immediately, it put my daughter and me on opposite sides of the firing line.

Liz was in full sympathy with the protesters, and only a glitch in her schedule kept her from being arrested. But she felt that the students who shouted "nigger lovers" should be dealt with harshly and was upset at my defending them. It was her view that black kids who had been subjected to racism all their lives were entitled to a protective atmosphere when they attended college. She also believed that since Brown was a private institution, it should be free to set its own rules and regulations with regard to speech.

I asked if she thought it fair that students who could afford to go to private colleges should be protected from racist speech while those who attended city or state schools were left without recourse. I also questioned the wisdom of creating an artificial environment for students who, upon graduation, would be obliged to confront the realities of a more hostile world. Her position softened a bit, particularly with respect to the distinction between private and public institutions, but for the most part she held her ground. She thought I was mouthing old-line liberal ideology that hadn't worked in the past, wasn't working now, and wouldn't work in the future. It was a dispute that reflected fairly typical generational differences, but it also raised a free-speech issue that cuts across ideological lines—the use of what is called "fighting words."

The term derives from a 1942 Supreme Court ruling that inflammatory references to race, ethnic background, sex, sexual orientation, or disability were not protected by the First Amendment. The decision has fallen into disuse by the courts but is being invoked with increasing regularity in the workplace and on college campuses around the country. The impulse to punish the use of offensive terms has often stifled expression, deadened the language with awkward euphemisms, and in some instances taken us to the brink of absurdity, where people refuse to utter a word even for the purpose of condemning its use.

This tendency was perhaps most evident during the latter stages of the O. J. Simpson trial in 1995 when it appeared the verdict might turn on the alleged racism of a prosecution witness, Detective Mark Fuhrman. Fuhrman had testified that he never used the epithet *nigger*, but tapes of an interview surfaced that caught him in the act. The issue, critical to the outcome of the trial, headlined the news for weeks, but reporters and commentators—even some attorneys and police officials who one might suspect were inured to the use of tough talk— declined to use the word *nigger*. They referred to it instead as the *N* word, often sounding like titillated schoolchildren indirectly summoning to use a word they had been forbidden to pronounce. Their disingenuous refusal to say the word *nigger* invested the term with a mystical power far greater than it had in ordinary usage. Here is a word, they seemed to say, so charged with emotion that its mere utterance can transform the texture of thought and action.

Decades before the advent of political correctness, Lenny Bruce understood that imposing taboos on language had the unintended consequence of mythologizing the very terms that were prohibited. Lenny, who often satirized our obsession with words considered obscene, probed the use of language with the devotion of a linguist. Occasionally, he would interrupt his act, look around the room, and ask, "Any niggers here tonight?" The question would land hard, the audience invariably responding with a stunned silence. Lenny wouldn't miss a beat. "Yeah, I see a few out there, come on, you niggers, raise your hands. How about kikes, how many kikes in the audience? Get your hands up. Spics? Micks? Wops? Let's see, I'm taking a census. Quite a few kikes; well, I'm a kike myself. Not too many niggers, some wops and micks, no spics. Hmmm, maybe I ought to *habla* a little *español* along with the Yiddish. Aright, we have kikes-niggers-micks-spics-wops." He would run the words together so they sounded like one. "Let's see, I have a poker hand here—two kikes, one nigger, and two wops. I'll take one card. Great! A full house, three kikes and two wops." Then, "Why don't you kikes go over there and introduce yourself to those niggers. You micks, say hello to the wops at the next table. That's it. Now, let's get the kikes together with the micks, the niggers with the wops . . ." He would go on that way until the repetition of the words seemed to blur their meaning and everyone in the audience was laughing. Then he would drive home his point.

"Why are you all laughing? You should be really pissed. You know why you're not offended? Because no one *meant* to offend you. Y'see, that's what is. It's not the words that are offensive, it's how you use them. The words themselves mean nothing; they're just words."

Chapter 8

I hadn't been to Mississippi since my journey to Mound Bayou in the midsixties, at the height of the civil rights movement. Now, nearly thirty years later, I found myself once again driving through the heart of America's Southland. I was embarked this time on a less turbulent mission, headed for a brief skirmish with a self-described ayatollah of the religious right who was attempting to suppress a documentary film about censorship. My return to a field of prior combat set loose a stream of memories and caused me to reflect on how much the South had changed while remaining, in many ways, essentially the same. It was not so alien to me now as it was then. I felt more comfortable with its slow, even tempo. But it still moved to rhythms that were quite its own, still seemed to thrive on the contradictory moods that defined its nature. Here folks conducted their affairs with a casual ease that banished haste and oozed good cheer; off their tongues rolled words as sure and sweet as if wrapped in honey. Yet now and then, one could sense beneath the surface the ticking of a more hostile mood, a subliminal violence that could explode on impulse without the slightest trace of warning.

Driving from the airport, across the flat roads heavy with the heat of August, I could not help but think back to the Mississippi summer of '64, to the Freedom Riders—Andrew Goodman, James Chaney, and Michael Schwerner—whose young bodies were plucked from this troubled soil, to James Meredith facing down hostile mobs as he integrated Ole Miss, to my own exploits in behalf of blacks who were arrested and beaten for no offense greater than trying to vote. This was the very same Mississippi, I knew, and yet it was marked by changes that could not escape one's notice: My route took us along a thoroughfare called Martin Luther King Boulevard, and we passed a street named for Medgar Evers. I was on my way to Tupelo, birthplace of Elvis Presley and home to the Reverend Donald E. Wildmon and his American Family Association, watchdogs of America's morality, who were bent on purging pornography from the nation's mainstream.

Wildmon, once the pastor of a small Methodist congregation in a residential section of Tupelo, had given up his practice in the late seventies and mounted an effort to bring religion to the rest of America. He formed the American Family Association (AFA), which he described as a "Christian organization promoting the biblical ethic of decency in American society," and took out after what he deemed to be the media's preoccupation with sex and violence. Threatening suits and organizing boycotts, he persuaded the Pepsi-Cola company to drop Madonna from its advertising campaign. He spearheaded a nationwide protest against *The Last Temptation of Christ,* a film based on the Nikos Kazantzakis novel. He pressured advertisers into withdrawing from *Roe v. Wade,* an NBC movie about abortion rights. He took aim at such television fluff as *Murphy Brown, Cheers, Roseanne, L.A. Law, The Simpsons,* and *Designing Women,* counting on computer-generated charts the number of times words like *damn* were uttered, calculating per show the percentage of allusions to sexual activity between unmarried partners.

His latest target heaped irony upon absurdity. He had filed suit to censor a documentary film about censorship in which he had consented to play a major role. What eventually would turn into a complex legal proceeding had begun simply enough. In October of 1990 Channel Four, a public-service television network in Britain, decided to do a documentary on censorship and the arts in the United States. The film, *Damned in the USA,* would present "the ethical arguments for and against censorship" in the arts. Filmmaker Paul Yule wrote to Wildmon requesting an interview. Wildmon wrote back asking assurance that neither "the interview nor any parts of the interview could be used for any other purpose nor sold or rented or given to any other source." He told Yule he was concerned that the interview might appear in a context other than the film, particularly in magazines such as *Playboy, Penthouse,* or *Hustler.* He did not, however, ask for any limitations on the distribution or exhibition of the film itself.

At a preliminary meeting in Tupelo on November 7, Yule described the scope of the film, explaining that it would focus on the controversy surrounding such artistic works as the homoerotic photographs of Robert Mapplethorpe and Andres Serrano's image of a crucifix immersed in urine. Wildmon raised no objection. He said his only consideration was that he be portrayed fairly. He then handed Yule a copy of the contract containing his licensing terms, and Channel Four agreed to it.

A month later, on December 3, Yule and his production crew traveled to Mississippi and began filming the interview. Yule believed he and Wildmon got along well. They addressed each other respectfully. Their attitudes were mutually amicable. Before long, they were on a first-name basis. But during a break in the filming, Wildmon presented Yule with a new document to be signed if the interview was to continue. Yule examined it and was told by Wildmon it was essentially the same as the first agreement, with the language adapted for a film interview rather than one for print. He didn't think it was necessary to send it on to London; he signed it and the interview resumed.

Wildmon told Yule on camera that he believed the film

could benefit him and his cause. "If it is a fair, balanced approach," he said, "then it could be very helpful. I'm not saying a favorable approach. I never asked any journalist to be favorable; all I've ever asked of any journalist is to report the facts: Tell my side as well as you tell the other side."

The resulting film was sixty-eight minutes long and included the interview as well as a clip from a Wildmon promotion piece for which he held the copyright. Wildmon occupied the screen for ten minutes. He made his case clearly and calmly. He explained that he and the American Family Association were waging a campaign against anti-Christian values in the arts. He called it a "struggle for the very heart and soul of civilization." Other advocates spoke for and against his side of the argument. Serrano and Mapplethorpe made brief appearances, and their controversial photos flashed quickly on the screen. While the film was clearly anticensorship, Wildmon came across as a personable man whose beliefs were genuine and deeply held.

On April 15, 1991, the film was broadcast on national television in Great Britain and received good reviews. Two days later, at Yule's request, a copy of the film was sent to Wildmon. On May 2, with Wildmon's knowledge and without objection, the film was shown at the Selfuison Film Festival in France. On May 7, not having heard from Wildmon since he sent him the film, Yule wrote, informing him that *Damned* had been sold to television companies in Spain and Sweden and confirming that Wildmon had no objection. Wildmon responded that he had none. On June 24 the American Museum of Natural History announced that *Damned* had been selected to open the Margaret Mead Film Festival. The following day, more than two months after the film had been sent to him, Wildmon wrote to Yule, stating that "because of the graphic content of *Damned in the USA,* I cannot grant my permission for the film to be shown in the United States." He contended that the second document

Yule signed required his permission before the film could be shown in the United States, and he refused to grant it.

On that basis, Wildmon filed suit against the film's producers, Yule and Jonathan Stack, claiming they had violated the agreement. He later widened the suit to include Channel Four and the British and American distributors of the film as well as any other exhibitor who showed it. He also added libel to his charges of contract violation, saying he had been quoted out of context. Although the legal complaint was framed in the language of a contract dispute, it raised larger issues, for Wildmon was clearly concerned with the display of graphically sexual photographs that he judged to be "blasphemous and obscene." He described the movie as "sickness masquerading as art."

In addition to showing the controversial photos by Mapplethorpe and Serrano, *Damned in the USA* included clips of U.S. senators Jesse Helms and Alfonse D'Amato denouncing the use of the photos in exhibits supported by grants from the National Endowment for the Arts. Wildmon acknowledged from the start that he was portrayed fairly and accurately. He maintained, however, that his appearance, juxtaposed as it was with pictures of penises, whips, and men making love, would lead his followers to believe he was promoting the distribution of such images. Or, as Benjamin W. Bull, general counsel to the AFA, put it, people "will believe he agreed to participate in a film that shows Mapplethorpe's pornography and Serrano's . . . blasphemy."

Wildmon knew that simply by bringing the suit he already had achieved a small victory. Many television and movie outlets, aware of the litigation, were reluctant to risk suit by showing the film. He was certain that Stack, Yule, and Channel Four would not be foolish enough to file suit in Mississippi and expect a local judge to rule in their favor. He was not entirely wrong.

Channel Four, which had retained me, wanted to fight the case but not in Mississippi. Looking for a more favorable venue, we tried to find an issue that would give a federal court in New York jurisdiction and allow us to move the case out of Mississippi. In New York, I felt, we could more easily invoke First Amendment issues and not be forced to try the case as a narrow contract dispute. I reasoned, too, that Bull and Wildmon might not be as familiar with federal procedures as they were with those in Mississippi and would generally find their footing less certain in New York than in Tupelo.

As luck would have it, the Human Rights Watch Film Festival was to open at New York's Lincoln Center in two weeks. Its director, Gara LaMarche, agreed to show the film if we could get a court order that would prevent him from being sued. We filed a suit in the New York federal court seeking a declaratory judgment that would give LaMarche the right to show the film and requested an expedited hearing so that the case could be resolved promptly. The suit was joined by a coalition of some twenty civil liberties and arts organizations.

As it developed, we earned a split decision. U.S. District Court judge Lawrence M. McKenna granted our motion for a hearing, forced Bull and Wildmon to come to New York to argue the merits of their case, and granted the declaratory relief that would allow the film to be shown at Lincoln Center on May 13. But he declined to move the entire case to New York or rule on its merits. He sent the case back to Mississippi, where a trial date was set for August 11.

John Willis, the London-based deputy director with Channel Four, was perplexed by the intricacies of the American legal system and uneasy about the prospect of a trial that might result in punitive judgments running into the millions of dollars. Channel Four, which was then competing not only with BBC television but with major film studios as it tried to expand into the motion-picture field, could not easily afford the expenditure of time and money it would take to try the case. I approached Bull in New York to see if we could reach a settlement. Only, he said, if the film was not shown in the United States. Willis said let's go to trial.

Damned in the USA opened the Mead Festival on September 20. Wildmon learned about it and commenced his legal action on October 14. His suit originally asked for two million dollars in damages, but the sum grew to eight million over the next few months as new defendants were added. Our countersuit was filed with the U.S. District Court in New York in April. Now, nearly two years after the agreement was signed, more than a year since its television premiere, we were in the Holiday Inn in Tupelo, Mississippi, in the blistering August heat, preparing to try the case.

The district courthouse in which the case would be tried was located in Aberdeen, thirty miles south of Tupelo and smaller by a fair measure. It was what is often referred to as a two-light town, a reference to its total number of traffic signals. I had never been to a district courthouse in a town that small, and when we checked into its only motel I had a suspicion of how Clarence Darrow might have felt when he arrived in Dayton, Tennessee, for the Scopes "monkey trial" in 1925. I was accompanied by a small entourage—two attorneys from my staff, two lawyers from London representing Channel Four, and six potential witnesses for our side—and our predominantly New York and British accents coupled with our formal style of dress rarely failed to attract the curious attention of the good citizens of Aberdeen during the two weeks we spent there.

It was not long before we were introduced to the hazards of trying to bring down a local celebrity on his home turf. The case was front-page news in the local paper, and during the course of an interview one of my associates told the reporter that we were there to show these Mississippi judges that "they can't play fast and loose" with the First Amendment. I learned that the quote made page 1 the next day when Judge Glen H. Davidson, who was to hear the case, summoned us to his office. When I walked in I saw on his wall four photographs of the judge with Jesse Helms, one with the senator's arm around him, and I could smell trouble not far down the road. Helms was, after all, shown quite often in the film, railing against gays and "other perverts" and proclaiming that AIDS was God's way of punishing homosexuals. Worse, *Damned* included a clip from Deke Weaver's short film *Don't Be a Dick,* which shows a close-up shot of a caricature of Helms drawn on the tip of a penis. I immediately thought of asking the judge to recuse himself, but even as he admonished me about speaking too freely with the press, I sensed a strain of reserve in him; he communicated, I felt, the resolve that a judge, though offended, must yet be fair. I apologized for my associate's indiscretion, and the judge accepted it without further reproof.

Before the trial got under way, we learned that the plaintiff's attorneys had missed a step that would cost them dearly: They forgot to ask for a trial by jury. I was certain that we would benefit if the case were to be tried before a judge, because I felt that a jury drawn from Wildmon's hometown would be disastrous for us. The case was, in its way, a complex one involving narrow distinctions, gradations of meaning, and it was therefore likely to turn on the fine nuance of interpretation. Twelve citizens, perhaps somewhat confused by the intricacies of the testimony, were likely to allow their identification with Wildmon to override any technical argument I might make.

Bull, by contrast, could not have been unaware that his case needed a jury and that he had a right to one if he asked for it. However, when the case was moved from state to federal court in Mississippi, he failed to file the necessary documents. He was not familiar enough with the procedures of federal practice to realize that U.S. courts required that such a request be made at the start of litigation. The day before the trial began, Bull petitioned the court for a jury, but the court ruled it was too late. It was a critical mistake on Bull's part, but he did not think it was necessarily fatal. After all, this was Mississippi, and Wildmon was one of its most distinguished citizens.

As for the judge, in whose hands the case now rested, I grew increasingly assured that we had made the right decision in not seeking his recusal. The buddy-buddy photo of him with Jesse Helms notwithstanding, he seemed to be cut from a different mold. He did not fit the stereotype of the xenophobic, Bible-pounding, right-wing conservative who would have suited Wildmon's ends. He was not the type of judge I had encountered on my last visit to Mississippi, one who would have allowed hoses to be turned on demonstrators or barred the way against blacks trying to pass through university doors. Judge Davidson seemed more a product of another aspect of Southern culture. One could easily see him as an Ole Miss fraternity alumnus, quaffing a beer or two at a pep rally before cheering on Saturday's heroes, a back-slapping, hail-fellow-well-met type whose social conservatism fell short of embracing the rigid constraints that would put the damper on another man's pleasure. I felt comfortable with Judge Davidson; he gave every sense of being committed to applying the law fairly, to ruling on each issue as he felt justice required.

I told Judge Davidson when we first met that I saw the case as a First Amendment issue clothed as a contract dispute because that was the surest way to bring it to trial. Assaults on freedom of speech often come disguised as meat-and-potatoes claims that damage has been done to one's image or reputation. This, in fact, was the substance of Bull's argument. "I'm trying to protect the value of someone's image placed on film," he told the judge. "It's only censorship when the government itself issues content restriction." It was a common enough argument but one that failed to take into account a century's worth of Supreme Court decisions that prohibited individuals or organizations from treading on rights the government was bound to protect. Calling Wildmon's action a simple contract dispute was like describing the Ayatollah Khomeini's action against Salman Rushdie as a dispute over scripture.

In structuring his case, Bull relied chiefly on the clause in the second agreement signed by Yule. It stated: "Mr. Yule and Mr. Stack agree specifically to refrain from making the interview available to any other media outlet including any portions that are not used in the television presentation. . . . In addition, Mr. Yule and Mr. Stack agree that any material obtained from this interview shall not form the basis of any other media presentation [in] England, the United States or any other country without written permission from the American Family Association."

The operative terms on which I believed the judge's decision would turn were "the interview" and "other media presentation." Wildmon contended that "the interview" was synonymous with the film as a whole and that "other media presentation" meant that the film could not be shown by any outlet other than Channel Four in Britain. I read "the interview" as referring to that portion of the film in which Wildmon was interviewed and "other media presentation" to mean that the material could not be lifted out of context and sold in another form. With respect to his copyrighted material, I contended that he did not have the right to stop his critics from making "fair use" of his image and his words.

I made these distinctions in our opening argument, asking as well whether it was reasonable to assume that a major TV network and a noted filmmaker would invest close to $300,000 in a documentary with the understanding that it could not be shown elsewhere without the consent of one of the participants. I then moved the argument onto First Amendment ground, noting that Wildmon had attempted to seize control of the film, offering to grant his permission for wider distribution only if the images he considered offensive were deleted. I also argued that the use of the film clip for which Wildmon held the copyright was protected by the doctrine of "fair use"—that since

Wildmon was a principal in a national debate it was fair to use a clip illustrating his position in that debate. In short, he was not entitled to maintain a lock on history; whatever he said could be used either for or against him.

Bull, of course, proffered his own interpretation. In a very brief opening statement, he suggested that neither I nor my clients should be believed against the word of Mississippi gentlemen. He maintained that no issues of censorship were involved and that the case was simply a matter of contract and copyright law, which turned on the question of credibility. Bull closed by saying that "with all due respect to my colleague, Mr. Garbus, . . . I think you will see that he's the best witness against his case, because his credibility won't be very strong once I think this case is over." Bull chose to call no witnesses on his own, relying solely on his reading of the clause in the agreement.

I found it interesting that Bull thought I would be the best witness for his case, because I thought the best witness for our case would be his client. As soon as Bull took his seat, I called the good reverend to the stand. It was an unorthodox maneuver, but I thought it would work to our advantage. Since Wildmon was an adverse witness, I would be able, in effect, to cross-examine him before his attorney had the opportunity to lead him gently through direct examination. I suspected that he would be unprepared to testify under oath, and I was eager to see just how surefooted he would be once the boat began to rock.

Under ordinary circumstances, Wildmon could have made an effective witness in his own behalf. Though the very image of moral rectitude, he came across as earnest and sincere. He did not thunder hell's fire and brimstone with the sentimental passion of Jim Bakker or Billy Graham. He did not ooze unctuous certainty with the glibness of Pat Robertson or other apostles of the religious right. Reverend Wildmon expressed himself calmly, quietly, in dulcet Southern tones as soothing and serene as a bedtime lullaby, his manner that of one who had rehearsed his lines well and was always in control. By calling him as the first witness, I intended to tip him off balance a degree or two.

Bull was not pleased with my decision. Rising from his chair, he proclaimed that I had no legal right to call his client as a witness. "This is embarrassing for Reverend Wildmon," he told the court. Having no legal basis for raising an objection, he staked his claim on medical grounds. He noted that Wildmon had suffered a heart attack several months earlier and was taking medication that required him to visit the "men's facility about every twenty minutes." In fact, Bull said, he was supposed to see his doctor in about an hour. He asked for and was granted a short recess to confer with the doctor. Wildmon then agreed to take the stand, and Judge Davidson offered an early lunch break to allow him to prepare to testify.

I made a conscious effort to be firm but respectful in my examination of the reverend. Basically, I wanted to elicit the salient facts from him before having them confirmed by my own witnesses. I also wanted the court to see that he was uncertain of the implications of his own agreement, that it did not say explicitly what he wanted it to say, and that, since the agreement was drawn up by his own lawyer, any ambiguity should be construed in our favor. I took him through the relevant parts of the contract phrase by phrase, clarifying the distinctions between such terms as "the interview" and "the presentation." He acknowledged telling Yule that he had been treated fairly in the film. He conceded that he never told Yule directly that the film could be shown only on Channel Four. He admitted that he knew "the interview would be public" and "could wind up anyplace in the world." Gradually, his lack of preparation began to shade the clarity of his responses. He appeared confused. "That is an area where I'm still not clear in my mind," he answered at one point. When I tried to get Wildmon to admit that the real reason for his suit was that he felt his side had lost the censorship argument in the film, Bull objected and accused me of trying to badger the witness into offering legal conclusions.

In overruling Bull's objections, Judge Davidson seized the opportunity to outline the principles governing the case in a manner that favored our side. Under Mississippi law, he explained, if the language of the contract is clear, the document speaks for itself. However, if the document is found to be ambiguous, the intent of the parties when the contract is signed becomes the court's basis for deciding the case.

Although I believed Wildmon's testimony alone would be enough to persuade the court of the contract's ambiguity, I called five more witnesses: John Willis, deputy director of programming for Channel Four; Donald Christopher and Janis Tomalin, the network's attorneys; and coproducers Yule and Stack. Each testified to their understanding of the contract's intent, emphasizing that they had never in the past ceded control of a film's content and distribution to one of the participants. Then, with Bull again protesting, I recalled Wildmon to the stand.

In his earlier testimony, Wildmon had stated that his only objection to *Damned* was its use of "pornographic" images. Now I showed him a press release issued by his office imploring the American public to watch a PBS film containing the very same photos. "By watching this film," the release said, "the taxpayers will have a better knowledge of what the debate . . . is all about." It points out that few people "have been able to actually see any of the art in question" and concludes, "We hope millions of Americans will watch this film." I asked Wildmon if he recognized the release as having been sent out by his office. He said he did. To my surprise, Bull chose not to examine his client to try to soften the weight of his testimony, which, even in the best light, could only be seen as damaging to his case.

But if Wildmon proved to be our most effective witness

while on the stand, he was even more convincing in the outtakes of the interview that the court viewed while he was being examined. There, on camera, the judge heard Wildmon tell Yule that he understood he had no right to control Yule's use of the interview in relation to the film. If he felt he had been portrayed unfairly, he said, his only recourse would be to turn him away if Yule ever requested another interview.

Four weeks after the trial ended, the judge decided the issue in our favor. He determined first that the contract was indeed ambiguous and therefore it remained for him to judge the intent of the parties based on the evidence presented in court. He also pointed to the rule that ambiguous agreements are construed more strongly against the drafter. In consideration of our First Amendment arguments, he said that an interpretation that favors the public interest should be chosen over one that does not, and he did not reject our claim that we had a fair-use right to Wildmon's copyrighted material. Finally, he concluded: "The most reasonable interpretation of this whole agreement is that 'the interview' meant the interview alone and that Wildmon did not have control over the distribution of the entire film."

Since the judge ruled in our favor on every point of law, we were startled when, citing the "irreversible effect" of the film's being released, he "invite[d] the plaintiffs to immediately move for a stay pending appeal." The plaintiffs so moved and the stay was granted, which meant that the film could not be shown until the case was decided.

The judge's action was gratuitous and sent mixed signals. On the one hand, he granted our request for declaratory relief allowing the film to be shown. He then issued an injunction barring its distribution until an appeal could be heard. It was the first time I had ever lost a decision after winning the case. It was, I think, the judge's way of ordering the baby to be cut in half. He was telling us, "As a jurist I must decide the case on the basis of the law and facts. However, I happen to live in this community and I'm not going to be the one to cut against its grain. Take it up on appeal; let the higher court shoulder the responsibility."

The appeal, expedited because of the injunction, was to be heard by the Fifth U.S. Circuit Court of Appeals in New Orleans, which is one of the great historic courts in the country. It is housed in a magnificent, turn-of-the-century building that looks the way a courthouse is supposed to look, with a brilliant white exterior and spacious, dark-paneled courtrooms, dimly lit, emitting an aura at once portentous and grave, as if to suggest that the judgments handed down here derived from a source even higher than the bench. Some of the landmark civil rights cases of the sixties were heard in that courthouse, and I was looking forward to appearing there again. It would not, however, be as soon as I had hoped.

Within two weeks of the lower court's decision, the appeals court determined that the likelihood of a successful appeal was "slim" and vacated the injunction that barred the film's distribution. Nevertheless, oral arguments on the appeal would have to be heard, and no television station or movie house would show the film while the appeal was pending.

Perhaps prematurely, civil rights organizations, including the ACLU, declared the ruling a "major First Amendment victory." Remarkably, Wildmon, who insisted from the start that the case was a contractual dispute with no First Amendment implications, claimed in his appeal that the district court had violated his own First Amendment rights by "compelling him to speak" on film.

Oral argument on the appeal was held several months later, and based upon "a reading of the district court's careful and lengthy opinion," Wildmon's appeal was denied. There was, at first, some talk about taking the case to the U.S. Supreme Court, but there clearly was no record on which to base an appeal. The case was over.

Wildmon and his forces had suffered their first defeat, and the timing of the decision was, in some respects, as significant as the ruling itself. It came just one month after elements of the Christian right, spearheaded by presidential candidate Pat Buchanan, had tried to turn the 1992 Republican National Convention into a religious crusade. Now, for a while at least, their momentum was slowed, but the movement was far from dormant.

Four years later, in the midst of another presidential campaign, the American Family Association was out in force again, waving the banner of a private morality they sought to impose on public behavior. Early in 1996, a conservative Christian forum was held in Memphis, Tennessee, not far from Tupelo, in an indoor arena whose entrance is guarded by a statue of Pharaoh Ramses II. Each session of the two-day conference was opened with a pledge that began, "I pledge allegiance to the Christian flag and to the Saviour for whose Kingdom it stands." The meeting was addressed by five candidates for the Republican presidential nomination including, again, Pat Buchanan, who told those assembled that his goal was not only to win the election "but to make this country what it used to be, God's own country." Among others who spoke in God's behalf, to no one's surprise, was the Reverend Donald E. Wildmon, who was serving as cochairman of Buchanan's campaign.

When *Damned in the USA* was finally distributed, shown on public television and in small art houses, it was preceded by a short preamble describing its odyssey through the judicial system. The introduction featured guitarist Randolph Briggs singing a satirical ode to the techniques used by Wildmon and the American Family Association to suppress the film. It ended with Briggs chanting: "The fundamentalists went, 'Sue, sue, sue, sue-sue-sue, sue, sue, sue-sue-sue' . . . And they lost."

PART IV

The Big Chill

Chapter 9

The laws of libel, whose roots are grounded firmly in the traditions of common law, have evolved in recent years into a numbing instrument of suppression. As a weapon brandished by public officials, the threat of a libel suit can be as inhibiting to free speech as government injunctions or physical threats. For the first question that emerges in such an action often has little to do with the truth of the charges; it centers instead on which party has the time, the will, and, most critically, the financial resources to pursue a case that might take years to wind its way through the labyrinth of the judicial system at a cost likely to be prohibitive to most citizens. Such considerations are rarely of concern to those who occupy seats of power and privilege. But the threat of a libel suit chimes like the bells of doom to a writer, reporter, or publisher who is obliged to weigh that unhappy prospect against the impulse to tell the truth as he sees it.

The 1980s was a watershed decade for blockbuster libel suits against the media. In nearly one hundred media libel actions won by the plaintiff, the average damage award was in excess of three million dollars. About forty such cases resulted in awards of more than a million dollars. By contrast, from 1960 to 1980, there were only three libel cases settled at the million-dollar level. But those figures tell only part of the story. Winning a libel suit can be almost as crippling as losing one. Two of the most dramatic, highly publicized cases of the eighties were won by the defendants but at great cost. General William Westmoreland lost his suit against CBS and Israeli general Ariel Sharon was unsuccessful in his claim against *Time* magazine, but each case cost the defendants well over a million dollars, not to mention staff time lost in the effort. With the threat of multimillion-dollar suits clouding the horizon, the decision to publish a story depends too often not on whether a libel suit can be won but on whether the defendants are prepared to bear the burden of defending it. The question of truth has given way to one of expedience: "Will they sue?" In the case of Peter Matthiessen, they did.

In the late seventies, Matthiessen, a well-known and highly respected writer, took it upon himself to investigate and tell the story of the 1973 siege at Wounded Knee and the case of Leonard Peltier, an American Indian convicted of murder in the shooting death of an FBI agent two years later. The author of eighteen previous books, Matthiessen came to the task with imposing credentials. He was a member of the National Institute and American Academy of Arts and Letters and was a cofounder, with George Plimpton, of *The Paris Review.* His book *The Snow Leopard,* a first-person account of his trek through the Himalayas, had recently earned him a National Book Award. Having written chiefly about the cultures of indigenous people and their environment, it was natural enough that his attention was drawn to the unique position occupied by American Indians and life on the reservations. The conviction of Peltier, on evidence many believed to be inconclusive at best, served as the trigger to an investigation that grew more intensive as the years passed. He interviewed hundreds of people, pored over thousands of pages of newspaper clips, trial transcripts, and briefs. He concluded finally that Peltier was convicted on the basis of fabricated evidence and tainted testimony. He decided to tell the story as he saw it.

The result was a scrupulously documented 628-page book called *In the Spirit of Crazy Horse,* published by Viking Penguin in 1983. It was publicized widely and rewarded with critical acclaim. While the book contained no new charges, it offered an exhaustive analysis of events leading up to the shoot-out and the prosecutions that followed. Government officials did not fare well in Matthiessen's account. He had dug deep and uncovered roots that stretched a long way back. The first of 35,000 copies of the book were fresh on bookstore shelves when Matthiessen and Viking were hit with a $24 million libel suit. The plaintiff was William J. Janklow, the governor of South Dakota.

In his suit, Janklow claimed that Matthiessen portrayed him as a rapist, a racist, a drunk, and an enemy of American Indians. These were not light charges to be levied against a governor, and it was not the first time he had heard them, but then, Wild Bill Janklow, as he was affectionately known, fit no one's idea of how a governor should look or act. Now in his second term, Janklow projected the image of the poor hometown boy who made good, the self-styled populist who did not need opinion polls to find out what the people wanted because he was of them. His office in the state capitol was no ivory tower; it was an ordinary affair, as unpretentious and workaday as the man who occupied it. And the governor himself blended nicely with his surroundings. Short, stocky, his belt tugged tightly beneath a belly that suggested he knew a good time when he saw one, the governor made his way around the state with little fanfare. He was just plain Bill to those who knew him, and his reputation as something of a high spirit in high school and college served to enrich the perception of him as a man who kept faith with his roots. Bill Janklow had the common touch, and he knew how to use it.

Janklow had launched his public career in the late sixties, right out of law school, as head of the Rosebud Sioux tribe's legal-services program. He quickly earned recognition as an excellent poverty lawyer who had come to the aid of many destitute members of the Rosebud tribe. But Janklow had a taste for greater glories, and he gave up on the practice of Indian law and, in effect, switched sides. He left the reservation, proclaimed himself an "Indian fighter," and became an assistant prosecutor for the state attorney general's office. A tough prosecutor, relentless and unsparing, he sensed that the path to higher office could be paved most smoothly with the promise of Indian scalps.

On his way to election as attorney general in 1974, he began issuing statements aimed at endearing himself to white, anti-Indian voters. "The only way to deal with the Indian problem in America," he admitted saying, "is to put a gun to the AIM [American Indian Movement] leaders' heads and pull the trigger." Such remarks, combined with the almost certain prospect of his election, stirred the Indian community to resurrect a number of accusations that had been leveled against Janklow in the past. The most serious was the charge that he had raped a fifteen-year-old Indian girl named Jancita Eagle Deer on January 14, 1967, when, as director of Rosebud's legal-services program, Janklow was serving as her legal guardian.

Jancita, a student at the Rosebud boarding school, told her principal the following morning that she had been raped by Janklow. The principal escorted the girl to the hospital, where it was determined that evidence suggested an attack had occurred. However, the FBI, after a two-day investigation, concluded that it was "impossible to determine anything." Six weeks later, they closed the case due to "insufficient evidence" and allegations that were "unfounded." Shaken and embarrassed as the story spread, Jancita fled the reservation. Her stepmother, Delphine Eagle Deer, swore she would prove that Janklow had raped her daughter. She never got the chance. Mrs. Eagle Deer died after being severely beaten, in all likelihood by BIA (Bureau of Indian Affairs) police, who left her lying unconscious in a winter field.

Seven years later, one month before the 1974 election in which Janklow would go before the voters as a candidate for attorney general, a petition to have him disbarred was filed in the Rosebud Reservation Tribal Court. Rape was not the only charge for which Janklow was called to account. The tribal court also heard testimony that he had been arrested in February 1973 for driving drunk through the Crow Creek reservation while nude from the waist down and that he had been seen riding a motorcycle through a residential area, shooting at dogs with a handgun. The critical testimony to those offenses was contained in sworn affidavits from eyewitnesses, two of them BIA policemen. There was, however, no such evidence to be offered in behalf of Jancita Eagle Deer.

The young woman, now twenty-two years old, had been located a year earlier in Des Moines, Iowa. She agreed to return to South Dakota, where she repeated her accusations in court. No other help was forthcoming. Janklow refused to answer his summons. The BIA declined to deliver the subpoenaed file. The FBI refused to cooperate in any way. Nevertheless, Rosebud tribal judge Mario Gonzalez found enough evidence to charge Janklow with "assault with attempt to commit rape, and carnal knowledge of a female under sixteen." As a white man, however, Janklow was outside the jurisdiction of tribal law. With no greater weapon at its disposal, the court disbarred him from further legal practice on the Rosebud Reservation. A month later the citizens of South Dakota elected him to the office of attorney general. Four years later they sent him to the state house.

When *In the Spirit of Crazy Horse* was published, Janklow was nearing the end of his second term as governor, and since state law barred him from running again, he cast an eye toward a seat in the U.S. Senate. What he did not need at such a time was a rehashing of charges now more than ten years old. A tra-

ditional libel suit, therefore, would not entirely suit his ends, for
he would be obliged to publicly address charges that he thought
had been laid to rest. Janklow wanted the book taken out of circulation immediately. He sought a court injunction to keep the
book from being distributed anywhere in the United States on
the grounds that it contained material that was known to be
false. He also took the unprecedented step of calling bookstore
owners in South Dakota and neighboring Minneapolis, threatening to sue them if they did not remove the book from their
shelves. Most of those who refused were named as codefen-
dants in his libel suit.

It was a maneuver doomed to failure in the courts, for it had
long been established that booksellers were not to be held
accountable for the contents of every book they stocked. But
Janklow didn't fail completely. With a $24 million libel action
against the author and publisher pending, Viking ceased printing additional copies of the book. Seven years of litigation, in
both state and federal courts, would ensue and more than $2
million would be spent defending the case before *Crazy Horse*
was put back in circulation.

It seemed natural enough that Viking would ask me to represent them. I had done a good deal of work for them in the
past, and Wounded Knee would not be virgin territory for me.
Still, there were arguments to be made against my getting the
case, and there were other defense attorneys ready to take it.
Among them was Gerry Spence, the renowned "cowboy attorney" from Wyoming, who had earned a reputation for winning
huge judgments and for the magic he could bring to bear upon
a jury. Spence had recently won a $25 million award represent-
ing the plaintiff in a libel action and was eager to prove he could
do as well working for the other side. The arguments he and
others made against my defending the case were not entirely
frivolous.

The first was that an associate of mine, Richard Kurnit, had done the libel read on the book in behalf of Viking. He had sat down with Matthiessen, checked all the facts, and told Viking that the book was libel-free. Therefore, the possibility existed that Kurnit, who would be part of the defense team, could be called as a witness by the plaintiff. Also raised was the question whether Viking and Matthiessen should be represented by the same attorney, for their interests, though clearly wedded, were not in every sense identical. If a libelous error was found, for example, Matthiessen could make the claim that Viking and its attorneys had been negligent, that he had relied on their expert judgment, which now proved faulty.

Spence was quick to raise that issue with both Matthiessen and Viking, at the same time pointing out that my previous involvement in the Wounded Knee trials suggested that I came to the case with a bias, while he could view it with a more objective eye. Even more to the point, Spence would be playing on his home field. He knew the people out there, he knew the judges, and the members of any jury in that part of the country were sure to be familiar with the legend of Gerry Spence. It was Spence's notion, therefore, that justice would best be served if the case were put in his hands or, at the very least, if he looked to Matthiessen's interests while I represented Viking. But in the end it was Matthiessen's call, and he didn't feel the need for separate counsel. While he understood the dangers of trying the case before juries that would be more sympathetic to Janklow than to him, he felt secure in his relationship with Viking and me and confident of the merits of his case.

Indeed, recent case law on libel supported his view. Since 1964 the operative decision in any libel action involving a public figure was the U.S. Supreme Court's ruling in *New York Times* v. *Sullivan*. For the first time in the nation's history, the Court had invoked First Amendment protection in a libel case, holding that public officials must bear a higher standard of proof than the average citizen in order to be awarded damages.

In addition to showing that a statement was false and harmful, Justice William Brennan wrote, a public official must also demonstrate that it was made with "actual malice" or in "reckless disregard" of the truth. Noting that "debate on public issues should be uninhibited, robust, and wide-open," the Court further held that erroneous statement is inevitable in free debate and that it must be protected if freedom of expression is to survive. As a public official, then, Janklow would be obliged to shoulder no small burden of proof.

Subsequent court decisions broadening the reach of *Sullivan* also promised to serve the defense well. In particular, an evolving First Amendment doctrine called "neutral reportage" had been advanced in 1977 by Chief Judge Irving Kaufman in the Second Circuit Court of Appeals in New York. In a case called *Edwards* v. *National Audubon Society,* Judge Kaufman ruled that the First Amendment protects the reporting of serious charges against a public figure without regard to the reporter's views of their truth. The decision had the effect of placing such reports within the scope of historical writing, and it fit our case precisely.

Matthiessen had, in fact, made no new charges against Janklow, nor had he affirmed the truth of those he reported. *Crazy Horse* was in its essence a documentary chronicle in which historical events were reviewed, commented upon, and buttressed with supporting evidence. Matthiessen was also careful to note that Janklow had disputed the charges and maintained his innocence. Of course the author had approached his subject with a point of view, which he made clear at the outset. In a twenty-two-page introduction, he expressed his sympathy for the American Indian Movement and dedicated his book to ". . . all who honor and defend those people who live in the wisdom of Indian way."

Though we felt well armed legally, we were nonetheless eager to avert a costly and protracted jury trial in South Dakota, particularly when it was the popular governor of the state who claimed to be the wounded party. We preferred, if we could, to take our chances with the trial judge. So, given the broad protection of *Sullivan* and the narrowly crafted decision in *Edwards,* we asked circuit judge Gene Paul Kean to dismiss Janklow's charges as being without legal foundation. An attorney's motion to dismiss is always more a product of wish than expectation, but much to our surprise, Judge Kean granted it, relying chiefly on our claim of neutral reportage. We knew, however, that our victory was tenuous, for Janklow immediately announced his intention to appeal, and he had appointed nearly every judge in the court that would hear the case.

In any event, there would have been little time for celebration. For while Judge Kean had been pondering his decision, we were named in an even larger libel suit, this one filed by David Price, who had been an FBI agent on the Pine Ridge Reservation during the seventies and was a key player in the events described by Matthiessen. Price was seeking $25 million in compensatory damages and an unspecified amount in punitive damages. We had hardly begun to lay our strategy for the new suit when we learned that the Supreme Court of South Dakota had in fact upheld Janklow's appeal.

Now we had to ready ourselves to wage the battle on two fronts. Janklow's case was to be reheard by Judge Kean in the state court in Sioux Falls, South Dakota. Price's suit, as it turned out, would be tried in federal court in Minneapolis. I packed my bags and headed west. A brutal winter on the Western plains would turn to spring before my return.

Flying into Sioux Falls in the dead of winter, one is filled immediately with a sense of utter desolation. The landscape, which appears to roll on forever, lies beneath a shroud of white that obliterates all detail; space appears endless while time seems compressed into a single clockless moment. The spell is broken by the appearance of the state capitol, which, also white, seems to be poking its dome through the vast expanse of an ice floe. The building is a small replica of the Washington Capitol but far more versatile, serving all three branches of government: The state legislature convenes in the main hall, while one wing houses the governor's office and another serves as the court-room for the Supreme Court of South Dakota.

In the months ahead I would become intimately familiar with the terrain around Sioux Falls and the unforgiving relent-lessness of a South Dakota winter. The state supreme court's re-versal of Judge Kean's decision had rendered no judgment on the merits of the case; it simply held that there were no legal grounds for dismissal. "This appeal is not a case of deciding whether Janklow is right or wrong . . . or whether Janklow was or was not libeled;" Judge Henderson said, "it is only to decide, in law, if his complaint states a cause of action for libel." Find-ing that a cause of action existed, the court ruled that the out-come of the case must rest upon the facts that supported it. In sum, the author's right to recount historical facts was not in dis-pute. What remained to be determined was whether he re-ported those facts accurately and fairly. Therefore, we were required to embark on a long, tedious process of discovery— interviewing witnesses, taking depositions, peeling back the cover that often separates fact from fancy.

Time is never your ally in such a quest. People forget, they disappear, their attitudes change. I spent three solid months out there, snow-blind in fields of white, finding my way across In-dian reservations in search of houses that no longer existed or were empty when I found them. The case of Jancita Eagle Deer was particularly difficult to reconstruct. Not long after she had testified before the tribal court, she had been killed when struck by an automobile on a deserted stretch of road in Nebraska. In order to establish the facts of her case I had to locate the princi-pal of her school, the doctors and nurses who had examined her, and Judge Gonzalez, who had heard her case. Gonzalez, for his part, now had a successful law practice and was not eager to delve into events that had occurred long ago.

The lives of others who had been involved had also changed with the times. Some who were deeply committed to the Indians' cause ten years earlier had since entered the mainstream. Lawyers who had represented them now had their former adversaries as clients. Many Indians who had lived in abject poverty now held government jobs with the BIA and were reluctant to jeopardize their positions. Some had moved and could no longer be located; others had died. Among those I was able to find, few welcomed my appearance. I cajoled some witnesses and persuaded others, gathering testimony that could be used as evidence when the case was reheard. At various times, I lived in a motel room in Rapid City, with Indian families on the reservations, and with local attorneys who had taken part in the original litigation.

All the while, Price's suit was never far from my mind. He had filed his claim in the South Dakota State Circuit Court in Rapid City, and our first priority was to obtain a change of venue. It was not for nothing that Price chose Rapid City as the site to make his case. Western South Dakota was where most of the events cited in the book had taken place, and it remained hostile territory for American Indians. However, Price was now a resident of Minnesota; Viking and Matthiessen were located in New York. We argued, therefore, that a state court in South Dakota lacked jurisdiction, and Judge Merton B. Tice, Jr., agreed. He ruled that Viking did not do enough business in South Dakota to establish a legal presence there and that if Price, no longer a resident of the state, had been harmed, he had not been harmed in South Dakota. Not easily dissuaded, Price then filed his suit in South Dakota's federal court, hoping to keep it within the state. We responded by filing claims seeking to move the case to New York, a jurisdiction that would be far more hospitable to the defendants and to the claims we were defending. Price's attorneys did not wish to come east, and we were equally disinclined to go west.

After three months of court arguments, negotiations, and legal maneuvering, both sides agreed to move the case one state east, to Minnesota. It satisfied Price because it was, after all, his home state. We were more than satisfied because we knew that Minneapolis, where the case would be heard, was one of the best cities in the United States in which to defend such a suit. A Minneapolis jury was likely to be more sympathetic to the plight of American Indians than to the FBI, and judges there had been traditionally skeptical of government claims. Perhaps most important, the Minnesota federal court was the source of a number of libel rulings that would prove favorable to our cause.

Although Price, like Janklow, had claimed defamation, their cases were very different. For while Janklow's charges concerned specific incidents of personal conduct, the allegations made by Price were of a broader nature and therefore less easily defined. Price contended that Matthiessen had libeled him by repeating serious accusations that amounted to little more than rumormongering while omitting more basic facts that would tend to exonerate him. These accusations, most of them growing out of the gunfight in which an Indian and two FBI agents were killed, involved FBI misconduct in the investigation of the murder of a key Indian witness and the tainted testimony of two government witnesses. Matthiessen, scrupulously precise with his documentation, noted that Price seemed always to be near center stage when such events occurred and that he would be "soiled for the rest of his days by deeds done in the belief that the end justified the means." It was upon remarks just so general in tone that Price pinned his suit, stating at the outset that he was suing in behalf of all FBI agents who were defamed by the charges.

Indeed, there could be little doubt that the FBI played a role in pressing the suit, for how else could Price have paid court costs that almost certainly exceeded a million dollars? He was represented by Roger Magnuson, a partner in Dorsey & Whitney, Minnesota's largest and most prominent law firm. Magnuson was a fundamentalist minister and a noted defender of right-wing causes, but it is not likely that he would have taken a case of this magnitude on a contingency basis simply to embellish his reputation. The FBI had as much a stake in the outcome as Price had, and it is not too far a stretch to think that the Bureau was ready to set up a fund to pay for the suit.

Whatever its degree of participation, however, the involvement of the FBI, if we could prove it, would not necessarily aid Price's case. For when it came to events at Wounded Knee, the agency had a cross to bear. Among those quoted in *Crazy Horse* was Minnesota federal court judge Alfred Nichol, who had tried the case of Russell Banks and Dennis Means in 1974. Having himself heard in that earlier trial accounts of FBI activity that Price now claimed were libelous, a visibly angry Judge Nichol expressed his disapproval in open court. "If that's the kind of arrogance that's going to exist down there in that Minneapolis office of the FBI," he said, "I can dismiss this case entirely on the ground of government misconduct, which apparently appears to be deliberate." The judge, himself a former assistant U.S. attorney for South Dakota, cited the FBI as being particularly responsible. "It's hard for me to believe," he said, "that the FBI, which I have revered for so long, has stooped so low."

As it developed, no trial was forthcoming. After four years of diligent investigation and discovery, we filed for a summary judgment on the grounds that the facts of the case did not support Price's claim of libel. Our plea was heard by U.S. District Court judge Diane E. Murphy, the first woman ever named to the federal bench in Minnesota. In her brief tenure, Judge Murphy already had earned a solid reputation on First Amendment issues. Now, armed with a massive public record detailing the charges against Price that were recounted in the book, she handed down a thirty-three-page decision, dismissing Price's claims with a point-by-point analysis that upheld the First Amendment at every turn.

Judge Murphy's ruling broke new ground, stamping the imprimatur of the federal court on an author's right to report historical events in a one-sided manner. "As is stated explicitly numerous times in the book, and as would be apparent to any reader," she wrote, "this book has a thesis and presents a one-sided view of people and events." She added that the author has the freedom to develop such a thesis, conduct research in an effort to support it, and publish it without feeling compelled to balance his account by presenting other points of view.

Noting that a large part of *Crazy Horse* was devoted to examining the actions of public officials, Judge Murphy stated that the "conduct of such agents in exerting their federal authority is a matter of legitimate public interest. Speech about government and its officers, about how well or badly they carry out their duties, lies at the very heart of the First Amendment . . . and it is this form of speech which the framers of the Bill of Rights were most anxious to protect. As criticism of government," she concluded, "the statements are entitled to the maximum protection of the First Amendment. They cannot provide the basis for a defamation action."

The decision, of course, was subject to appeal, and Price was a man not quickly discouraged. We believed we had established a persuasive case in the trial court, and Judge Murphy's opinion was unequivocal. Still, given the effect the outcome would have on the freedom of writers to address history from their own perspectives, we felt the need to strengthen our position wherever we could. We obtained an amicus curiae (friend of the court) brief signed by dozens of writers and publishers, including William Styron, Kurt Vonnegut, John Irving, Alfred

Kazin, and Susan Sontag. The case was submitted to the U.S. Court of Appeals for the Eighth Circuit in October 1988.

Now, along with a hopeful but understandably anxious Peter Matthiessen, we found ourselves awaiting the decisions of both the state trial court in South Dakota and the federal appeals court in Minnesota. Word came first from South Dakota, where Judge Kean, after four years of legal wrangling, was ready to rule on Janklow's suit for the second time. I was not optimistic. We had asked the court for a summary judgment, and I did not think a state judge would be eager to dismiss a suit filed by the governor of his state two times running. Having been rebuked once, he was not likely, I thought, to jeopardize his chance for higher appointment by risking another reversal. I was wrong.

In a display of rare courage and judicial integrity, Judge Kean granted the summary judgment and dismissed the case. Bypassing the doctrine of neutral reportage, which he had relied on in his original decision, the judge ruled that Janklow had failed the *Sullivan* test; he had not shown that the statements in question were made "with actual malice or reckless disregard for the truth." He found *Crazy Horse* to be an "accurate account" of historical statements, noting: The "evidence shows that the statements in the book concerning Janklow are not based upon a fabrication by Matthiessen. Nor are they the product of his imagination, or based wholly on anonymous sources, or allegations so inherently improbable that only a reckless person would have published them. Matthiessen has shown that some individuals believe these statements reflect actual events. . . ." Kean also addressed the charge that *Crazy Horse* was not a balanced account of what had occurred, noting that "lack of objectivity does not create a cause of action. A publisher is held liable for what it does print, not for what it does not. First Amendment privileges of expression do not hinge on the basis of objectivity." The judge thus affirmed an author's right to interpret historical events as he sees them.

Kean's decision was all we could have hoped for. Janklow, of course, felt otherwise. Clearly enraged at having his suit twice thrown out by a court in his own state, upset at being deprived of a trial by jury that he thought he could not lose, the governor declared he would appeal again and vowed to carry his case to the U.S. Supreme Court if his appeal was denied.

Price, we soon found out, also had the Supreme Court on his mind. Two months after the Janklow decision came down, the Eighth Circuit Court of Appeals in Minnesota denied Price's appeal in a ruling that was even broader than the trial court's decision. Writing for a unanimous court, Judge Gerald W. Heaney resurrected and applied the doctrine of neutral reportage. He held that an author must be free to report the charges and countercharges in a controversy involving public figures regardless of his own subjective beliefs or whether the charges are true or false. The question to be determined, then, was not whether all the allegations were true but whether the writer "believes, reasonably and in good faith, that his report accurately conveys the charges made."

Judge Heaney concluded by articulating a creative and original test balancing the rights of an injured party against First Amendment privilege. "Sometimes it is difficult to write about controversial events without getting into some controversy along the way," he said. "In this setting, we have decided that the Constitution requires more speech rather than less. Our decision is an anomaly in a time when tort analysis increasingly focuses on whether there was an injury, for in deciding this case we have searched diligently for fault and ignored certain injury. But there is a larger issue to be considered, the damage done to every American when a book is pulled from a shelf, as in this case, or when an idea is not circulated. . . .

"In its entirety, *Crazy Horse* focuses more on public institutions and social forces than it does on any public official. The sentiments it expresses are debatable. We favor letting the debate continue."

Price, as good as his word, took his case to the U.S. Supreme Court. The Court refused to hear it. Janklow, already a two-time loser, chose to press his case no further. And so, finally, one of the longest, most bitterly fought libel cases in publishing history was over. It had begun in 1983 and ended in 1990. During that time, seven separate decisions were issued by five different courts in two states. More than two million dollars was spent to defend the suits.

In the Spirit of Crazy Horse was returned to the shelves in 1990. A year later, Penguin published a paperback edition with a lengthy epilogue by Matthiessen and an afterword in which I described the court actions. Matthiessen has continued his career as a writer and naturalist. David Price, recently retired from the FBI, still lives in Minnesota. William Janklow lost his bid for the Republican nomination to the U.S. Senate in 1986. In 1994 he was reelected governor of South Dakota.

Chapter 10

Allesandro Bianchi was a world-famous Italian industrialist, one of the richest men in the world. His picture had graced the covers of both *Business Week* and *Fortune* magazines. Now, however, his empire had become a shambles. A poor investment of almost a quarter of a billion dollars had pushed Industria Bianchi, his international conglomerate, to the edge of ruin. Still, men of vast wealth are somehow immune to financial disaster; no matter how dire their straits, they seem never to be without means. Allesandro Bianchi was no exception. His resources were many, and he numbered among his assets an American mistress whose attention was much in demand by those who could afford her.

Lisa Blake was a high-priced call girl who maintained herself in fine style between occasional visits from Bianchi. She owned a lavishly furnished co-op apartment in the Olympic Tower on New York's Fifth Avenue, drove a BMW, and had a tax-free income of $75,000 a year back in the seventies, when that kind of money meant something. Her lifestyle suited her well, and she looked every bit the part. Lisa had a fresh-scrubbed look, with blond hair, bright blue eyes, and a pair of strong, well-formed legs. Nor was she without her special talents. She had a taste for the novel when it came to plying her trade, and her inventiveness could awaken even the most jaded spirit. All told, there was no finer oasis at which a man might

slake his thirst or shed his woes for a spell. So when Allesandro
flew to New York to spend a night with her, he was treated to a
sexual extravaganza that reminded him, once again, of the pleasures that lay beyond the reach of fortune. Yes, it seemed to
him, Lisa Blake was too good to be true. And, in fact, she was.

Lisa Blake and Allesandro Bianchi are characters in a novel
called *State of Grace,* a tale of financial intrigue and assassination set mainly in the Vatican. Allesandro is a central character
in the book; Lisa has only a bit part, but her presence has had a
longer reach. For she became, in effect, "the other woman" in a
precedent-setting libel suit when the author's former girlfriend,
Lisa Springer, claimed to be the thinly disguised model for the
fictional Lisa.

Springer and the author of the novel, Robert Tine, had met
in 1974 as freshmen on Columbia University's Morningside
Heights campus in Manhattan. Springer was a psychology
major at Barnard College; Tine had entered Columbia as an aspiring novelist. Throughout their college careers, they were an
item on and around campus, enjoying what appeared to be an
idyllic and lasting relationship. But in 1978 they parted ways.
Two years later Viking Press published Tine's first novel. After
reading it, Springer charged that she was instantly recognizable
as the fictional Lisa Blake and that Tine was guilty of defamation for portraying her as a prostitute. She sued him and Viking
for libel, asking $160 million in damages.

Suits alleging libel in fiction were not unusual at the time,
and the factors that determined their outcome were even more
elusive than those that governed more conventional libel actions:
How well known is the plaintiff? Are the offending statements
held to be fact or opinion? Are the charges in any way true, and
if so, can they be validated? If the charges prove to be false, were
they made intentionally and with malice? Even if the charges are
false and malicious, has the plaintiff actually been damaged by
them? When a suit alleges libel in a work of fiction, the difficulty

of resolving such questions is compounded. Since the offended party has not been named or depicted visually, the plaintiff is obliged to show that he or she is in fact the person in question. The defendant in the suit, conversely, must offer a preponderance of evidence suggesting that a reasonable reader would be able to distinguish the fictional character from the real.

As a matter of course, attorneys in my office always ask an author, particularly when vetting a first novel, if the characters are drawn from real life. If the answer is yes, we tell the author to disguise the characters as much as possible. However, Tine's book was not vetted for such similarities even though his editor knew of Lisa Springer and Tine's relationship with her.

All the same, the similarities between Springer and Blake were in the main of a physical nature. Both were small, blond, blue-eyed, with good strong legs and small, firm breasts. They also had a common educational background and shared some recreational interests. Both Lisas spoke fluent French and had graduated with honors in psychology; they had been known to go skiing in Vermont, had vacationed in the Bahamas and Switzerland, and both always wore two pieces of jewelry— a watch and a diamond on a gold chain. Their lifestyles, however, had followed sharply divergent paths. While Blake lived in luxury at one of the classiest addresses in the city and told friends she paid her way by producing television commercials, Springer occupied a modest apartment on the West Side and worked as a part-time tutor and teacher of statistics. She was not known to be acquainted with any of the world's wealthiest men, professionally or otherwise.

Still, it was Springer's contention that friends who had known both her and Tine in college might know nothing of her life after graduation and thus might assume that Blake represented what she had since become. "Since the publication of *State of Grace,*" she said, "my life has been shattered, as all my friends and acquaintances have read it. While there have been overt outpourings of sympathy, I do not know what they actually feel inside toward me. Am I a whore in their eyes?"

Springer said she had read the novel in manuscript form and had been flattered by the similarities between her and the heroine, "a well-traveled, beautiful, olive-skinned Sicilian noblewoman." The character of Lisa Blake, she said, had not yet been invented. Tine had added the ten-page chapter in which Blake appears for the first and only time, she claimed, in "a vicious attempt to avenge his bruised ego" after she ended their relationship. In fact, Springer said she first learned of the new character from a mutual friend, Hugo Cassirer, who happened to be the son of the world-famous South African novelist Nadine Gordimer. Gordimer, who had met Springer and Tine while a guest lecturer at Columbia in 1977, had received a pre-publication copy of the book. In a letter to her son, Gordimer wrote: "I have read Robbie's book and am absolutely amazed that he has put Lisa into it—under her own name!—as a psychology student who has become a high-class prostitute. What a childish revenge! . . . I wonder if L. has read it?" She had not but soon would, and her suit was not long in coming.

Representing both Tine and Viking, I was a bit uneasy about our prospects. Since the facts of a case are seldom in dispute in a libel action, judgment tends to be subjective, and juries are inclined to identify more closely with the plaintiff. The trend in recent years was nothing less than alarming. A former Miss Wyoming, Kim Pring, had won an award of $26.5 million from *Penthouse* magazine for an article recounting the fantastic sexual exploits of a fictitious Miss Wyoming. That verdict was later overturned, but the U.S. Supreme Court had let stand a California decision in which a jury awarded $75,000 to Dr. Paul Bindrim, a psychologist who ran nude encounter sessions and claimed to be libeled in *Touching,* a novel by Gwen Davis Mitchell. Mitchell had attended one of the nude group-therapy sessions and clearly had used Dr. Bindrim as the model for the psychiatrist in her novel. Nonetheless, the differences between the real and the fictional doctors—in appearance, education, and background—were vast and apparent to even the most casual reader. The California Court of Appeals had affirmed the jury's finding and, with the Supreme Court's imprimatur, *Bindrim* emerged as a chilling decision that could be used as a precedent in other states, including New York.

Of course an appellate court's review of a jury's verdict is limited by law to a consideration of the facts presented at trial. If we were to keep *Bindrim* law from being applied in the Tine-Springer case, our best chance, I thought, was to preempt a jury trial and lay the facts of our case before a trial court early in the litigation. We therefore entered a motion to dismiss and left it to the court to decide whether the author and publisher should be forced to go to trial. Unfortunately, the state supreme court found that they must.

Judge Richard Lee Price ruled that Springer had established a firm enough connection between herself and Lisa Blake to make it appear that she was the person about whom the defamatory statements were made. He concluded therefore that she should be given the opportunity to prove at trial whether the similarities between the two were merely coincidental or libelous statements "of and concerning" Springer.

In reaching his decision, however, Judge Price failed to consider whether the novel, taken as a whole, could support his conclusion. The central plot of *State of Grace,* after all, centered on the death of a fictional Pope Gregory XVII, the election of Pope Anthony I, and the plot of a group of cardinals to assassinate the new pope. Since the novel could not be read as anything but fiction, no reasonable reader could conclude that it was making a factual statement "of and concerning" a real person. The court's decision, we believed, was seriously flawed, and although the lower-level appeals court refused to reverse, the appellate division did.

By a 4-to-1 vote, the court ruled that the similarities between the real and fictional characters were superficial, while the differences were "so profound that it is virtually impossible to see how one who has read the book and who knew Lisa Springer could attribute to Springer the lifestyle of Blake." To sustain a defamation claim, the court said, the fictional and real characters must be so closely related that a reader would have no difficulty connecting the two. But the heart of the ruling was yet to come. Even such close identification, by itself, would not be sufficient, the court continued, proceeding to break new ground with a landmark, precedent-setting decision. A reasonable reader must also find it credible that the negative traits of the character could be attributed to the real person.

In the Springer case, therefore, the attribution test meant that readers who identified her with the Lisa Blake character would also have to recognize in her those aspects of behavior that were found objectionable; to wit, they had to be ready to believe that the Springer they knew could indeed be a high-priced prostitute, the mistress of an internationally renowned industrialist, and a woman whose lifestyle was steeped in the trappings of high-tone fashion and luxury. In sum, the court found that similarity alone does not equal identification and identification alone does not satisfy the "of and concerning" test for linking a real person to a fictional character.

The court added yet another obstacle that plaintiffs would have to clear in future libel-in-fiction suits. It stated that it is for the court, not a jury, to decide whether any allegedly libelous statements are "of and concerning" the plaintiff. That determination, it said, should be made, as a matter of law, at the outset of litigation. The court's decision, then, was broad and far-reaching, making it more difficult to sustain a libel claim in a fictional work than in a work of nonfiction. It protected scores of authors who drew their characters closely from real life. Springer took her claim to the court of appeals, but New York

State's highest court gave it short shrift, affirming the appellate division's ruling and dismissing the case in a brief, one-page opinion.

While the *Springer* decision did not create a new standard nationally, it redefined libel law in the publishing capital of the country. In rejecting *Bindrim,* it gave federal and state courts throughout the country a respected precedent on which to rely. The two-pronged test of identity and attribution, which became known as the Springer rule, enabled courts to dismiss unjustified claims promptly, sparing defendants the costs and risks of a jury trial. It was a ruling that made the world safer for writers of fiction, but it appeared that at least one of them was not inclined to applaud my efforts.

In an interview with David Margolick, who was reporting the Tine-Springer case for *The New York Times,* I explained that most, if not all, novelists use real people as models for their characters. "If you look at all other books of fiction," I said, "by Saul Bellow or Philip Roth or Bernard Malamud, what Tine did was modest. Every fiction writer does this. They rely on their own life experiences and build on it. They just don't totally make up people." It was an innocuous enough remark, I thought, and certainly true of those I mentioned. But Bellow took exception. He wrote me a letter insisting that the characters in his stories were entirely the product of his imagination and had no real-life sires. He said I had tarnished his reputation by implying that he was something less than a totally creative writer of fiction.

I was utterly astonished. The tone of the letter was too grave to be treated whimsically, yet too improbable to be taken at face value. Bellow, more than most writers, draws upon his personal experiences in his work. The protagonist of *Humboldt's Gift,* for example, clearly is modeled upon the poet Delmore Schwartz. I did not know what to make of the letter or how to respond. I chose to ignore it.

About three weeks later, a second letter came from Bellow, saying he would sue me for libel unless I offered an apology and asked the *Times* to print a retraction. On the heels of that came a letter from Bellow's agent to the president of Viking Penguin, which was Bellow's publisher and one of my principal clients. The agent, Harriet Wasserman, expressed surprise that Viking's attorney would try to discredit the publisher's most notable author and suggested that Bellow might have to review his relationship with Viking. It was an *Alice in Wonderland* scenario in which events kept getting "curiouser and curiouser." I refused to apologize or offer a retraction, but I did write to Bellow, elaborating on my remarks in as cordial a manner as possible, and that finally put the matter to rest.

The issue of libel in fiction, however, did not disappear so quickly.

Seven years after the *Springer* decision, a budding young novelist named Terry McMillan found herself the defendant in a similar suit. McMillan, who was later to write *Waiting to Exhale,* was on her way to literary and commercial success with her second novel, *Disappearing Acts,* when she was cited for defamation by Leonard Welch, her former lover and the father of her child, who claimed to be a thinly veiled, real-life version of Franklin Swift, the male lead in the novel.

Though in many respects his claim mirrored Springer's, there were two critical differences between them. The first was that Welch raised the possibility of financial damages in the form of lost income: Noting that both he and the fictional Swift were black construction workers, Welch claimed that an identification of the two might make it difficult for him to find work, since Swift was portrayed as a rapist, a racist, a drunk, and a swindler. The other was that a year before the suit was filed McMillan candidly acknowledged that her story of the love affair between Zora Banks, a college-educated music teacher and aspiring singer, and Swift, a high-school dropout and often un-employed construction worker, was based on her relationship with Welch.

In an interview published in the *Detroit Free Press,* McMil-lan said: "The story is autobiographical in a sense. Franklin is a composite of a number of men I know, but he sprung out of one man in particular, based on an ex of mine, with a lot of exagger-ations." She also had sent a copy of the book to Welch with the inscription: "Please read it with the same love and compassion that forced me to write it. But try to read it as fiction because I took liberties in order to make the story more plausible."

In writing the novel, McMillan endeavored to describe the relationship from dual perspectives, each of the characters hav-ing their say in alternating chapters. "I wanted to put myself in this man's shoes," she told an interviewer, "to see his side of the story. In every relationship, there are two sides to every story. When you're honest, you don't have anything to lose."

But in this case she did have something to lose, and it was no small sum. Welch asked for $4.75 million in damages. He might as easily have asked for ten times that amount, for Leonard Welch had no case. Since the suit was brought in New York State Supreme Court in Brooklyn, the *Springer* test would control, and there was virtually no chance that Welch could meet the burden of proof. Strangely enough, he and his attor-ney seemed at times to be unaware of the *Springer* decision. They based their case largely on two federal-court rulings that preceded *Springer,* apparently overlooking the fact that it was New York law that governed their action. They submitted a batch of affidavits in which people who knew Welch swore that they could *not* attribute the defamatory aspects of Swift's char-acter to Welch when such attribution was precisely what was required to establish their claim. In fact, their supporting evi-dence appeared to do more for our case than for theirs.

State supreme court judge Jules L. Spodek wasted little time in addressing the issues. Citing the court's *Springer* decision, he dismissed the suit, recognizing "the obvious and implied constitutional repercussions of a libel-in-fiction claim." The court found that, on the one hand, it is "accepted fact that writers create their fictional work based on their own experiences," so that actual persons are often "prototypes" for fictional characters. On the other hand, the court said, works of fiction carry with them a "presumption of invention," which makes it impossible for reasonable readers to assume that they are truthful biographies. In order to make such an assumption, therefore, the identity of the real and fictional persons "must be so complete that the defamatory material becomes a plausible aspect of the real life plaintiff or suggestive of the plaintiff in significant ways." Then, as if counseling those who might be inclined to trouble the court with such claims in the future, the judge advised: "[I]t must be a requirement of an action for defamation that the reader be totally convinced that the book in all its aspects as far as the plaintiff is concerned is not fiction at all."

If the prospect of identifying fictional characters with real people is freighted with legal problems, the burden is yet greater when real people inhabit works of fiction. For one must then decide whether the character in the novel is meant to actually represent the person he is named for or if the writer intended merely to create a caricature in the way a cartoonist exaggerates certain physical traits of his subject without pretending to produce an exact likeness.

Is, for example, the Norman Mailer who enjoys the feel of cold steel on his anus before being fatally shot with his pants down in a novel called *American Mischief* meant to depict the author of *The Naked and the Dead* or simply a namesake who ended up both naked and dead in Alan Lelchuk's 1972 novel? Mailer, who had read the galleys prior to publication, took exception to his being portrayed as a man who would die with his

pants down. I represented Lelchuk at a meeting in my office
that was as fittingly bizarre as the scene in Lelchuk's book.

Mailer, as indignant as one would care to see him, opened
the discussion by pounding on the conference table and shouting, "By the time this is over, Lelchuk, you ain't going to be
nothin' but a hank of hair and some fillings." Since the book, he
said, made it appear that he was a man who enjoyed homosexual pleasures, it could make him a target for those who might
take it literally. "Guys will go after me," he said. "They'll think
you know about me and that what you're saying is true. You
shouldn't do this to me, a fellow author."

Lelchuk, an assistant professor of English at Brandeis University, responded, "This is my first book, and I'm not going to
change it because of your pressure."

Mailer's lawyer, Charles Rembar, a distinguished First
Amendment attorney and author of a fine history of American
law, had raised the possibility of a suit to stop publication, but
as the discussion grew heated he seemed to take a more conciliatory posture. Calmly and clearly, he explained his client's objection. The scene, he said, "might give people who didn't know
Mailer the impression that he would submit to the worst indig-
nities out of physical fear. That is just not Norman Mailer."

Lelchuk and I brought to Mailer's attention his writings
about Fidel Castro and Jack Kennedy, Martin Luther King and
Robert Kennedy, about assassinations real and imagined, and
the dangers with which public figures are obliged to live.

"But I'm not a fucking politician," Mailer said. "I'm not
supposed to be out there. I'm a writer. You guys have made me
fair game for every nut who's out there." He then lunged across
the table, trying to grab Lelchuk by the neck, but Lelchuck
eluded his grasp.

Finally, following a brief but raucous period of warnings
and accusations, the encounter evolved into a philosophical dis-

cussion about honor, dignity, and death. At one point, Lelchuk, unyielding but obviously respectful of Mailer, told him: "Listen, you're the father of us all; you're the one who taught us to go as far as you can with literature." To his credit and true to his code, Mailer did not try to suppress the book, nor did he ask to see any revisions prior to publication. In the end, Lelchuk made some minor adjustments, the scene remained, and the book was published as scheduled several months later.

The trip was not as smooth for Robert Coover's fantasy novel *The Public Burning*. Coover, who described his book as a satirical re-creation of American history, knew from the start that he might be headed for trouble. Despite the author's high literary standing and the obvious quality of the manuscript, a number of major publishers had shied from accepting it. Their concern was the possibility, even the likelihood, of a libel suit that could come from any of a number of directions, for the novel was studded with real-life characters from the recent and long-ago past—former presidents, judges and prosecutors, political heavyweights, notables from every corner of American life—and many of them were seen acting in a manner that would do little to embellish their reputations.

The plot centered around the execution of Julius and Ethel Rosenberg, who were convicted as Soviet spies in the early fifties. In Coover's novel they are the victims of the "public burning," which takes place in New York's Times Square and is attended by a who's-who cast drawn from American history. Among those present were George Washington and Abraham Lincoln, surrounded by a supporting cast that included Judge Irving Kaufman, who had sentenced the Rosenbergs to death, and prime-time cold-war players like Senator Joseph McCarthy, Roy Cohn, and, most notably, the commander in chief of the cold war, Richard Nixon. Each prances in and out of the story in flights of satiric fantasy as remote from reality as an Aesop fable.

Yet, while *The Public Burning* could not be read as anything but fiction, there remained nonetheless the unhappy prospect that one or another of the characters depicted in the book might be offended enough to bring suit. Viking Penguin decided the book was worth publishing despite the risk but took the unorthodox precaution of muting any attempts at publicity. It chose not to announce a publication date and shipped the first of its 250,000 copies to bookstores in plain brown envelopes, concerned that those who reacted unfavorably might try to keep the books from reaching the shelves.

The book eventually was published to enthusiastic reviews, and we waited for the first round to be fired. Months passed without the suggestion of a claim being filed. Then, at about the time we thought the danger point had passed, we were served with papers from a most unlikely source: The children of the Rosenbergs, who were the tragic heroes of the novel, sued for libel, claiming that their mother had been degraded in a scene that shows her in sexual union with Richard Nixon. The eight-page episode depicts Ethel Rosenberg being buggered by Nixon and gradually, reluctantly, yielding to her own passion in a frenzy of heat and desire. It is a scenario that summons an altogether preposterous vision—a sexual assault by a man who, by every sense and intuition, was at odds with his own body, neither sexually alert nor given to physical gymnastics. Nixon, it would appear, was the most improbable of buggerers; yet the metaphor may not have been entirely misplaced. For the case could be made that he, more than anyone, had fashioned a national presence by attacking from behind those who opposed him. Ethel Rosenberg, Coover tells us, was perhaps the last in a line that followed from Jerry Voorhis, Helen Gahagan Douglas, and Alger Hiss—the last to feel and the first to respond in full measure to the headlong assault that was the trademark of an otherwise sexless assailant.

But metaphor and fantasy notwithstanding, the children of the Rosenbergs were deeply offended at seeing their possibly martyred mother being sexually ravaged by a man she despised—and enjoying it. Still, they understood that Coover was, in a way, their advocate. His novel was sympathetic to their parents, portraying them as victims, and contemptuous of the homespun paranoia, whipped to a froth by Nixon, that sent them finally to Sing Sing's electric chair. After some lengthy and congenial discussions, they agreed to drop the suit in return for Viking's making a modest contribution to a charity of their choice.

The lesson to be sifted from the Coover case, however, was not its happy ending but the narrow margin by which his book escaped suppression. It demonstrated just how fragile the framework of open expression can be when publishers contemplate the prospect of libel. With no First Amendment to afford protection, the covert censorship imposed by private companies or pressure groups can be more oppressive than governmental action, for there are no standards that individuals are obliged to meet. At its heart, it is an undercover operation that works best in the shadow of anonymous intent, as insidious as a blacklist, governed only by its internal imperatives. While the First Amendment cannot be applied directly in such instances, First Amendment values should guide private entities no less than agencies of government. Unfortunately, publishing houses, among others, often feel free to play the role of censor.

In 1996 St. Martin's Press abruptly stopped publication of a book called *Goebbels: Mastermind of the Third Reich,* a biography of the Nazi propagandist that was not without sympathy for his cause. The book's author, the English historian David Irving, had a well-earned reputation as a Holocaust revisionist and an apologist for Hitler. He had been convicted of race hatred and defamation of the dead in Germany, where denying the truth of the Holocaust is a crime. In previous works, Irving had called the Holocaust a "blood lie," described Auschwitz as merely a "slave labor camp" with an unusually high death rate, said that the gas chambers were "ugly rumors" erected by Poland as a tourist attraction, that the Anne Frank diary was fraudulent, and that European Jews were largely responsible for their own fate. His latest effort, a 640-page tome based on Goebbels's diaries, suggested no change in his views. St. Martin's chairman, Thomas McCormack, described the book as "inescapably anti-Semitic" before notifying Irving by fax that he was canceling publication. By that time, however, jacket copy had already been written, galleys circulated, and orders sent for a first printing of thirty thousand copies.

It was remarkably late in the day for a publisher to pull a book, but the pressure on St. Martin's had been fierce. Protests came from a broad spectrum of the Jewish community, from the Anti-Defamation League, the Jewish Defense League, and, perhaps most influential of all, Elie Wiesel, Nobel laureate, survivor of Auschwitz, and the undisputed "conscience of the Holocaust." St. Martin's, it could be said, was in a particularly vulnerable position because it is partly owned by German interests, but its quick capitulation nonetheless came as a surprise. A few years earlier, Salman Rushdie's book *The Satanic Verses* was published, distributed, and sold despite bombings, killings, and murderous threats. Yet, with Irving's book, a small unofficial lobby succeeded where the head of a state had failed by exerting the right type of pressure in exactly the right place.

Irving originally threatened to sue, and I was asked to represent him, but in the end there was no suit because he had no case. A private company has no legal obligation to publish a book so long as it meets the terms of the author's contract, and since St. Martin's allowed him to keep his advance, Irving was left without a cause of action.

The circumstances were very different, however, when Simon & Schuster killed a six-figure book deal to publish Robert Sam Anson's exposé of the inner workings of the Walt Disney Company. There were no social issues involved in that decision, no pressure from outside groups, no one questioning the integrity of Anson's thesis or the accuracy of his account. Anson, after all, was a writer whose reputation was more than secure. He was a highly regarded investigative reporter who had covered politics and war for such publications as *The New York Times, The Washington Post, Time, Esquire,* and *The Saturday Review.* He had written well-received books on Richard Nixon and Vietnam. His latest work, not yet complete, was pulled because Simon & Schuster was part of a conglomerate owned by Paramount Communications and Paramount's chairman, Martin Davis, was going to be roughed up in the telling.

Anson had signed the $400,000 contract in 1991 at the behest of Alice Mayhew, the editorial director of S&S. He had been given $160,000 as a first payment on his advance, had moved his family to Southern California, and had hired a research staff of six. Over the next two years he and his assistants had conducted more than four hundred interviews, and Anson had begun putting the pieces together. Tentatively titled *The Rules of the Magic,* the book was to tell the inside story of Disney's corporate growth under Michael Eisner and Jeffrey Katzenberg, both of whom had been spirited away from Paramount in 1984. Eisner and Katzenberg had worked under Davis at Paramount, and apparently, they had a tale to tell.

Early in 1993, just months before the manuscript was due for delivery, Anson called Mayhew and told her he needed more time, at least another year. Mayhew said it was no problem. He also told her that Davis was going to be a character in the book and that he would not fare well. She told him not to worry about it. But about two months later Anson was notified that his contract was being canceled because the book was behind schedule.

The story had a bogus ring to it. Extensions of delivery dates are routine in the publishing industry, particularly when the book's content does not lend itself to a particular time of publication. As Anson's attorney, I had no doubt that he was a victim of corporate censorship, part of the cost of doing business when publishers barter their independence and slip under the control of conglomerates whose concerns are sometimes less than literary. We filed a breach-of-contract suit in U.S. District Court in Manhattan, charging that S&S was seeking to suppress publication of the book because of pressure from its parent company, Paramount Communications. We asked for damages of one million dollars and a declaratory judgment releasing all rights to the manuscript so that it could be published elsewhere. The Authors Guild and the writers' organization PEN submitted affidavits in our behalf. Judge Kimba Wood was quick to grant our request that a trial date be set immediately, and S&S was eager to cut a deal. The company relinquished all rights to the book and agreed to allow Anson to keep the money he had already been paid.

Less than a month later Anson sold the book to Pantheon, a division of Random House. His choice of a publisher was not an idle selection; Random House is one of the few major book publishers that has no ties to the motion-picture industry.

PART V

Who Owns an Idea?

Chapter 11

In 1988, after a quarter of a century spent fighting court actions aimed at stopping books from being published, I found myself for the first time on the other side of the issue. I was trying to prevent the publication of a book of short stories by John Cheever, the Pulitzer Prize–winning writer who had died six years earlier. It was a complex and bitterly fought case, involving the thorny questions of ownership that often arise after an author's death. Before it was resolved I appeared in four courtrooms in New York and Illinois before twelve state and federal judges in a litigation that spanned three years.

It all began innocently enough, in 1987, when Academy Chicago, a small, specialty publishing house, entered into an agreement with John Cheever's estate to publish some of his uncollected short stories. The deal was the brainchild of Academy's East Coast representative, Franklin Dennis, a young man who had long admired Cheever's work. Over the years, Academy had earned a reputation as a quality small press chiefly by publishing out-of-print classics of nineteenth- and twentieth-century English language literature. Dennis believed that a volume of Cheever's early stories, previously published in magazines but never given life in a Cheever anthology, would be a coup of no small magnitude. He knew that *The Stories of John Cheever,* an omnibus collection published in 1978 by Alfred A. Knopf, had won a Pulitzer Prize and sold more than 100,000 copies. He reasoned that a subsequent volume held the promise of both financial success and critical acclaim.

Dennis took his idea to Anita and Jordan Miller, the couple who owned Academy. The Millers, who had operated without pretension and in relative anonymity since 1975, were understandably captivated by the prospect of a John Cheever book carrying their imprint. Through a mutual friend, Dennis obtained an introduction to Benjamin Cheever, the author's son, and proposed a joint venture. Dennis would gather some of the Cheever stories, published as early as 1930, and Academy would produce *The Uncollected Stories of John Cheever.* Those selected for the book, Ben was told, would be approved by the Cheevers, particularly John's widow, Mary, the executor of the estate.

A contract was soon drafted, calling for a small advance of $1,500 with all subsequent royalties to be split evenly between Mary Cheever, designated as the author of the book, and Dennis as editor. Upon signing, Mrs. Cheever received half of her $750 share of the advance, less her agent's 10 percent commission, for a total of $337.50. By contrast, the initial advance for Cheever's previous book of stories brought the author $40,000. By all indications, given the size of the advance and Academy's history of publishing books of modest length for a limited audience, both the Cheevers and Millers envisioned a slim volume that would appeal mainly to students and scholars.

When the search for the stories began, in August of 1987, neither Dennis nor the Millers could have foreseen the mother lode of material that awaited them. Within a few months, they uncovered sixty-eight stories that had not been included in Cheever's seven previous collections, and they were better than expected. Anita Miller, who held a doctorate in English literature from Northwestern University, had originally been skeptical about the quality to be found in Cheever's earliest work, but as she read some of the obscure stories from the 1930s, she "began to get excited," she said. "It's interesting, because it's political, it's the Depression, it's people, it's stuff you don't associate with Cheever, and some of them were awfully good. . . . I realized I was wrong when I thought we'd get second-string, leftover Cheever."

It was at this point that the lights started flashing and the bells began to chime. Dennis and the Millers decided that the book should contain all the stories they had located. While Academy's initial print runs normally averaged between five and ten thousand copies, they now planned a first printing of ten times that number. *The Uncollected Stories of John Cheever* would be by far the biggest book they had ever published.

Now, with a breakout book apparently just over the horizon, Academy began to move swiftly. Dennis sent Ben a typewritten list of the story titles. In December, on a trip east to a sales conference, the Millers decided to show photostats of sixty of the stories they had collected and fastened in two ring-bound volumes to Ted Chichak, their representative at the Scott Meredith Literary Agency in New York. They told him they expected to publish the book in the fall of 1988. Chichak said he would plan to auction the paperback rights to the book in May, following the convention of the American Booksellers Association. After meeting with Chichak, Dennis took the photocopies of the stories to the Cheever home in Ossining, New York, where he showed them to Mary Cheever. It was the first time they had met; it would also be the last.

Dennis left the binders with Mrs. Cheever. As "author" of the book, she was to read the stories and decide which would be used. The sheer heft of the binders alarmed her, for she had not anticipated a project of this magnitude. Her discomfort grew as she read the stories and deemed many of them unsuited for publication. Furthermore, she found Dennis's introduction and commentary, written as though he were acquainted with the intimate details of Cheever's life, offensive. She regretted having signed the contract and feared she would not be able to stop publication of the book.

When two weeks passed without having heard from Mary Cheever, the Millers did not trouble themselves to call and get her reaction. With Dennis as the driving force, they decided to set sail on their publishing venture with as little interference as possible. On January 3, 1988, just three weeks after Dennis's meeting with Mrs. Cheever, the *Chicago Tribune* carried an article noting that Academy Chicago had scheduled for October publication "more than sixty stories that did not appear in [John Cheever's] 1978 collection." When the article came to Ben Cheever's attention, the alarm was sounded.

Ben was no ingenue when it came to the business of publishing. He had been a senior editor at *Reader's Digest* until leaving to edit a book of his father's letters and pursue his own writing career. He was, and still is, married to Janet Maslin, film reviewer for *The New York Times,* and her colleagues at the *Times* suggested that he get professional advice. Ben turned to his high-powered literary agent, Andrew Wylie. Together they met with Dennis at the Algonquin Hotel in New York. As far as Wylie was concerned, the project had already proceeded too far and in the wrong direction. Three days after the meeting, he phoned Anita Miller and asked her to terminate the contract. Ben, in his turn, called the Millers and offered to meet with them in Chicago. When they refused, Wylie suggested that the Cheevers consult an attorney. He gave them my name.

By the time Ben called me he had already spoken with two other attorneys. They told him the contract was valid, that the book couldn't be stopped. I thought otherwise. The contract, it seemed to me, was too vague, its language too ambiguous for it to be deemed a valid agreement. Certainly there was nothing in it that could be construed as granting Academy the rights to all of Cheever's uncollected stories. Mrs. Cheever, the contractual author of the book, had never been given the opportunity to produce a manuscript, no less deliver one to the publisher. Besides, having worked the other side of the issue for many years, I knew from painful experience just how potent the laws of copyright were. While libel laws cannot be enforced until after the fact, a justifiable claim of ownership can stop a book in its tracks; courts will issue an injunction halting publication until the dispute over ownership is settled. Since copyright infringement is, in some instances, considered a form of theft, laws governing copyright enjoy a degree of immunity from First Amendment protection. It is, in fact, the only ground other than national security on which prior restraint is permitted.

Confident that the law would work in our favor, I met with Ben and then with Mary Cheever and told them I would take the case. On February 17, 1988, I wrote to the Millers explaining that I thought the contract was invalid and that we were prepared to go to court to prevent publication of the book. I also returned the uncashed check for Mrs. Cheever's $337.50 advance. A week later Academy filed suit in Chicago, seeking a declaration that it should be permitted to publish the manuscript immediately, with all sixty-eight stories included. Without waiting for the court's decision, the Millers proceeded to put the book on the fast track for publication. They ordered a first printing of 100,000 copies, announced a September publication date, and developed their own advertising campaign, featuring a full-page photo of John Cheever on the cover of their catalogue and heralding the importance of the book as offering valuable new insights into Cheever the man and the author. Galleys were printed and distributed to the media, including *The New York Times, The Washington Post,* and *The New York Review of Books.* Mrs. Cheever received only a table of contents, an introduction, a preface, and a cover letter stating that "these documents are not being sent to you for your approval or disapproval."

On May 16, in an effort to stop publication, we moved for a

nationwide preliminary injunction in the U.S. District Court for the Southern District of New York. Academy responded by arranging to auction the paperback rights to the book, without so much as notifying the Cheevers. I informed the six publishers who were to bid on the book that Academy did not have the right to sell it. My attempts for a court order to stop the auction were unsuccessful. It went forward, and Dell won with a bid of $225,000. Mrs. Cheever was upset at having lost the first court battle, but I told her it was of no consequence; there would be no book.

The hearing on the injunction was held before district court judge Gerard Goettel in White Plains, New York, not far from Mrs. Cheever's Ossining home. I called as witnesses several agents and representatives of publishing houses who testified that the vague language of the contract rendered it unenforceable. All the same, the contract could be a problem simply because it existed; Mrs. Cheever had signed it. I did not wish to trust our case entirely to a judge's interpretation of a document so ambiguous. There was a greater issue involved, I felt: the moral right of an author to determine the fate of his own work.

My key witness, therefore, was Robert Gottlieb, the noted editor who worked with Cheever on his 1978 story collection. Gottlieb, at the time editor of *The New Yorker,* took the stand attired in his trademark outfit of white sneakers, shirt open at the collar, and no jacket. He testified to the critical eye with which Cheever had appraised the stories to be included in that omnibus volume, that Gottlieb had often tried and failed to persuade him of the merit of works the author considered less than distinguished, and that the author had deliberately chosen not to have the stories in question published in previous collections. He addressed the need to protect an author's reputation and warned against publishing an "authorized" version of a book that the author's estate did not wish to authorize. It was compelling testimony but of a clinical, literary nature that did not seem to move the judge; Mrs. Cheever, after all, had signed a contract to publish at least some of these stories.

The hearing promptly turned in our favor, however, when Mary Cheever was called as a witness. Nervous and uncertain before taking the stand, once sworn, she quickly gained her composure, and from the very start she and the judge connected in a profound and unusual way. Mrs. Cheever was a woman of seventy at the time, petite, soft-spoken, and articulate, with an elegant bearing and, we made clear, literary credentials of her own. She held a bachelor's degree from Sarah Lawrence College, she had taught composition and creative writing for ten years at Briarcliff Junior College and for three years at the Rockland Country Day School, and she had published a book of her own poems entitled *The Need for Chocolate.* For several hours, appearing diminutive on the witness stand in the huge new federal courtroom, she chronicled the sequence of events that had brought her there. She explained that she had been given to believe that the book would be a slim volume of carefully chosen stories that she herself would select, stories she was certain her husband would have wanted to see in print. She spoke of her devotion to her husband and how she felt herself to be the caretaker of his literary reputation. The publication of this book would be her final service to him.

The emotional impact of courtroom proceedings is too often underplayed. I've always believed that, in many instances, judges make decisions in accordance with their own sense of justice and their private perceptions and then find the legal precedents to support their conclusions. The law is the law, but it is a malleable instrument that rarely fails to bend a degree or two when a witness appears authentic enough to touch the chords of judge or jury. Basing his decision largely on Mrs. Cheever's testimony, Judge Goettel halted publication of the book, pending the outcome of the Millers' suit in Chicago. He concluded that Mrs. Cheever "envisioned a rather modest work

containing only a limited number of stories with a small printing. She believed that, as the author who was supposed to deliver a manuscript, she would have control over which works
would be included. She was aware that her husband considered
his early stories inferior and did not want his literary reputation
sullied by their collected publication."

Then, addressing the validity of the contract directly, he
noted, "It is simply unreasonable to conclude that the intent of
the publishing agreement was that Mrs. Cheever would license
all of the uncollected stories of John Cheever to [Academy] for
publication." But he said that the case must first be tried in
Chicago, where Academy had filed suit. Finally, looking beyond
the contract dispute, he gave our case a boost as it headed
toward the Illinois courts. Even if the contract were found to be
valid, the judge said, he would be likely to rule against Academy
as a matter of copyright law, since the agreement conveyed no
specific rights to Academy.

Although the court's granting the injunction to stop publication was a victory of substance, I was not looking forward to a
trial in Chicago, where a state court could undo much of Judge
Goettel's decision. The proceedings in Illinois also promised to
be time-consuming, and Mrs. Cheever, who had proved an im-
pressive witness, was not inclined to make the trip. Furthermore, I cautioned her that the cost of litigation and transporting
witnesses from New York to Chicago would be high, and even
if we won the case, she might find herself in the ironic position
of having to sell her husband's stories to cover expenses. But
she was determined to see the case through. The issue involved,
she believed, transcended both cost and convenience.

At this point, I was obliged to make a critical decision:
whether to insist on bringing the Cheevers—Mary, Ben, and
Susan, the author's daughter, who had testified in federal
court—to Chicago or to try to have the transcripts of their depositions admitted as evidence. Academy, of course, could have

compelled their appearance in court, so the Millers and their attorney also had a say in the matter. I opted to force their hand. They seemed eager to match their live witnesses against our impersonal array of documents, depositions, letters, and motions. It was a mistake.

The Millers and Franklin Dennis were the kind of witnesses on which opposing attorneys could build a reputation. Although they were on their home turf in Chicago and had the support of local journalists as well as the Association of American Publishers and the literary establishment, they chose to shy away from the testimony they offered in New York and concoct new arguments to support their case. Aware that the Cheevers would not be in court to refute their stories, they testified about conversations that the Cheevers said never took place and played fast and loose with the chronology of events. Jordan Miller, clearly ill at ease with the tale he was telling, chain-chewed antacid tablets throughout his entire stay on the stand; Anita seemed to balk at every question put to her under cross-examination; and Dennis, the principal witness for their side, had to be his attorney's worst nightmare. He responded to questions haltingly, in a small, uncertain voice, sounding as though even if he was telling the truth, he wasn't sure he could make you believe him. In a *Chicago* magazine article otherwise favorable to the Millers, Dan Santow described Dennis this way:

[I]n his ill-fitting navy-blue suit and little-boy side-part haircut, he looks woefully uncomfortable, constantly drinking from his plastic cup of water, wiping his face, squirming in his seat from right to left. He never sits up straight. When the Cheevers' lawyer, Martin Garbus, gets close—and Garbus gets close often—Dennis's voice creaks considerably; he nervously wipes his face with his hand, and he shifts uneasily in his seat. When Garbus points his finger at Dennis—and this, too, he does often and very close to Dennis's nose—the witness is clearly and understandably uncomfortable. . . . Dennis just seems to be wilting up there.

After three days of testimony, the Millers rested their case. We spent one day reading our depositions and Mrs. Cheever's previous trial testimony to the court. Illinois Circuit Court judge Roger J. Kiley, Jr., took just a few weeks to hand down his ruling. Not having heard Mrs. Cheever, he was apparently affected chiefly by the inconsistencies in the testimony of Dennis and Miller. He turned in a decision that narrowly favored our side. Contradicting Judge Goettel, Judge Kiley ruled that the contract was valid but that Mrs. Cheever, as the author of the book, had the right to select which stories should be included. Her contractual obligation would be fulfilled, he said, if she chose ten to fifteen stories covering no less than 140 pages. He described as "inexplicable" Academy's contention that it had the right to all sixty-eight of the uncollected stories but ruled that Academy could include its own introduction and comments by Dennis preceding each published story.

We told the Millers that, under the circumstances, we were prepared to live with the decision in order to end the dispute. But the Millers were not ready to settle the issue on a give-and-get basis. Although Mrs. Cheever agreed in writing to provide them with fifteen stories, they appealed the trial court's decision. That was their second mistake. The appellate court affirmed the lower court's decision. Academy then appealed to the Illinois Supreme Court. This would prove to be their biggest mistake of all.

Not satisfied with the prospect of publishing a slim volume of Cheever stories with their own introduction and comments, the Millers chose to play double-or-nothing, and nothing was what they got. On June 20, 1991, more than three years after the battle was joined, a seven-judge panel ruled that the contract itself was invalid. In a brief, four-page opinion reversing both the trial-court and the appellate-division decisions, Judge James D. Heiple declared that the agreement "lacks the . . . essential terms required for the formation of an enforceable contract." After enumerating the specific provisions that should have been covered in the agreement—the minimum number of stories and who would decide which were to be included, the dates for delivery and publication of the manuscript, the price at which the book would be sold—Judge Heiple concluded: "A contract may be enforced even though some contract terms may be missing or left to be agreed upon. But if the essential terms are so uncertain that there is no basis for deciding whether the agreement has been kept or broken, there is no contract."

Academy briefly considered applying for a rehearing of its last appeal but finally conceded. They resigned themselves to waiting for the inevitable publication of a hefty volume of John Cheever's uncollected stories, which, they were certain, would soon be in bookstores. Throughout the course of the litigation, Academy had contended that the Cheevers' primary motive for trying to back out of the contract was commercial rather than literary. Having discovered a gold mine of material they did not know existed, the reasoning went, the Cheevers were hungry to place the book with a major publisher. The Millers also said they believed the family was trying to keep aspects of John Cheever's past from being made public. They were wrong on both counts; the stories have never been published.

As circumstance had it, Academy Chicago was not the only casualty in the case. The outcome left its scars on the publishing industry as well and damaged my standing with the influential Association of American Publishers. The AAP, a trade group of more than two hundred book publishers, which had submitted an amicus curiae brief in the Illinois Court of Appeals in behalf of the Millers, expressed alarm at the breadth of the court's decision. They noted that the disputed provisions in Academy's contract were "not substantially different . . . from the terms

contained in many other publishers' contracts." The final decision on what goes into a book must remain with the publisher,
they contended, as is currently provided in all publishing contracts. After wavering a bit, the Authors Guild, representing
6,500 book authors, finally weighed in on the Cheevers' side of
the argument, asserting that the author should have the final say
on every word in his book.

The dispute left me in the uncomfortable position of opposing the group that fed a large part of my practice. A number of
my book-publishing clients were quick to make their feelings
known. I had, it seemed to them, built a practice on the fees
they had paid me, and now, at a critical turn, I had been instrumental in obtaining a legal decision that worked against them.
Not for the first time, I heard myself described, though in much
softer terms, as a traitor. My allegiance, however, was never to
one side or the other, publisher or author, but rather to the idea
that an author's right to control his own work is absolute and
includes not only the right to publish but the right *not* to publish.

A few years later, in 1994, I took a case that some of my critics
said violated precisely the principles I espoused in the Cheever
case. I represented a publisher in an attempt to have a play published over the objections of the author's estate. There was,
however, an essential distinction between the two cases: In this
instance I concluded that the executor of the estate was not representing the wishes of the author. The matter was of some concern to the literary community, for the estate in question was
that of Samuel Beckett, the Gaelic/French existential playwright who had won the Nobel Prize for literature in 1969.

The play, *Eleutheria,* was among Beckett's earliest works,
written in 1947 just prior to his enigmatic masterpiece, *Waiting
for Godot.* From its inception, *Eleutheria* had followed a long,

circuitous, and often troubled route on its way to publication nearly half a century after its completion. Yet, except for a turn of chance here or there, it might well have preceded *Godot* into production. Jean Vilar, of the Théâtre Nationale Populaire, had expressed interest in the three-act play as early as March 1947, but he wanted the play cut and woven into one long act. Beckett declined and turned his attention to completing *Waiting for Godot*. He then asked his live-in companion and future wife, Suzanne Deschevaux-Dumesnil, to circulate the two plays among producers and publishers. The noted French director Roger Blin liked them both. He decided that he should probably produce *Eleutheria* first because it was more traditional than the darkly foreboding *Godot,* which Blin said he "frankly did not understand." There were, however, other factors to consider.

"*Eleutheria,*" Blin noted, "had seventeen characters, a divided stage, elaborate props, and complicated lighting. . . . I thought I'd be better off with *Godot* because there were only four characters and they were bums. They could wear their own clothes if it came to that, and I wouldn't need anything but a spotlight and a bare branch of a tree."

Upon considerations so mundane was experimental theater given its seminal play and its author sent on his way toward the pantheon of Europe's postwar existential elite. Within the next three years, Beckett completed his trilogy of novels, *Molloy, Malone Dies,* and *The Unnamable,* and they were prepared for publication in France by Jérôme Lindon's Editions de Minuit. In the United States, Barney Rosset, of the avant-garde Grove Press, agreed to publish translations of all of Beckett's work. His literary future now assured, Beckett turned once again to the theater and began work on a new play, *Endgame.* The manuscript of *Eleutheria* was laid away in a trunk and, for the next three decades, largely forgotten.

In the spring of 1986, on the occasion of Beckett's eightieth birthday, he, Rosset, and some mutual friends celebrated over drinks in a Paris bar. Rosset, however, offered up a piece of news that darkened the mood of the festivities. He had been discharged from Grove Press after thirty-three years of building and running the company. During that time, Rosset had been responsible for publishing more than twenty volumes of Beckett's work as well as approving performances of his plays in the United States. The two men had grown very close; some described Rosset as Beckett's spiritual son.

Rosset now spoke of forming his own publishing company, and it came as no surprise that the author was eager to help. He would search his trunk for something that might get Rosset started again. He came up with his first full-length play, *Eleutheria.* He inscribed a copy of the play to Rosset and began revising and translating it from French to English. But he soon abandoned the task. Well on in years and in failing health, he found he could not give his attention to a work now nearly forty years old. Instead, not long before his death in 1989, he wrote his final prose piece, *Stirrings Still,* dedicated it to Rosset, and gave it to him in gratitude for not having insisted on publishing *Eleutheria* before his revisions were complete.

Rosset, however, never gave up on the idea of publishing Beckett's first play. While possessing literary merits of its own, *Eleutheria* had the added appeal of foreshadowing themes and attitudes that in the years ahead would become so closely identified with the author. The play, whose title is Greek for "freedom," is a dark comedy about a young writer named Victor Krap (sire, no doubt, to the title character of *Krapp's Last Tape*) who has decided to spend the rest of his life doing absolutely nothing. To an audience now familiar with the shadows that slip in and out of Beckett's work, the early play could conceivably illuminate a nuance or two of the author's intent. It certainly was a play worth publishing, Rosset thought.

On March 3, 1993, he wrote to Jérôme Lindon, Beckett's literary executor and French publisher, informing him that he planned to publish the work Beckett had bequeathed to him in 1986. Then, together with copublishers John Oakes and Dan Simon, he formed a new company, Foxrock, named for Beckett's birthplace outside Dublin, for the specific purpose of publishing the play. Lindon, however, had reservations. He wrote back saying he thought the play should be published first in French, but not quite yet. "When?" he asked in his letter. "I cannot possibly tell you for the time being." The reply was not good enough for Rosset, who believed Beckett had given him full sway to do with the work as he wished. Now the two most important figures in Beckett's literary life were ready to cross swords, each firm in the conviction that he was acting in his friend's best interests. And indeed, both Lindon and Rosset had legitimate claims to knowing the heart and mind of the author.

Lindon, after all, had been named literary executor of Beckett's estate. He had accepted the Nobel Prize in Beckett's absence at the award ceremonies in Stockholm. He believed that if the playwright had wished to have *Eleutheria* published or performed, he would have seen to it during his lifetime.

Rosset, for his part, had served as Beckett's dramatic agent and publisher in the United States and had in his possession a manuscript inscribed by the author signifying his approval to have the play published. He believed the work was of great importance, and few men had struggled as valiantly or successfully in behalf of suppressed literary endeavors as had Barney Rosset. It was his Grove Press that had broken new ground in the fifties by publishing the works of Henry Miller and D. H. Lawrence along with dozens of other authors whose books had been banned in the United States until Rosset cleared the way. Now he sensed the irony of abetting the censor if he did not do all he could to bring *Eleutheria* to public attention.

Rosset asked if I could help mediate the dispute or, failing that, represent him as he published the play. I had worked with him on publishing issues in the past and had represented Beckett ten years earlier in a copyright claim. I decided first to speak with a few people who knew Beckett and could help me assess the author's wishes. Deirdre Bair, a friend of his who had spoken with him at length while writing her prizewinning biography of Beckett, was unambivalent. "Beckett trusted Rosset completely," she said, "and he was very generous to his friends. He would have done everything he could to help Barney if he was in trouble. He had begun translating and revising the play so that Barney could publish it, and only his failing health kept him from completing it. I have no doubt that he would have wanted to see it published."

I also spoke with several French publishers and was growing increasingly skeptical of Lindon's claim that he, and he alone, spoke for the author. Nonetheless, it was a claim that the law entitled him to make. Litigation would be difficult, I knew, and I thought it best that we try to settle the issue outside the courts. I suggested a variety of alternatives to help resolve the dispute, ranging from informal procedures to formal mediation or arbitration to simplified principles of litigation. Lindon rejected them all.

Rosset, growing impatient, decided to force the issue. He arranged for a private reading of the play to be given on September 26, 1994, at the New York Theater Workshop. However, when we arrived at the East Village theater, we found the actors on the street and the door locked against us. Word of a threatened lawsuit had come to the attention of the theater's trustees, and they were not inclined to take the risk in a not-for-profit venture. They asked Rosset to post a $25,000 bond, which he was unable to do. Undeterred, he marched us all the few blocks to his apartment building on Fourth Avenue, converted a loft area into a makeshift theater, and the play was given its reading by thirteen actors before one hundred invited guests seated on wooden folding chairs.

Still, the performance did not go unnoticed. Mel Gussow and Herb Mitgang, both of *The New York Times,* were in attendance, and in the following day's edition Gussow gave the play a favorable if not rave review, observing, "Philosophical points were made about everyday madness, fathers and sons, and suicide," subjects Beckett explored more fully in later works.

Now the play had penetrated the theater world's mainstream, and some of America's most noted directors and theater owners expressed interest in producing it. Their letters were forwarded to Lindon, but he remained unmoved. In letters to Rosset and his copublishers, he warned that if *Eleutheria* was published, he would "prosecute not only the publishers but all those . . . who have been accessory to that illicit action."

Such a suit would have introduced the unpleasant prospect of involving us in French criminal and copyright law, which, by every measure, favored the estate's executor. In the United States, the First Amendment often tips the balance in favor of publication. Unless the issue of ownership is clear-cut, there is a tendency to apply constitutional values: Publish the book and let the readers judge the value of the work. Under French law, the executor speaks with a more powerful voice, and since the copyright decisions of one nation are generally honored by others, we chose to move first. At the request of Rosset and Foxrock, I prepared to seek a declaratory judgment in the U.S. District Court in New York, freeing the play to be published. Lindon, however, backed off, and the papers never were filed. Rosset and the publishers then decided to proceed with publication. In order to avert a claim that they were interested primarily in turning a profit, they chose to publish a limited, not-for-sale edition of *Eleutheria.*

At this point, realizing he could not stop the book, Lindon grudgingly offered his consent. In a letter to Rosset, he wrote, "The one thing I am sure of is that Sam would not have liked us to fight against each other about him in a public lawsuit."

Eleutheria, translated by Michael Brodsky, was published by Foxrock, Inc., in a regular edition in May 1995. At about the same time, Lindon published the play in its original French version. It has yet to be produced.

It was some years earlier, during the production of another of his plays, that I first spoke with Beckett about the control of his work. We were trying to prevent an adaptation of his play *Endgame* from being produced by the American Repertory Theatre (ART) company at the Loeb Drama Center in Cambridge, Massachusetts. The issue here was not who owned the work but the degree of liberty that can be taken in adapting it for the stage. Beckett, who was as meticulous with his directions for staging as he was in writing dialogue, included specific instructions concerning set design, lighting, and the movement of the performers, even prescribing pauses and periods of silence. For *Endgame,* Beckett described the set as a bare, cell-like room with two small windows. The ART production, directed by JoAnne Akalaitis, offered instead an underground, abandoned subway station layered with trash and occupied only by a gutted subway car. When the change in staging was described to him, Beckett's response was unequivocal. "This has nothing to do with my play," he said. "They can't do this. They have no permission to do this."

The change in set design was not merely cosmetic; it shifted the play's focus, crossing what Edward Albee once described as the "fine line between interpretation and distortion." Like all of Beckett's work, *Endgame* probed the depths of internal despair, the hopeless resignation of the spirit confronted by an indifferent world, and Beckett's empty room reflected that sense of desolation. A set suggesting a bombed-out bunker after a nuclear holocaust, by contrast, altered the play's dynamics, for it grounded the individual's despair in an external event that was shared by all. It was as if Ahab's quest for Moby Dick were driven by motives grander than personal revenge. The version of *Endgame* directed by Akalaitis and produced by ART's artistic director, Robert Brustein, had merits of its own, but it was not Beckett's play.

Brustein described his production as bringing "new values to an extraordinary play." His position was unambiguous: "I revere Mr. Beckett above all living playwrights and would never tolerate any disrespect for his work in my theater," he said. But, he added, "A playwright cannot serve as the designer, director and actor of his own play. He has to collaborate."

The terms of the contract, however, suggested otherwise, for permission to produce the play had been granted on the condition that no changes be made, and ART did not deny making changes. As a matter of contract and copyright law, there appeared to be a clear violation of the agreement. But the dispute raised a broader, more critical issue, which was the right of the playwright to control the production of his work. If the playwright is contractually entitled to limit the changes that can be made in his play, who, then, should be the judge of whether those limits have been exceeded, the director or the playwright?

Beckett was in France at the time, and Rosset and I consulted with him on the phone. Barney described the production of the play, and I explained to Beckett that if we filed suit to prevent its opening, he could be compelled to come to the United States to testify. It was a prospect he found distasteful, but he said he would rely on Rosset's judgment. "If Barney says I should file the suit and come to New York, I will," he said.

On the day the play was to open, December 12, 1984, I filed for an injunction in the U.S. District Court in Boston to stop that night's production. The suit charged violation of contract and copyright law as well as of the federal Lanham Act, which protects authors against the misappropriation of their work. Confronted by the possibility of a public courtroom dispute with Beckett and the likelihood of an aborted opening night, ART agreed to a settlement that was nothing less than extraordinary. The play would open on schedule, but attached to each playbill would be a disclaimer by the author, an unprecedented compromise.

The disclaimer consisted of the first page of the text of *Endgame,* including the author's detailed stage directions and a message from the playwright, which read: "Any production of *Endgame* which ignores my stage directions is completely unacceptable to me. My play requires an empty room and two small windows. The American Repertory Theatre production, which dismisses my directions, is a complete parody of the play as conceived by me. Anybody who cares for the work couldn't fail to be disgusted by this." Brustein, in turn, was permitted his own say, in which he stated that ". . . to insist on strict adherence to each parenthesis of the published text not only robs collaborative artists of their respective freedom, but threatens to turn the theatre into waxworks."

The dispute underlined the irony that copyright laws, no matter how scrupulously crafted, contain within them an element of paradox, for they are designed to guarantee the ownership of words and ideas that become the property of an author only when he makes them public. Once in circulation, they are freely cited, adapted, and often quoted at length. They were written, after all, in the hope that they would prove memorable enough to insinuate themselves into the consciousness of those they reached. If, however, a reader is sufficiently enamored of the author's work to make a substantial part of it his own, he will have committed the ultimate copyright infringement; it is called plagiarism and is tantamount to theft.

David Leavitt, a talented young writer, was accused of such an act by the eminent English poet Stephen Spender when Leavitt's third novel, *While England Sleeps,* was published in 1994.

Spender perceived the novel to be little more than a thinly disguised, often salacious version of his 1951 memoir, *World Within World,* the tale of a doomed homosexual relationship set against the backdrop of the Spanish Civil War. While Leavitt acknowledged using the memoir as a "springboard" for his own story of a love affair between two men, also set in the late thirties, Spender thought he had crossed the bounds that separated inspiration and expropriation.

The eighty-five-year-old poet filed a suit against Leavitt and Viking, the publisher of the book, claiming breach of copyright and arguing that his "moral right" to control his own work had been violated. In its essence, breach of copyright is a charge of plagiarism, which is usually enough to stop publication or distribution of a book. The "moral right" claim is more difficult to define. It was based largely on a new British law, still untested in the courts, that was designed to protect authors from having their work adapted against their will. Its inclusion in the suit was a measure of Spender's outrage, his sense of the covers being peeled back on the most private corners of his life, the intimacies he had so carefully sheltered now laid bare to public scrutiny.

By the standards of the fifties, *World Within World* was remarkable for its candor, daring to explore attitudes that were sometimes suggested but rarely proclaimed. Writing of his relationship with a man called Jimmy, Spender spoke of "friendship," of "paternalistic feelings," of "someone I love." Romantic involvements with men were hinted at but never openly declared and certainly not described in intimate detail. *While England Sleeps,* by contrast, left little to the imagination. Leavitt provided the reader with vivid, almost clinical descriptions of homosexual lovemaking. It was the explicit nature of these scenes, with Spender a presumed participant, that particularly offended the poet. "I don't see why he should unload all his sexual fantasies onto me in my youth," Spender said. "If he wanted to write about sexual fantasies, he should write about them as being his, not mine."

Given Leavitt's open concession that he had used Spender's memoir as a source, and a subsequent statement that he had considered including an acknowledgment to the poet, the suit was not easy to defend. The whole question of plagiarism is an elusive one, and to complicate matters, British copyright law favored the litigant. The First Amendment gave writers greater leeway in America than they enjoyed in Great Britain. There was more of a recognition here that if you wrote about a mother-son conflict, you were not necessarily stealing from *Oedipus Rex.* British courts tended to look at the similarities between two works; American courts looked at the differences. As Viking's attorney, I thought it best to settle the suit rather than enter into a prolonged litigation.

In a good settlement, neither side gets to claim victory, nor do they suffer badly or alone. It could fairly be said that the settlement reached in the Leavitt-Spender dispute hurt neither author. All thirty thousand copies of Leavitt's novel printed for the U.S. market had already been shipped to bookstores, and most of them had been sold. Since the agreement did not require bookstores to return the unsold books, the remaining copies, now considered collectors' items, were expected to move off the shelves quickly. In England, where the novel had been more recently distributed, the books were recalled pending the publication of future editions with the questionable passages deleted.

As for Spender, a poet of the thirties whose reputation had become better known than his work, he enjoyed a brief new wave of recognition. *World Within World,* out of print for more than a decade, was reissued in the fall of 1994 with an introduction about the Leavitt affair, along with a collection of Spender's poems. "It's ironic, isn't it?" Spender said.

Leavitt wrote his own account of the copyright case in an introduction to the new edition of *While England Sleeps*. He said that the principal lesson he learned from the experience was: "If you're going to write a historical novel, base it on the life of someone who's dead." Ironically, Spender died several months later.

Chapter 12

It was a Saturday night, March 2, 1991, but George Holliday had gone to bed early. He was looking ahead to a big day. Holliday was planning to attend the Los Angeles Marathon on Sunday, and an early start would assure him a good vantage point along the route. So he went to bed at ten o'clock hoping for a good night's sleep. He could little have suspected that just a few hours later he would be rudely awakened, summoned by chance to a cameo role in American history.

Not long after midnight, Holliday was jarred from sleep by the sound of sirens and helicopters hovering over his apartment in the San Fernando Valley. He went to his window and saw police cars forcing a motorist to the side of the street. Holliday picked up his newly purchased video camera and focused on the scene. He saw a cadre of Los Angeles police officers haul a big black man from the front seat of his automobile and knock him to the ground. When the man tried to rise, the police began clubbing him with their nightsticks. The victim of the attack was Rodney King, and Holliday's homemade video, only eighty-one seconds long, would soon become one of the most widely viewed and controversial clips of tape in television history.

Holliday brought the footage to Los Angeles television station KTLA, a CNN affiliate, and granted the station the right to broadcast it for five hundred dollars. KTLA aired the video on March 4 and sent it by satellite to CNN. Within hours, it was seen in every city and town in America. The police officers caught on film were arrested, tried, and, the graphic video evidence notwithstanding, found not guilty. In a city where racial unease was never far from its flash point, their acquittal served to light the fuse. For days the streets of Los Angeles were besieged by rioting that stirred memories of the sixties. The Rodney King tape had become a staple of television news shows, shown night after night, now preceded by scenes of stores burning, cars being overturned, a white truck driver pulled from behind the wheel and beaten by rampaging blacks. And George Holliday, a plumber by trade, amateur video cameraman by inclination, suddenly found himself an unwitting player in a Grade B drama that defined a part of the nation's conscience.

Holliday's troubles began almost immediately. His telephone was ringing at all hours of the day and night with menacing voices on the other end. A stream of hate mail carried threats. Unable to bear the strain, his wife retreated to Argentina, where both she and Holliday were born, to live for a while, he said, "in peaceful obscurity." The furor subsided after a month or two, but it was brought to a boil again a year later when the trial of the policemen charged in the beating got under way. The videotape, which was the principal evidence against the officers, was being aired almost nightly, and George Holliday was back in the news. When the officers were acquitted, it was as if Holliday himself had been rejected. He viewed the scenes of Los Angeles burning while rioters and looters stormed the city's streets with a feeling of guilt mingled with despair. In an interview with the *Los Angeles Times,* he said, "The question still pops up in my mind: Did I cause this?" It seemed now that his year of travail had all been for nothing. Eighty-one seconds of home video, filmed on the trigger of the instant, without plan or future intent, had transformed his life. And it was not over yet. Just a few months later, Holliday was back in public view. This time he occupied center stage, the plaintiff in a legal struggle in which his adversary was one of the nation's most prominent film directors, Spike Lee.

Lee, no stranger to controversy, was putting the finishing touches on his most ambitious film project, a three-hour-and-twenty-minute biographical treatment of Malcolm X, when it occurred to him that he might make use of the Rodney King footage in the opening sequence that ran with the credits. In the spring of 1992, Lee's attorney obtained permission to use the tape from an agent who had been representing Holliday. The licensing agreement granted Lee nonexclusive rights to the tape for fifty thousand dollars. It was a routine, unambiguous contract except for one detail: Holliday's agent, Stanley Martin, had been dismissed prior to entering the agreement and had no authority to close the deal. When Martin tried to persuade him to sign the agreement with Lee, Holliday balked. He said he had never agreed to license the tape to Lee. When he learned that it was to be used in a montage with the burning of an American flag and that Lee had urged students and workers to take a day off to see the movie, he became adamant.

"Such statements," he said, "are . . . indicative of the racial divisiveness that his movie will likely promote, and that his film is intended to provoke violence." Lee, for his part, had already woven forty-five seconds of the footage into his opening, counterpoising symbols of what he saw as the failed American dream against a background soundtrack of Bruce Springsteen's "Born in the USA." The technique worked well, and Lee did not wish to remove it. The film, *Malcolm X,* was scheduled to open nationally on November 20. Completed prints were needed for distribution to exhibitors by early October. On September 10 Holliday filed suit in U.S. District Court in Los Angeles, asking for an injunction barring Lee from using the King footage in his film and seeking damages of up to $120,000.

Lee had long been a client of my firm's, but although I had

spoken with him on occasion, I had never represented him in litigation. Other attorneys in the firm generally handled the business affairs and contract disputes of clients in the arts and entertainment field, which made up a large part of our practice. But I felt there was an important First Amendment issue here that transcended ordinary contract considerations. Free-speech rights often run on a collision course with those of copyright, and we would argue that the King tape had been shown often enough and was significant enough to be treated as part of the public record; it had become a piece of the documented history of race relations in America, and it was essential to an understanding of what the country was like in the 1990s.

Lee and I went to a studio and watched the film together. He had done a brilliant job of integrating the tape with other effects to create a powerful prologue. It began with a full-screen image of the American flag, then cut briefly to the black-and-white footage of King being clubbed to the ground by police. As the images on the screen pulsed repeatedly, in quick snippets, from the flag to the King tape and back, the flag started to burn slowly at its edges. With Springsteen's song in the background, the voice of Denzel Washington, playing Malcolm X, was heard: "We've never seen democracy; all we see is hypocrisy." The flag was becoming engulfed in flames as the policemen continued to beat King. "We don't see any American dream; we've experienced only nightmare." Finally burned away at its four sides, the flag then burst into a giant *X* as the credits ran and the body of the film opened with Malcolm X at a railroad station in Boston.

The opening sequence ran a little more than two minutes, but it was enough to leave a viewer feeling emotionally drained. It constituted, in its way, an overture that struck precisely the right chord for the more than three hours of film that would follow. Spike and I spoke for a long while, and he explained why he developed the footage and felt so strongly about retaining it. His remarks would later be included in an affidavit submitted to a California federal court.

"I needed a powerful graphic image," he said, "to demonstrate that the struggle that Malcolm X waged for equal human rights for African-Americans was far from being won. I also felt that the footage stated eloquently why Malcolm's observation that no African-American is 'an American or patriot or a flag-saluter or a flag-waver' is legitimate even today, thirty years later. It is imperative that I use the Rodney King footage to make these points. There simply are no other images or materials with comparable impact and historical importance. The Rodney King footage stands alone as one of the most significant documents in recent American history."

I found Lee vastly different from his public image. In discussing his work, he seemed to mix the fierce commitment of the artist with a critic's cool eye for every shading of nuance. He was not merely the impish firebrand who traded barbs with opposing players from his courtside seat at Knicks games, nor was he the race-baiting provocateur whom his critics accused of reveling in pointless controversy. He was thoughtful and measured in his approach, polite, even somewhat diffident.

I considered the merits of his case and weighed our options. While it was true that he had obtained permission to use the tape, the validity of the agreement was open to question. It was unlikely that the courts would be ready to accept Martin as representing Holliday's interests when Holliday insisted he had dismissed the agent weeks before the deal was struck. I was eager to use a First Amendment defense, and Spike, ever the public person, understood that assuming such a position would likely do him and his film no harm. I would argue that Lee had a First Amendment right to use the footage and put his own interpretation on it, that a claim of copyright did not extend to an individual's right to control a slice of American history that was documented nowhere else. For example, the photographs of the young Vietnamese girl running down the road naked after a napalm attack and of a man, blindfolded and kneeling, about to be shot to death were essential to an understanding of the Vietnam War and the antiwar movement and therefore superseded the photographer's copyright claim.

The argument was a bit unorthodox but not totally without precedent. Federal courts in both California and New York had taken up similar conflicts between copyright law and First Amendment rights, and each had ruled in favor of the constitutional position we were taking. The question here was whether the court would view the case as a First Amendment issue or solely as a contract dispute and, given the time pressure for the film's release, whether it would grant an emergency hearing.

In the New York case, the court had agreed to look at the First Amendment issue and held that the publisher of a book about the assassination of President Kennedy could reproduce frames from the Zapruder home video of the event even though Zapruder held the copyright. The court concluded that the public's need for the information and analysis supplied by the author outweighed any infringement of copyright.

The language in the California decision, I thought, could prove even more helpful. It was handed down less than a month earlier in the Ninth Circuit, which was where our own case would be heard. There the court cited photographs of the My Lai massacre in Vietnam as an instance where ordinary copyright protection is limited by the First Amendment nature of the material being used.

"No amount of words describing the 'idea' of the massacre could substitute for the public insight gained through the photographs," the court said. "The photographic expression, not merely the idea, became essential if the public was to fully understand what occurred in that tragic episode. It would be intolerable if the public's comprehension of the full meaning of

My Lai could be censored by the copyright owner of the photographs."

We structured our case along much the same lines. The Rodney King videotape was precisely the type of material in which the expression could not be separated from the idea. There was simply no other way for Spike Lee to use the fact or the idea of the incident without using the tape. Therefore, normal tests for copyright infringement and fair use could not be applied. Since copyright law allows greater latitude for fair use if the material is educational rather than strictly commercial, we emphasized the educational nature of the film. The fact that it was a forty-million-dollar production by a major studio should not be permitted to overshadow its broader value. Taking a cue from defenses I had made in obscenity cases, I argued that the film must be viewed as an artistic whole and that its social relevance warranted the stretching of the fair-use doctrine.

Holliday, for his part, built his case on practical grounds. He claimed, not without justification, that he was being deprived of his rights of ownership because the pictures he took were socially significant. Under my argument, he said, he, like Zapruder or the photographer who took the picture of Jack Ruby shooting Lee Harvey Oswald, would lose the right to control the use of his work. He was making the case, he said, not just for himself but for all copyright holders. In sum, he contended that this was a case not about First Amendment principles but about money. Pay me enough, he said, and you can use the material.

That, in essence, was the substance of the conflict. However, we never got to argue the issues in the California trial court. To my utter amazement, our motion for an expedited hearing, filed two days after Holliday's request for an injunction, was denied by U.S. District Court judge Terry J. Hatter.

An early hearing, of course, was more than a matter of convenience. Warner Bros., the studio that financed the film, said that if the issue was not resolved by October 1, the King footage would be excised from the movie. Warner Bros. was not about to book the film into thousands of theaters and spend millions of dollars on advertising if it was not certain the film would be shown.

In full knowledge of the time constraints, Judge Hatter set a hearing date of October 13, in effect peremptorily deciding the issue against Lee and Warner Bros. without hearing the arguments.

I could not recall another instance of a judge denying a request for an expedited hearing in similar circumstances, and I was at a loss to explain it. Judge Hatter was one of the few black judges on the federal bench in California, and I thought at first that might work in our favor. There were those, however, who suggested otherwise. I was told that Hatter's politics were very different from Lee's, that as a black man who had mastered the machinery of the mainstream power structure, Hatter resented Lee's outspoken activism, his appeal to a mass minority culture that scorned a system that had proved no obstacle for the judge.

But it is one thing to lose a case on its merits, quite another to lose without having been heard at all. We had little choice but to appeal the decision although we knew our chances of success were close to zero. While aggressive litigation often produces the unexpected, appeals courts rarely reviewed the discretionary rulings of a lower court when the matter in question was not decided on a substantive issue. So it came as no surprise when the U.S. Ninth Circuit Court of Appeals denied our petition for an early hearing. What was a surprise, however, was a dissenting opinion in the 2-to-1 decision that was worth every bit of effort that went into the appeal. The opinion was written by Judge Stephen Reinhardt, whose father happened to be a movie producer whose credits included *The Red Badge of Courage*. Reinhardt was a forthright, independent-minded jurist who, a few years later, would earn his own badge of courage when he raised his voice in defense of a federal bench that was being criticized by members of Congress as being too liberal on civil-liberties issues.

Here, in a four-page opinion, Judge Reinhardt agreed with the defense we filed before Judge Hatter. He argued that Lee's film should be afforded greater protection under the First Amendment because of its political content and subject matter. *Malcolm X,* he said, "is not merely ordinary entertainment but the dramatic expression of a highly controversial point of view on an extremely important subject—a point of view the public is entitled to hear. It is political speech in a raw though dramatic form."

Then he addressed the legal questions of speech and copyright issues, which, he noted, were of extraordinary public concern. "Time is always of the essence in speech cases," he said. "Courts must resolve them promptly. The failure to do so is often a resolution in itself. Here, the unwillingness of the courts to act in a timely manner may have a direct impact on the content of important political expression. The public may never see *X* in the form its creator intended—in the form that delivers the message Spike Lee sought to convey. There is no explanation before us, and none comes readily to mind for the district court's unwillingness to act."

He rejected Holliday's argument that Lee could use a different image, saying that Lee felt that the image he had chosen best expressed his view that the American dream was, like the flag, being consumed by racial polarization. The artist's choice of how to deliver his message to the public must be protected by law, he said, and it is not for the court to decide whether it is appropriate.

Though Reinhardt's dissent would resonate in future court decisions, it would be of little use to Spike Lee. The court's refusal to grant an early hearing was indeed "a resolution in itself." The appeals court's ruling had come down on September

29, just two days before our deadline for distribution, and there was nowhere else for us to go. We considered going back before the California federal trial court and trying to get the case heard by a different judge, but there was not enough time. The Rodney King footage would have to be deleted unless we could reach an out-of-court settlement with Holliday. As it turned out, Holliday was not averse to doing business. For while the courts' decisions had the effect of preserving his copyright, nothing had been decided in his favor. The merits of his suit had not been considered, and all he was due to receive was a bill for legal expenses. After demanding several million dollars, Holliday said he would grant Lee nonexclusive rights to the footage in exchange for $100,000—twice the sum his former agent had agreed to—and recognition that he owned the copyright. It was a settlement, then, in which each party got what it wanted, but the larger issue of First Amendment protection remained unresolved.

The majority opinion of the appeals court did not comment upon the constitutional question; it merely followed the judicial protocol of declining to overturn the discretionary decisions of a lower court. Only Judge Reinhardt felt compelled to view the case in a wider context. His opinion marked the first time a judicial distinction had been made based upon the quality of the product, and while his dissent did not rewrite law, it offered the possibility of influencing future cases in which First Amendment rights ran up against the protection afforded by copyright. Years later other judges relied on his opinion to help move the law in that direction.

Indeed, the laws of copyright, as well as libel, were already entangled in a snare of legal controversy. They were in the process of being rewritten and applied to the rarefied atmosphere of cyberspace. The growth of the electronic media had begun to raise new questions for which there were no ready answers. Who owned an idea? When a piece of information moved across the Internet, who was responsible for its accuracy? Was the on-line company the equal of a publisher and therefore accountable for its network's content, or merely the distributor who was free of liability? Just how complex these issues were and how uncertain the ground on which they rested was illustrated in a 1995 test case when an investment-banking firm challenged one of the three leading on-line providers, Prodigy Services, Inc., in a $200 million libel suit.

The suit turned on the pivotal question of whether on-line services such as Prodigy were legally liable for the truth of statements carried across their lines, as a publisher would be for remarks made in his newspaper or magazine, or whether such services were no more than conduits of information, like a telephone company, which bears no responsibility for the actions of its users.

The case took root early on the morning of Sunday, October 23, 1994, when an anonymous subscriber posted a series of messages about Stratton Oakmont Inc., an investment-banking firm in Lake Success, New York, on Prodigy's "Money Talk" bulletin board. The messages accused Stratton and its president, Daniel Porush, of committing criminal and fraudulent acts in connection with the initial offering of the stock of Solomon-Page Ltd. earlier that month. The subscriber, who claimed to be a lawyer, said Stratton was a "cult of brokers who either lie for a living or get fired" and that Porush was a "soon to be proven criminal." Similar remarks were posted for the better part of two weeks before they came to Porush's attention. Porush then made the first move in an improbable scenario complete with an unlikely cast of characters and misadventures worthy of Molière.

With orders to get the defamatory messages off the system, Porush chose to represent him an attorney by the name of Jacob

Zamansky, who had spent most of his career as a securities litigator. Zamansky had represented Stratton before but was a stranger to First Amendment law, and he responded much like a character actor who had been given his first starring role. "This is the best thing that's ever happened to me in my life," he told the press as the case continued to draw public notice.

For its part, Stratton Oakmont would have been no one's first choice as a plaintiff in a case that could make new law and echo with constitutional vibrations. Specializing in penny-stock issues, Stratton, which was founded in 1989, had been on the wrong end of legal proceedings almost from its inception. The Securities and Exchange Commission had sued Stratton in 1992 for what it called "boiler room" brokerage activities. Following extensive investigation, the SEC had charged that Stratton "was systematically engaging in . . . high-pressure, fraudulent sales tactics: improper price predictions, refusing to allow sales, crossing customer orders, failing to advise customers of the risks and speculative nature of the investments." Without admitting or denying the SEC's findings, Stratton agreed to be censured and to submit to an audit by an independent investigator, whose recommendations the firm agreed to follow. Porush, one of three principals named in the suit, was suspended from acting in a supervisory capacity for a year and fined $100,000.

Now Stratton filed a libel claim against Prodigy seeking $200 million, claiming it had lost customers, suffered immeasurable harm to its good reputation, and was unfairly being subjected to state and federal investigations brought on by the statements posted on Prodigy's bulletin board. Porush charged that the public had been led to think he was a crook and that he would never be able to work again in the securities business.

Doubtless aware of Stratton's vulnerability, Zamansky, with the instincts of a street fighter, surprised everyone by going for a preemptive strike. He moved for a partial summary judgment

on the question of whether Prodigy was to be considered a publisher and therefore liable for what appeared on its bulletin
board. Prodigy's attorney, John Kinzey, Jr., of LeBoeuf, Lamb,
Greene & MacRae, did not take Zamansky's motion seriously.
Given Stratton's questionable reputation, he probably expected
at worst a small out-of-court settlement. In any event, he certainly could not have anticipated a judge's granting Stratton's
request for a speedy judgment—which is precisely what the
judge did, before Kinzey had even begun to examine Stratton's
or Porush's alleged fraudulent conduct.

There had, at that time, been only one precedent case addressing on-line services, and that had resulted in a ruling favorable to the defendant. In 1991 a federal district court in
Manhattan found that CompuServe was the electronic equivalent of a library or bookstore and so could be held liable only if
it knew or could be expected to know that it was distributing
defamatory material. With no other case law to go by, how, one
might have asked, could a judge summarily find that Prodigy
acted as publisher?

Zamansky, however, had done his homework. He discerned
a distinction between CompuServe and Prodigy that LeBoeuf,
Lamb failed to find. When Prodigy went on-line, in 1989, it
billed itself as the family-safe service. Unlike its competitors,
Prodigy monitored every message before it appeared on its bulletin boards. Material that was deemed offensive was deleted;
statements that were potentially libelous were verified before
being sent into cyberspace. But as its membership grew to more
than two million subscribers in 1993, Prodigy's monitors found
themselves unable to screen the more than 75,000 messages that
were funneling through the system each day. So the company
decided to split the difference. It implemented an automated
scanning device that rejected messages containing profanity,
racial or ethnic slurs, or clearly obscene content. It continued to
employ monitors, but they intervened only after a user com-

plained about a note that had appeared. Prodigy no longer maintained total control over what was shown on its bulletin boards, and it had advised its users of the change in policy.

But attorneys for LeBoeuf, Lamb neglected to document the shift in the company's operation. Also, since they had never attacked Stratton's practices, the court record showed Stratton to be dirt-free. Worst of all, LeBoeuf, Lamb filed a woefully inadequate set of papers, and state supreme court judge Stuart L. Ain ruled accordingly. While acknowledging that, in general, on-line services should not he held accountable for the truth of the messages on their bulletin boards, Prodigy's claims of editorial control, he said, exposed it to a higher degree of liability. The judge further noted that "no documentation or detailed explanation" of changes in Prodigy's editorial policies had been submitted as evidence. It was a devastating decision for the entire industry, opening the way for countless libel suits that would turn on the question of how much control an on-line service could be expected to exercise. Concerned with the possible consequences, Prodigy fired LeBoeuf, Lamb and asked me to represent it.

Persuading the court to rehear the case would be no easy matter. Courts do not grant motions to reargue at the whim of the petitioner. One must first show that there is new evidence to be presented. But the party who enters the motion also must provide a justifiable excuse for not having placed those facts before the court in the first instance, and we were unable to explain why previous counsel had failed to document Prodigy's change in policy. Zamansky, derisive of our predicament, later told Judge Ain, "They're looking for what we used to call in stickball a do-over; there are no do-overs in court."

Zamansky thought he had us, and the entire on-line service industry, backed into a corner. As he viewed it, we would either have to settle or take our chances on appeal. But an appeal, he reasoned correctly, involved substantial risk, for if we lost, the

ruling would have behind it the force of a highly respected appeals court rather than that of a lower-court judge, and such a
precedent would have far-reaching consequences.

Circumstances called for an unorthodox strategy, and my
associate David Atlas and I developed an aggressive, two-
pronged approach that we thought might prove effective. First,
we would make it clear that we would not talk settlement; there
would be no negotiations with Stratton Oakmont. Second, we
would put on hold a First Amendment appeal and focus instead
on the absolute defense against libel—truth. The case had gotten a great deal of publicity, and Prodigy's initial defeat had
brought cries of anguish from the First Amendment bar and the
computer industry. We decided to use the publicity to our advantage. We stated publicly that we planned to prove beyond a
doubt that the statements made about Stratton were not libelous because they were true. Every newspaper article an-
nouncing our plans also repeated the charges made against
Stratton.

In accordance with our "truth defense," we served a set of
discovery demands on Stratton Oakmont asking for, among
other items, the confidential SEC report on the firm's "boiler
room" activities. One had reason to infer that Stratton's eager-
ness to settle its differences with the SEC had been motivated at
least in part by its desire to keep the report from reaching the
public. Now, once produced in the process of discovery, it
would become part of the public record. Yet, how could Stratton Oakmont balk at the request? A firm that claims its reputation has been damaged can hardly contend that information
about its reputation is irrelevant. Stratton was now trapped, and
Zamansky knew it.

Almost immediately, he began calling our office and suggesting a settlement. He started at $4 million and slowly, over
several weeks, adjusted the figure downward. We refused every
offer. "We want to get that decision reversed," we said, "and

we'll need all those documents for discovery." His calls became more frequent, and with each call his settlement demands grew smaller. What started as a $200 million claim shrank to $100,000 and a full-page apology in *The New York Times* and *The Wall Street Journal*. A few weeks later Zamansky was ready to settle for the apology alone, but we remained adamant. Finally, he called and said his client wanted out of the case and was ready to walk away without a formal apology; a simple "I'm sorry" would suffice.

We structured a statement saying, "Prodigy is sorry if the offensive statements concerning Stratton and Mr. Porush, which were posted on Prodigy's Money Talk bulletin board by an unauthorized and unidentified individual, in any way caused injury to their reputation." We did not, as such, admit to any wrongdoing. Our statement was tantamount to telling someone, "I'm sorry to hear that your mother died." In return, Stratton agreed to join us in urging Judge Ain that it would be in the best interest of the on-line industry for him to reverse his earlier decision and agree to rehear the case. Then Stratton would drop its suit and we would both walk away, leaving behind a record entirely void of precedent.

It appeared at the time to be a total triumph. In just a few months, Stratton, the victor in the early stages of an important libel suit, had agreed to forfeit a $200 million claim, drop all charges, and join in a petition asking the judge to reverse his decision. For a client who had been in a losing position it didn't get any better than that. But the impulse to celebrate was premature. We entered Judge Ain's chambers with an air of utter confidence; we left stunned, with the sense of disbelief one feels when defeat comes unexpectedly and with no predictable cause.

I knew a little about Judge Ain before I met him but not nearly enough. I knew he was a staunch Nassau County Republican, that he had been appointed to the state supreme court by

Senator D'Amato, who had virtually total control over such appointments in Queens and Long Island, and I knew too that there was a disquieting connection between D'Amato and Stratton Oakmont. Stratton had been a big contributor to the senator's campaigns, and it was fairly well known that D'Amato had made a great deal of quick money through the firm's penny-stock offerings. So the possibility of an unholy alliance suggested itself, but there still seemed to be little need for concern. My request for a rehearing was, after all, uncontested. What cause could a judge have for denying such a request when it was joined by both parties to the lawsuit?

But my sense of assurance was shaken the moment I entered Judge Ain's chambers. The judge seemed strangely out of place in his own office. The Nassau County Courthouse is an old building, with cavernous, elegantly appointed rooms, and here sat Judge Ain, a short, squat, unprepossessing man nearly inconspicuous in an office that seemed to have been designed to deprive its occupant of context. The room was as large as a main conference room in a corporate headquarters. Its walls were paneled with fine wood and covered with books. The judge's desk was of a deep mahogany hue and scaled to the dimensions of his chambers. I barely had time to fix the judge in his surroundings when he offered a greeting that upset my balance completely. He came around his desk, placed an arm across my shoulders, and said, "You have a lovely wife."

It was not the kind of greeting one expects from a man one has never met before.

"How do you know that?" I said.

The judge responded with a reassuring smile. Then it occurred to me that an announcement of my recent marriage had appeared in *The New York Times* along with a photo of my wife and me, and it had doubtless been brought to the judge's attention. But as he led me to a chair near his desk, the judge demonstrated that that was not the only detail of my background with which he was familiar.

"We have a mutual friend," he said, naming Ken Gribetz, the former Rockland County district attorney whom I had gotten to know rather well during the two-year trial of Kathy Boudin. "He thinks very highly of you."

Clearly, the judge had been doing some research. It wasn't as though he was hoping to find something untoward in my past; I think he was trying to get a sense of me, of what manner of man I was, because when we got to discussing my request for a rehearing he said, in a very friendly tone, "You don't want to embarrass me, do you? If you want me to reverse my decision, you have to find a way for me to do it without embarrassing myself. This was a big case, it got a lot of press. I'm often interviewed about it, people around the courthouse comment on it, I go to conferences, people ask me to speak. I can't just turn around now and say I was wrong."

Right then I knew for certain that I was in for a difficult time. For while the law is a sturdy instrument, it is rarely strong enough to pry a man loose from the public image he wishes to project. And Judge Ain, now well on in years, had discovered his image at a time of life when reconstruction would not come easily. A respectable though undistinguished judicial career had suddenly turned into something special. Judge Ain had written his name into the books of legal precedent. Out of nowhere he had become the Brandeis and Cardozo of cyberspace, and he was not about to relinquish that slim claim to judicial renown.

In subsequent meetings with the judge I did my best to explain how he could reverse his decision without embarrassment. Look, I said, you don't have to say you were wrong the first time. All you have to do is say, "On the set of facts I was presented with initially, my decision was correct. But now I am given a new set of facts, which both parties concede to be true, and based upon this new evidence, which was not available to me before, I am changing my decision." There is no disgrace in that, I told him. "Your statement can be written in broad enough terms to make it a standard-setting decision for the whole industry." But he would not relent.

We filed our motion, we argued it, and we lost. In his ruling denying our request, Judge Ain cited the lack of guidance concerning the Internet and noted that "this is a developing area of the law (in which it appears that the law has thus far *not* kept pace with technology) so that there is a real *need* for some precedent. To simply vacate that precedent . . . would remove the only existing New York precedent in this area leaving the law even further behind the technology."

It was a foolish and disingenuous statement. In effect, Ain said that the laws governing the Internet needed clarification and a bad precedent was better than none at all. For there is little doubt that his was a bad decision. Even as he was hearing our request, the Communications Decency Act was moving through Congress with a stipulation that would override the Stratton Oakmont–Prodigy ruling. The CDA contains a safe-harbor provision that says no on-line computer service can be held liable for the statements of other parties.

Stratton Oakmont was finally and permanently expelled from the securities industry in December 1996 by the National Association of Securities Dealers for defrauding hundreds of customers. In a last-ditch effort to remain afloat, Stratton filed for Chapter 11 bankruptcy protection and sought to reorganize as a merchant bank. A federal judge in New York quickly ended that attempt and ordered the firm to be liquidated.

Nonetheless, Judge Ain's decision that Prodigy alone among on-line services was vulnerable to libel suits still stands and has been cited as precedent in lawsuits in other states. The dangers inherent in that ruling are, of course, enormous. There are perhaps ten million people or more who have the ability to put allegedly libelous statements on the Internet today, and if the on-line services are held liable, they will be driven out of business.

The question of who can or should be held responsible will not be decided quickly. Cyberspace is the next frontier at which the great First Amendment battles will be fought. In the sheer vastness of its reach, the Internet holds out the possibility of taking America back to its roots, of reviving the mystique of the town forum where every citizen has the opportunity to have a say. Those who wish to make their views known will no longer need to persuade a publisher of their worth or own their own printing press or gain access to the airwaves. The spectrum of political debate will be greatly expanded. Those with unpopular beliefs who once mounted soapboxes in New York's Union Square to address their fellow citizens by the handful will now be able to reach millions. As with all speech, guidelines will evolve, limits will be set regarding such issues as obscenity, defamation, libel, copyright. In the early decades of the next century, dramas small and large will be played out in court-rooms, the decisions will fill volumes of new case law, and exactly where those limits are drawn will determine what we can and cannot say, and define the content of our national character.

PART VI

Stretching the Limits

Chapter 13

During the early years of my practice, all through the sixties, free speech had come under siege from many directions. Political speech, always the first casualty in time of crisis, was being muffled in the name of national security. The pornography patrol, which was being neutered by a spate of court decisions, was in a frenzy to seek out and mute the peddlers of obscenity before the constitutional curtain fell. Libel suits seeking astronomical awards were being used as instruments of suppression. The First Amendment seemed to need all the protection it could get, and my concern was to lift the restraints wherever I found them. It was not a time for musing upon the subtleties of nuance. The antidote to bad speech is always better speech. I had given little thought to the notion that the zealous protection of certain types of speech—speech whose message was bought and paid for—could actually subvert the intent of the First Amendment.

The case that first focused my attention on the broad latitude of discretion granted to commercial speech was a suit brought by the actor Robert Redford against a tobacco company that was test-marketing a new brand of cigarettes bearing his name. Redford, a personal friend and client, called one morning in 1973 to tell me he had received in the mail a package of cigarettes called Redford. It was manufactured by the Lorillard tobacco company, certainly no stranger to the indus-

try. The package was attractive enough, with white block letter-
ing on burnt red set against a background of the sun rising
above rugged mountain terrain. Beneath the name Redford was
the message "Fresh as the wind." If the setting and the name
were not enough to conjure the film star's image, the promotional material appeared to reinforce it. The Redford version of
the Marlboro Man was a hardy outdoor type with a shock of
dark blond hair and a trim mustache. He was shown working in
the field alongside his pickup truck and pausing to light a "fresh
as the wind" Redford cigarette.

The intentional identification with the Robert Redford of
Sundance fame seemed clear enough. His reputation as an envi-
ronmentalist was already well established. His movie persona as
a fresh-faced outdoorsman with the pioneer spirit had been
communicated in his roles in *Downhill Racer* and as the Sundance Kid. If a man so devoted to the dictates of clean living
found cigarette smoking compatible with the good life, perhaps
the dangers were not so great after all, the message seemed
to be.

We filed suit in federal court in Manhattan, making two
claims: first, that the advertising was false, since it implied, contrary to all evidence, that cigarettes enriched a healthy lifestyle;
and second, that the use of the name Redford led the public to
believe that the actor either owned the product or endorsed it.
Lorillard, of course, denied both allegations. Redford was the
name of two old towns in England, the company noted, and it
was seeking to evoke the aura of British dignity and elegance
found in cigarette brands such as Chesterfield, Marlboro, and
Parliament, while combining it with a sense of rugged American
individualism. When the name was test-marketed, they said,
few of those surveyed identified the name with the actor; most
thought it referred to a large tree.

But it was on the first claim—the claim of false advertising—that the company was truly vulnerable, and I was eager to

test the limits of the First Amendment as applied to commercial speech, for it was my growing belief that speech whose sole intent was the sale of a product was inherently different from political expression and should be held to a tighter standard. Toward that end, I began using the federal discovery process of depositions and interrogatories to ask some difficult questions. I wanted to know precisely what it was that made the cigarette "fresh as the wind." I also tried to compel John J. Bresnahan, the vice president of advertising and brand management for Lorillard, to address the health issues involved. Did the implication that cigarette smoking was consistent with good health constitute false advertising? And, more broadly, should such commercial claims be accorded First Amendment protection? I was ready to introduce a mountain of evidence regarding the hazards of tobacco use. I never got the chance.

In 1973, it was early in the day for suits seeking damages against tobacco companies. Cigarette advertising was still commonplace, and Lorillard apparently had little appetite for breaking new ground. Despite a huge investment of time and money spent researching, creating, and building a market for Redford cigarettes, the company decided to walk away from the suit. One year after the suit was filed, it agreed to withdraw Redford cigarettes from the market. The outcome, though a legal victory, was not the one I had hoped for. Calling to question the truth of cigarette advertising had seemed the ideal battleground to make the case for limiting the reach of commercial speech. But with the cigarette now off the market and Redford, a nonsmoker, unable to claim personal injury, we had lost all grounds for pressing litigation. Lorillard, in effect, had chosen to forfeit its investment rather than defend the legitimacy of its advertising policies. In the process, I had lost the chance I was looking for. Nearly twenty years passed before another opportunity came my way.

During that time, commercial speech, nourished by the

phenomenal growth of media conglomerates and a Supreme Court that seemed to confuse speech with money, attained an increasingly broad level of protection. While the courts traditionally have recognized a distinction between commercial and political speech, that distinction has become blurred as the media barons, conduits for both types of expression, have gained greater influence and control. In a recent decision, for example, the Supreme Court ruled that placing caps on campaign spending by political parties infringed on their rights of free speech.

For the past two hundred years, the First Amendment has been a bulwark against government interference with freedom of expression. First Amendment advocates have resisted attempts to limit speech, recognizing that the government can hurl powerful resources against unpopular speakers and silence its critics. As the Supreme Court has said, the First Amendment rests on the premise that it is governmental rather than private power that is the major threat to expression.

Today the issue has become even more complicated because private power and money have an enormous impact on both the speaker and those who listen to the speech and because we have new methods of transmitting that speech. In rejecting the television cable companies' claim that "must-carry" restrictions (which require owners to transmit local broadcasts on their networks) violate their First Amendment rights, federal district court judge Stanley Sporkin said the cable companies "have come to court, not because their freedom of speech is seriously threatened but because their profits are; to dress up their complaints in First Amendment garb demeans the principles for which the First Amendment stands and the protection it was designed to afford."

Though the judge's point is well taken, the situation is not quite so simple. There are fine distinctions that still must be made. In a case involving cable television heard by the Second

Circuit Court of Appeals early in 1997, I argued, for the first time, that government intervention is necessary for the protection of free speech. The case, murky with other issues and allegations, saw devoted First Amendment advocates on both sides of the issue. Friend-of-the-court briefs by unwavering defenders of free speech argued against the cable owners' claim that the First Amendment barred the government from having any say in what programming they carried on their channels.

A few months later, the Supreme Court split 5 to 4 in a pivotal case called *Turner Broadcasting* v. *F.C.C.* Seeking to differentiate among the media and encourage free speech, the Court upheld restrictions on cable owners that no court would ever place on a newspaper or book-publishing company. In future cases, the courts will define specific rules for each of the media and other rules for various consumer products because of their growing tendency to identify speech with economic power. That association already has resulted in commercial speech being granted a wider berth.

The courts, like the Constitution, are structured to balance competing interests. The protection accorded individual rights is obliged to live side by side with an economic system that puts a high premium on the freedom to turn a profit from commercial transactions. The two are not always the most congenial partners. During the Industrial Revolution, the rights of individuals to decent working conditions and fair wages clashed head-to-head with the property rights of those who owned the instruments of production. Now, in the midst of what might yet be called the Informational Revolution, individuals' rights to information untainted by private interest are often at the mercy of those who control the outlets of communication.

The only legal restriction on commercial speech is that it make no false claims. Manufacturers have the right, even the obligation, to try to sell their products. Tobacco companies are required to inform the consumer that cigarettes are harmful to one's health, but that does not prevent them from concealing evidence regarding the habit-forming qualities of nicotine. It does not prevent them from fashioning advertisements aimed at a fertile teenage market. Their subliminal message is that the hazards of smoking are offset by the fresh-as-the-wind freedom of spirit enjoyed by the rugged individualists who use their products. The right to deliver the message is bought with money and given First Amendment protection by courts that seem unable to differentiate between the government's attempt to censor speech and its right to regulate power.

My next chance to test the use of the First Amendment in the interests of such speech did not come until 1991. The product at issue this time was malt liquor, a high-octane version of beer that was being marketed principally in black ghetto areas. My client was an entertainer who had little in common with Robert Redford. Chuck D was the hard-edged, controversial leader of a popular rap group called Public Enemy. With a voice like a boom box and a manner rough as gravel, Chuck would have been no one's first choice to set sail into high winds in the name of public virtue. He was a social activist in the sixties tradition of the Black Panthers, a disciple of the young Malcolm X, a defender of the Reverend Louis Farrakhan. He took few pains to deny charges of anti-Semitism. He cranked out lyrics that offended gentler sensibilities, while fashioning an image described by one admirer as Public Enemy Number One, a title he wore proudly enough to share it with his rap group.

There was, however, another side to Chuck D, known better to his fans than to his critics. He was aggressively protective of black urban youth, outspoken in his opposition to alcohol, drugs, and violence. He and Public Enemy were particularly critical of the malt-liquor industry, which, they felt, targeted and exploited the black teenage market. Malt liquor, which is not brewed but injected with alcohol at a ratio half again as potent as beer or ale, had long been considered a "black" drink. G. Heileman Company sold an estimated 75 percent of its Colt 45 malt liquor to black consumers, largely with the commercial help of the actor Billy Dee Williams.

Chuck D, never timid about expressing his views, had left little doubt where he stood on the subject. During his concerts, he was known to go into the audience and lecture his listeners on the dangers of the product. In a public statement carried in the press, he was quoted as saying, "This shit is destroying us. Malt liquor has fifty percent more alcohol than beer, and they sell it to *us* without caring what happens. A lot of times when you see brothers fighting, they're drunk." Reaching an even wider audience and one at which his message was aimed directly, Public Enemy produced an album called *Apocalypse 91 ... The Enemy Strikes Black,* which includes a track entitled "1 Million Bottlebags," a takeoff on the body bags used to carry away the casualties of war.

Imagine, then, Chuck's sense of disbelief when he heard himself singing the praises of St. Ides malt liquor in a radio commercial. In a lyric taken from "Bring the Noise," a cut from Public Enemy's hit album *It Takes a Nation of Millions to Hold Us Back,* there was his own unmistakable baritone chanting, "The incredible Number One," with the words "St. Ides" inserted, in a voice other than his own, between "incredible" and "Number One." In all, more than one third of the sixty-second commercial featured Chuck's voice wrapped around a glowing endorsement of a product whose use he had consistently denounced. Beyond a clear case of copyright infringement was the damage done to Chuck D's reputation among his most devoted followers, who were not unfamiliar with the claims made by St. Ides in its carefully structured advertising campaign. By implication, he was now identified with such slogans as "Get your girl in the mood quicker and get your Jimmy thicker with St. Ides malt liquor" and "Heat up your brain and give it a suntan."

Chuck translated his outrage into a five-million-dollar lawsuit against St. Ides malt liquor and the McKenzie River Corporation, which marketed the product. There was a host of claims, including copyright violation and invasion of privacy, but the principal one was defamation, charging that Chuck's reputation had been seriously damaged. As counsel for Public Enemy, I now believed I had the case that would allow me to pry commercial speech loose from full First Amendment protection. There were no questions here, as there were in the Redford case, of identification or intent. It was Chuck D's voice on the commercial. It was used, without his knowledge or consent, in the service of a cause he had publicly opposed.

Russell Smith, an attorney in my office, phoned Minott Wessinger, the CEO of McKenzie River, who played the recording for us from his office in California. He sounded as shocked as we were. He told us that the commercial had been independently produced, and he was unaware of its content, but he acknowledged it was Chuck D's voice on the tape. Wessinger agreed to withdraw the commercial, but the damage had already been done. By all accounting, it had been played at least five hundred times in more than fifteen major cities on MTV between July 4 and August 12, 1991. It also had been widely distributed on a promotional audiocassette called *Summer 1991.* We told Wessinger that we estimated the damages to Chuck's reputation at five million dollars and gave him a week to send us a check. At the same time, we began preparing a case that would be broad enough to place the abuses of commercial speech under public scrutiny.

Russ took it upon himself to document our case. He went into black communities in New York City in an effort to gather support for an offensive against the promotion of malt liquor. He spoke at church meetings and in community centers. He interviewed young people as well as their parents. It was at once a campaign of mobilization and education, in support of Chuck D and against the lies, illusions, and misconceptions employed by malt-liquor companies to exploit the unsuspecting and the vulnerable. Russ spoke with one youngster who said he ripped his Chuck D poster from the wall of his room when he heard the St. Ides commercial. A mother told him that her son refused to leave his room for two days because he felt betrayed by his hero, who turned out to be a fraud. In all, Russ compiled a list of seventy-five youths who assured us they were ready to testify in court to their loss of respect and admiration for Chuck D and the feeling of violation they felt at being made the prey of the malt-liquor industry. We also collected material on the company's promotional operation. We learned that they used focus groups made up of teenagers, testing them to see which types of advertisements they responded to most enthusiastically.

In the meantime, the case dragged on in the federal district court in Manhattan. St. Ides employed three law firms, and they filed an avalanche of motions on each of seven different claims. As each motion was denied, their settlement offer increased. They started with $75,000 and by increments went to $375,000. Finally, the judge provided some impetus. After reviewing their most recent set of motions, he threw them out without requiring us to respond. At that point, St. Ides's offer jumped precipitously, to $1.4 million. I don't know how much more we might have gotten, but I wanted to bring the case to trial, to give the entire issue a public hearing. The press had been covering the suit and was certain to give even wider coverage to a courtroom proceeding. But Chuck was a reluctant client. He was not particularly interested in the intrigues and strategies of the legal system, and he was more than a little put off by the grudging pace at which it moved. Nearly two years had passed since the suit was filed, and Chuck was impatient for a resolution. We took the $1.4 million.

All the same, while we did not get to test the limits of commercial speech to the degree I had hoped for, we certainly had taken it a step further. The publicity the case attracted didn't end with the settlement. ABC-TV devoted a segment of its prime-time *20/20* show to examining the malt-liquor industry and the validity of the claims it made in its advertisements. CNN also ran a hard-hitting piece that was shown at a nationwide conference on alcohol abuse conducted by the U.S. Department of Health and Human Services. It is perhaps more than coincidence that malt liquor commercials have virtually disappeared from television and are rarely seen any longer in the print media.

One of the hazards in seeking to set limits on commercial speech is that the line separating it from other forms of expression is not always clear. An advertisement for a candidate seeking election, for example, is protected as political speech, but few would deny that its intent is not strictly to inform the public. The candidate is seeking votes and perhaps a contribution or two to his campaign war chest. In like manner, defining the nature of satire when it is used in a commercial context can be equally troublesome, since by its very nature satire seeks to express truth by distorting reality. The courts traditionally have granted generous First Amendment shelter to the use of satire; it is not, however, entirely free of peril.

As satire is nothing without a target ripe for criticism, its terrain is mined with the prospect of suits charging defamation, libel, or invasion of privacy. When shadings of obscenity enter the mix, when one of the subjects of the satire is a little-known fashion model, when the satirist has a nationwide reputation as a purveyor of pornography, the terrain becomes even more treacherous.

Al Goldstein had spent a good part of his career in the

media stretching the limits of free speech while at the same time traducing every suggestion of good taste. A pioneer in the marketing of pornography, Goldstein was among the first to take advantage of Supreme Court decisions loosening the reins on obscenity. He began publishing *Screw* magazine nearly thirty years ago, and it is still the nation's best-known and most widely read sex publication. A few decades later Goldstein was just as quick to plunge into the late-night cable-television market as executive producer of the sexually explicit *Midnight Blue*. It was a brief, thirty-second segment of this show that landed him, not for the first time, in the snare of the legal machinery.

Goldstein, who has a quick eye for hypocrisy, particularly when it is employed in the interest of financial gain, had viewed a television commercial for Wasa crispbread, in which the implicit suggestion of sex was used to sell the product. The commercial opens with an attractive, statuesque model draped only in a towel, apparently after a morning shower, entering the kitchen where a man in a bathrobe is washing his breakfast dishes. As the two embrace, the camera cuts to pictures of various types of bread to the accompaniment of a voice-over that says: "Today, eighteen million eat this as bread [cutting to a picture of a bagel, then back to the couple], fifty-five million eat this [cutting to a picture of a croissant and back], two hundred forty million eat this [a slice of white bread and back], but only eight million eat this as bread [a shot of Wasa crispbread]." The commercial ends with the model leaning back seductively on the kitchen counter, embracing her companion as her elbow knocks a box of Wasa Crispbread off the counter.

Midnight Blue often featured segments satirizing the tacit use of sex in television commercials, and Goldstein recognized an opportunity when he saw one. He directed his staff to produce a parody of the crispbread commercial. The result was a clip that left the opening scene intact but proceeded to play havoc with the voice-over. Where the original version cut from the declaration of the number of millions who "eat this" to various types of bread, the adaptation flashed instead to scenes of couples engaged in imaginative varieties of oral sex.

To Goldstein, the adaptation fit neatly within the borders of classic, if perhaps tasteless, satire: By magnifying the manner in which the suggestion of sex was used to sell unrelated products, he had mimicked it into absurdity. A reasonable viewer, he was certain, would have little difficulty distinguishing the literal from the parodic. Moreover, it was clearly in the public interest to turn a bright light on the hypocrisy of vendors who had few compunctions about enticing consumers with the trappings of sex while pretending to scorn graphic depictions of the real thing. As Goldstein saw it, he was performing a public service.

The model in the original commercial, Angie Geary, a wife and a mother who resided in the quaint little town of South Kingstown, Rhode Island, saw it otherwise. Without her knowledge or consent, she had been given a starring role in a blatantly pornographic production. Her privacy had been invaded and her professional reputation sullied. The parody had been broadcast at least six times during October and November 1989. According to her complaint, a number of friends and business acquaintances in the advertising and entertainment industry had either seen or heard about her appearance on *Midnight Blue.* She also claimed that the company that produced the original commercial had withdrawn it from national television, cutting off the royalty income she received from its broadcast. Her career, she felt sure, was a shambles. Now, in papers filed in U.S. District Court in Manhattan, she was seeking restitution. The asking price was $29 million.

I found it difficult not to feel a degree of sympathy for Angie Geary. There was no question that she was badly served by Goldstein's self-indulgent adventure in parody. She could never have anticipated seeing herself cast in a film that featured graphic sexual acrobatics. She had, in every sense, the right to moral outrage. Unfortunately for her, however, she stood on weak legal ground, for New York State statutes and case law provided her with little protection.

Geary's suit stated two causes of action: invasion of privacy and defamation. We were ready to argue that she had no case on either claim. The adaptation, we said, was entitled to First Amendment immunity since it was satirical in nature and concerned a matter of public interest; to wit, the use of sexual innuendo to sell unrelated products. Just a few months earlier, a U.S. Supreme Court decision had included parody under the umbrella of protected speech. The justices ruled unanimously that the rap group 2 Live Crew's adaptation of the tune "Oh, Pretty Woman" enjoyed the same "fair use" protection as "criticism, comment, news reporting, teaching, scholarship, and research" even though parody was not directly cited in the law. Writing for the Court, Justice David H. Souter noted that parody "can provide social benefit by shedding light on an earlier work, and, in the process, creating a new one." Because parody's "art lies in the tension between a known original and its parodic twin," he continued, a parody must be able to use enough of the original to be recognizable to the audience.

One could not have asked for a precedent from a higher source or one more clearly crafted to the occasion. Furthermore, the New York statute under which Geary filed her claim specifically stated that the aggrieved party's name or portrait cannot be used for "advertising purposes or for purposes of trade," which certainly did not apply to Goldstein's parody.

The claim of defamation was even more difficult to support, for the adaptation made no statement about Geary, nor was she identified in any way. Although she appeared, unwittingly, in a pornographic production, she was not depicted in an unfavorable light, and, we argued, given the context of the show as a whole, no reasonable viewer would be led to infer that she had consented to her appearance in the film or derived any profit from it.

Consequently, Goldstein asked that the case be dismissed, contending that, as a matter of law, Geary's claims were without foundation. Federal judge Kimba M. Wood did not see it that way. She denied his motion to dismiss, saying that entertainment or comedic broadcasts did not constitute categorically protected speech. She also found that a channel-surfing viewer might not have been aware that the parody was part of a larger context and said it should be left to a jury to decide whether reasonable people would know if Geary willingly participated in the adaptation and if it was intended as editorial commentary. She concluded that the issue was not free speech, but rather whether one could be prevented from "exploiting without payment . . . the image of a non-public figure without the person's consent."

Judge Wood's decision set loose the arduous process of discovery. Long hours of depositions stretched into months during which testimony was taken from Goldstein, Geary, and members of the modeling agency for which she worked. Several trial dates were set and, for one reason or another, deferred. Goldstein, of course, was not pleased about the circumstance in which he now found himself. Never the most agreeable of clients, he made for a testy witness during depositions. At one point, he baited Geary's attorney. "I know you're a lawyer," he said, "I'm not expecting the greatest amount of honesty or ethics. . . . Why don't we try an honest question?"

The attorney, John Barton, from a stylish Boston law firm, protested politely. "I resent your suggestion that I'm in any way dishonest or unethical," he said.

"Let's read the question," Goldstein said.

"Sir," said Barton, customarily a soft-spoken advocate, "this is my deposition."

"It's my life," Goldstein snapped.

Barton had reached the end of his tether. Pointing his finger directly at Goldstein, he barked, "I ask questions, you give the answers, you got that?"

The exchanges between the two never grew more cordial. Goldstein, a man unaccustomed to restraint, had continued to comment on the case during the process of discovery in editorials in *Screw* and on *Midnight Blue,* providing Barton with useful ammunition. As part of the defamation claim, Geary was obliged to prove malicious intent or reckless disregard of consequences, no easy matter, since Goldstein did not know the plaintiff and had never heard of her before she filed suit. But Goldstein had made the task a bit easier. Barton now was able to play a videotape in which the defendant was seen saying, "This woman wanted me; I think she did. She may have wanted my cock." And later, "What I did to that stupid Rhode Island model, I'm proud of."

As if such indiscretions were not enough, Goldstein also took out after Judge Wood with the unmindful zeal of a craftsman using his tools to repair a guillotine that was being fitted to his neck. He ran a succession of editorials called "Educating Kimba Wood," assailing the judge in nonjudicial terms and depicting her in various sexual postures. Barton introduced them into evidence, raising the possibility of a motion to disqualify the judge from hearing the case. But Kimba Wood is one of the most respected judges on the federal bench, regarded highly enough to have been considered by President Clinton as a candidate for U.S. attorney general. We chose to take our chances.

When discovery was completed, we filed a motion for summary judgment, asking that Geary's claims be denied by the court without benefit of trial. While a request for summary judgment has the same effect as a motion to dismiss—in each instance the case is thrown out of court—the criteria for granting them are quite different. A motion to dismiss, often made but rarely conceded, asserts that the law cited by the plaintiff does not apply directly to the charges being made. By contrast, summary judgment is requested after an investigation has been conducted and contends that the evidence gathered is insufficient to support the plaintiff's claims.

Our motion sat with the judge for more than a year, but as it turned out, her decision was worth the wait. In an uncommon display of judicial candor, Judge Wood reversed her earlier ruling on both claims.

"Upon reflection," she said, "I have decided that it was error for me to have included . . . a 'channel-surfing' viewer in the category of 'reasonable viewers.' . . . In doing so, I believe I gave insufficient weight to New York precedent emphasizing that a court deciding whether a statement may reasonably be interpreted as defamatory must take into account the full context in which the statement was promulgated." She concluded that "it would be clear to any viewer who watched for more than a few minutes that both the parody and *Midnight Blue* were produced by Mr. Goldstein; that they arose from his particular set of beliefs; and hence that the parody was part of the larger work of the *Midnight Blue* program." Judge Wood also did an about-face on Geary's privacy claim, finding that in past cases, New York courts had excluded "the satiric and fictional uses entirely" from the privacy law's definition of "advertising or trade purposes."

Geary's prompt appeal of the decision was withdrawn six months later, leaving the lower court's ruling intact. More than five years had passed since she filed her complaint. By then, *Midnight Blue* had long since run its course. *Screw* magazine continues to be published regularly, a weekly testament to the doctrine that every freedom worth protecting has its cost. Angie Geary would be ready to certify that on occasion it is the innocent and unwitting who are obliged to pay the price.

Chapter 14

When I represented the estate of John Cheever, I drew the ire of some members of the Authors Guild and raised eyebrows among those in the Association of American Publishers. The negative reaction, however, was short-lived and, as it turned out, of no great consequence. Although I had taken the case of a plaintiff against a publisher, there were no damages sought and our posture was basically a defensive one. I was, after all, doing no more than protecting a widow's right to determine the fate of her husband's unpublished work.

The circumstances were entirely different and the reaction far more extreme some years later when, for the first and only time in my career, I represented the plaintiff in a libel suit. Now the stakes were much higher. I had filed a twelve-million-dollar claim against a big-name columnist for the country's most widely read tabloid newspaper. The newspaper was the New York *Daily News,* the columnist was Mike McAlary, and the response from the community of First Amendment defenders was, to paraphrase Thomas Hobbes, quick, nasty, and brutish. I was accused of being an apostate and betraying my professional trust. I was summarily suspended from the nation's most important organization of libel defense attorneys, and I felt obliged to offer my resignation to the partners in my firm, whose future I had placed in jeopardy.

My client was a twenty-seven-year-old black lesbian who,

after reporting to police that she had been raped in Brooklyn's Prospect Park, was called a liar by McAlary in three of his columns. The assault had taken place on April 26, 1994, but it was not until McAlary had published his third column, on May 13, that she decided to file suit. Jane Doe, as she would be known publicly for the next three years, sought the advice of several attorneys, and they referred her to me. I found her to be a gentle, soft-spoken young woman who had been severely wounded, both physically and emotionally. "I have been raped twice," she told me, "first in the park and then in print. I can understand the randomness of crime but not the malicious attacks in the *News.*"

Without prompting, Jane Doe provided me with a full and candid personal history. She had been raised in Cincinnati, the daughter of a schoolteacher and a city planner. In 1984, she had been awarded a scholarship to Yale, where she majored in African-American studies and was once taken into custody by police during a protest against the university's investments in South Africa. She also played in the Yale marching band and studied drama with an eye toward a career in the theater. In 1990 she moved to New York, where she shared an apartment in a Brooklyn brownstone with three gay men and women. She managed to get a small part in an off-Broadway play but earned her living at jobs with several gay and lesbian social organizations.

Then she offered a detailed, tearful account of her assault and rape. Though she rarely visited Prospect Park, just a few blocks from her home, a short jog seemed like a fine idea on that warm spring afternoon. She put on a pair of blue-and-white running shorts, a white exercise top with peace symbols, and a purple sweatshirt and headed outdoors. Having run to the far end of the park, she walked a block to a grocery store and bought two bags of vegetables, then started back through the park on her way home. It was about five o'clock, with the sun just beginning to fade. As she walked along a narrow path around the side of Lookout Hill, she heard a man's voice behind her. She glanced over her shoulder and saw a man carrying what looked like a walking stick. The man came up behind her and grabbed her around the neck in a choke hold. She blacked out for a second or two and fell to the ground. When she regained consciousness, she tried to break free, but the man tightened his hold and threatened to draw a knife. Then he forced her up the hill to the back of a tree with a hollowed-out trunk and raped her. He told her not to look back until he left.

When Jane Doe sensed he was gone, she ran down the hill. She tried to flag down a few joggers, but they ignored her. Out in the middle of the street, crying, she saw a police car about to pass her. She slammed her bag of groceries against the side of the car to get the driver's attention. The car stopped, and she told the officer she had just been raped. She gave the policeman a description of her assailant: a dark-skinned man in his thirties or forties, bearded, slightly over six feet tall, wearing a red shirt, a black jacket with lots of pockets, and a cap that was not a baseball hat.

Now, as she related her story, Jane Doe periodically choked back tears, struggling to retain her composure. "I think about it," she said. "There's no place I can go where I won't have to think about it. How can I come to terms with that?" She told me that she wanted to go back to Prospect Park to confront the scene, to exorcise the demons, but "I can't," she said, "because I'm afraid." Months after the incident, its recounting still left her badly shaken. Yet there was a quiet strength about her, a hard-edged resolve to restore balance and set the record straight. If the rape had made her fearful, McAlary's columns had the somewhat cathartic effect of stirring her anger.

"Right after the rape," she said, "the first couple of days, I sealed my mind off, as if it had happened in a dream. Then a [rape] counselor showed me the article, said it was better to see it from her. I couldn't believe it. It was like a sucker punch."

Her voice was no longer quavering. It had taken on a firmer, self-assured tone. She had been helpless against the brute, physical force of the man who had raped her, but now, having been savaged in print, she felt she had the resources to fight back. She showed me copies of McAlary's columns. The first one had appeared on April 28, a day before McAlary's regular column was scheduled to appear. He apparently had been in haste to get into print.

Under the headline "Rape hoax the real crime," McAlary wrote that the police "believe they are being lied to," that "everyone who heard the woman's story about the alleged rape was calling it a hoax. The woman, who probably will wind up being arrested herself, invented the crime, they said, to promote her rally." The rally in reference was to be held the following weekend by a gay and lesbian organization protesting crime against the gay population. Immediately after reading the article, Jane Doe called the lead investigator on the case, Special Victims detective Andrea Sorrentino, who assured her that the police had nothing to do with the story and were operating on the premise that a rape had occurred.

"I could not fathom why [McAlary would] say it," Jane Doe told me. "I can't fathom it now. And I don't know why. I've never hurt anyone in my life."

But McAlary wasn't through. The following day, even as police commissioner William Bratton was issuing an apology to the victim, on the same page in which the *Daily News* carried a regular news story saying that police had recovered evidence supporting her claim, McAlary, in his regularly scheduled column, titled "No easy task exposing lie," compared Jane Doe to Tawana Brawley, a proven rape hoaxer. "How can the cops in Brooklyn . . . prove that this week's supposed victim wasn't raped the other night in Prospect Park?" he wrote. "They believe she lied, but they are letting her fade away, worried that genuine victims might not come forward."

Still, Jane Doe was not prepared, psychologically or emotionally, to take action against McAlary. The experience had left her numb; she was hoping the incident would soon play itself out and vanish from public consciousness. "I wanted the media to go away," she said. "I was depressed. I did not understand the back-and-forth between the police and McAlary. I stopped reading the papers."

But then, on May 13, three weeks after the incident, McAlary struck again. "I'm right, but that's no reason to cheer," read the headline above his column. Despite the fact that every newspaper in the city, including his own, had reported that the police lab found semen on Jane Doe's shorts and in her vagina, he wrote that there "was no evidence . . . to support the alleged victim's claim of rape in a public place." One of his police sources, he said, had told him, "Stand your ground. The lab is wrong." But, as it turned out, it was McAlary who was wrong. On May 10 a police memo had been issued, correcting an earlier report, saying there was conclusive proof of the presence of semen. "We have physical evidence that a rape did occur," police said. McAlary's column, crowing that he was right and the lab was wrong, appeared three days later. It was the trigger that spurred Jane Doe to take legal action.

"I had thought it was finally over," she said. "The police had substantiated my story, the lab reports proved I had been raped, every paper in the city was reporting the case accurately. I had put the early columns behind me. I believed that at that point even McAlary understood he had wronged me and was ready to let it go. When the last column appeared, days after police confirmed the attack on me, I knew I had to do something." She asked me to help her.

The woman seemed entirely credible to me. She had by this time ample corroboration to support her story. As for McAlary, although I had never met him, I was well aware of his reputation as a quick gun who was more concerned with getting a story first than getting it right. It was an admission he had made more than once and a distinction in which he took some pride. Testifying in a legal action between the *News* and the *New York Post* a few years earlier, he had explained, "In a newspaper war there's really no fair or unfair. In a barroom fight you're allowed to hit somebody with a bottle." In a sworn affidavit in that case, McAlary justified a reporter's fabricating events as simply a "writing device." Asked by an attorney to explain "the difference between a writing device and perjury," McAlary replied, under oath, "I don't know the difference 'cause I don't know what the word *perjury* means."

I knew what the word *perjury* meant, and more than thirty years of practice had left me with a finely honed sense of a witness's devotion to the truth. I believed Jane Doe was telling me the truth, that her account of the events was as accurate as she could make it. Still, I felt the need to proceed with caution. I understood that in filing a libel action against a member of the press I would be entering a minefield. Specialists in any occupation tend over time to resemble a priesthood whose members' first injunction is to fend for themselves by protecting one another. It is a catechism among First Amendment attorneys that under no circumstances do they represent the plaintiff in a libel case. They are bound by their code, so the thinking goes, to defend the libelous statements of a journalist in the same manner that a criminal lawyer must defend a man he knows is guilty. So if I felt compelled to challenge that dictum, I wanted to be as certain as I could that I would be entering the list on the side of the angels.

After several conversations with Jane Doe, I began conducting my own investigation. I spoke with her parents in Cincinnati. I met with the police officers involved in the case. I reviewed their records and the reports of the hospital and police lab. I visited the site of the attack with Jane Doe, and she pointed out the tree trunk behind which the assault took place.

I found that the grade up Lookout Hill was not so steep that a woman of five feet two could not have been forced to the top by a man perhaps a foot taller than she was. I also discovered that the top of the hill was not visible from the paths below, which is why there were no witnesses to be found. It was an emotional two hours that we spent in the park. She was shaken and crying much of the time, but she was precise and accurate in her description. Every detail was consistent with what I had read in the police report, and nothing that I saw or heard bore any relation to what McAlary had written. I was totally persuaded that she was telling the truth, and I was not alone in my conviction that McAlary's version of the events was a mix of fantasy and invention.

On the day McAlary's first column appeared, three *News* reporters warned their editors that some of their police contacts disputed the accuracy of his account. Not long afterward, thirty members of the paper's staff, including crime reporter Jerry Capeci, signed a petition calling the column "a disgrace" and urging the paper to issue "a public apology" to the woman "as well as [to] all of our readers."

It seemed clear enough that McAlary had rushed to print with his hoax story on the basis of little more than a gambler's hunch. He made no attempt to speak with the victim, he did not consult the lab or hospital reports, he never contacted the doctor who examined her, he did not think it necessary to visit the site of the attack. His alleged police sources were as amorphous as his conclusions. He had, so far as I could determine, virtually no foundation on which to build his story. It was, pure and simple, a product of his own imagination. In late June, I filed a libel suit against McAlary and the *News* asking two million dollars in compensatory damages and ten million in punitive damages.

We began taking depositions several months later. Depositions are a part of the legal process of discovery that precedes

every trial, both criminal and civil. They afford attorneys an opportunity to gather information and documents by examining
witnesses for the other side. Perhaps most important, since all
testimony is given under oath and can be used in court, they
lock a witness into a set of facts from which he cannot easily depart; to try to alter his story later is to invite a suspicion of perjury.

However, while depositions are as legally binding as testimony given in the courtroom, they are conducted under a much
looser set of guidelines; standard rules of evidence do not apply.
Objections, for example, are for the record only, and a witness
will answer each question unless his attorney directs him not to
respond. With lawyers afforded greater latitude and no trial
judge present to mediate, such proceedings sometimes take on
the rough-and-tumble aspect of a prizefight in which there is no
referee. Each attorney knows the rules, but he is aware too that
an occasional head butt or a thumb in the eye will not cost him
points in the final reckoning.

My deposition of McAlary was anything but polite. In his
late thirties and with the build and swagger of a beefed-up light
heavyweight, McAlary proved to be every bit the part of his
tough-guy image. He responded to even the most perfunctory
questions with an air of defiance, his aggressive tone more befit-
ting a celebrity author being interviewed by a TV reporter than
a defendant in a high-stakes legal proceeding. It was a style he
had shaped carefully during his years in the newspaper business: the hard-nosed street reporter who knew where all the
bones were buried and did not hesitate to get some dirt beneath
his fingernails while digging them up.

McAlary, it might be said, was a man who was living his
dream. Right from the start, he sensed that he was cut to fit the
mold of tabloid journalist, and he set his sights on the top and
got there quickly. In 1988, after just three years as a general-
assignment reporter at *New York Newsday,* he signed on as a

columnist with the *News,* replacing Jimmy Breslin, who had taken his Pulitzer Prize–winning credentials to *Newsday.* It was, in its way, an informal swap, and McAlary, often regarded as a self-styled pretender to the Breslin throne, could not have been more pleased. However, his tenure with the *News* was a brief one. When the paper was struck in 1990, McAlary skipped to its chief competitor, the *New York Post.* It was just the first in a succession of seesaw moves between the two tabloids that earned him a reputation as a hired gun, a newsman mercenary for sale to the highest bidder.

In February 1993 he was back at the *News,* working for Mort Zuckerman, the publisher he had described in a *Post* column as "a power-mad Stalin wannabe" with "no decency," a "cheap dictator who shot his way to power." Seven months later, apparently unable to flourish under the thumb of a "dictator," he broke his contract with the *News* and jumped back to the *Post,* protesting that his column had not been displayed as prominently as he had hoped. This time Zuckerman sued and obtained a preliminary injunction preventing McAlary from writing for the *Post.* McAlary answered by filing an affidavit in state supreme court, which was then published in the *Post* as a quasi column. The affidavit, which became part of the public record, revealed more than a little about McAlary's creed regarding newspaper work.

"There is a great and glorious history of thievery in this business," he wrote. "That's the game we are in. . . . Yesterday's thief wants to be seen as today's victim. But it seems to me . . . the whole newspaper business is about 'stealing.' We 'steal' ideas. We 'steal' sources. We 'steal' advertisers. We 'steal' talent."

As if to prove his point, just five months later, after a period of convalescence from a near-fatal auto accident, McAlary was back at the *News* for his third tour of duty. In March 1994 it was the *Post*'s turn to sue for breach of contract. Before long,

McAlary was testifying under oath, providing evidence that to
him the newspaper business was about lying as well as stealing.
McAlary readily acknowledged that not everything he said in
his affidavit was true, that he recounted incidents and invented
conversations that never took place. He further testified that his
columns were not intended to be "read factually, word for
word." It was part of his technique, he explained, to make up
anecdotes and fabricate quotes to "illustrate" a story.

Now, as I questioned him in the Jane Doe case, he elabo-
rated on life in the fast lane among high-profile columnists. "It's
not nice to get beat," he said, referring to a newsman's distaste
for finding that a rival has beaten him to a story. "The general
rule in journalism: Knock down the other guy's story. If he beats
you on a case or story, you got to say he is full of shit."

"You call the other guy a liar?" I asked.

"The word *liar* is not right," he explained. "Usually what
you say, 'He is full of shit' or 'That can't be true' . . . 'It's bullshit.' "

"Have you said that about other journalists who have beat
you?" I asked.

"Of course," he said.

I couldn't shake the feeling that McAlary was not making a
reluctant admission, but was boasting, proud to declare his devotion to a doctrine he held to be universal but which was alien
to most others who practiced his trade. I was surprised that his
attorney, Kenneth Caruso, allowed his client to enter into evidence testimony that portrayed him as a confirmed liar in a case
in which his truthfulness was the heart of the matter, for there
were not many questions to which he permitted the witness to
respond. On no fewer than 132 occasions Caruso held up his
hand and intoned, "I direct the witness not to answer the question," then, eyebrows raised and index finger pointed high for
emphasis, adding, "in that form." It was clear to me that
McAlary would be a disastrous witness for his own cause. A

jury weighing his credibility against Jane Doe's would not hesitate to come down on the side of the plaintiff.

It also became clear during the questioning that the defense had decided to rely on a two-pronged strategy. In legal circles it is called substantial truth and opinion. First, McAlary would contend that his columns were based on factual, off-the-record information given to him by police sources whose identity could be kept confidential under New York's shield-law privilege. Second, he would maintain that the conclusions he drew from those "factual statements" were opinion and therefore merited First Amendment protection. We challenged the opinion defense first.

My associate, Gerald Singleton, led McAlary through his initial hoax column sentence by sentence, asking whether each statement was fact or opinion. It was a distinction with which McAlary was not quite comfortable. He described his assertions that "last night everyone who heard the woman's story about the alleged rape was calling it a hoax" and that the woman "probably will wind up being arrested" as opinion, adding that "it is difficult to fit one with a shoehorn into fact shoe or opinion shoe." He also characterized as opinion a sentence that read, "In fact, they believe they are being lied to." Singleton was incredulous.

" 'In fact' means opinion?" he asked. "Is that your testimony?"

"That's his testimony," Caruso interjected. "Read the next question."

Singleton was not quite ready to move on. "When you say 'in fact,' do you normally use those words to designate what is to come is opinion?"

"There is no ordinary or normal use," McAlary replied.

The deposition of John Miller, at the time the deputy police commissioner in charge of public information, proved to be more informative. Miller was new to the post, having previously worked as a news reporter for WNBC-TV, a position to which he has since returned. He and McAlary had known each other for several years. As colleagues in the news business, they shared a late-night preference for Elaine's, a trendy watering hole on Manhattan's Upper East Side that attracted showbiz types, jet-setters and their followers, and a who's who from the world of glitter and glitz whose fame derived chiefly from their being well known. Though not especially close, they were sometime buddies, and it was not unreasonable for McAlary to suppose that Miller might prove helpful when he was tracking a story.

Miller testified that on the day after the rape, he received several phone calls from McAlary. Earlier in the day, at an off-the-record briefing, Miller had told reporters that detectives on the case had expressed some doubts about Jane Doe's account and that they should approach the story cautiously while police pursued the investigation. McAlary, who had not attended the briefing, called and asked Miller to fill him in. Miller gave him the same information he had given the other reporters, with the same caveat that police doubts about the case were off the record. An hour or two later, McAlary called again, asking more detailed questions and inquiring who else in the press was onto the story. "By this time," Miller said, "McAlary had a great deal more information, including some information that I didn't have." It also occurred to him that, despite his warning, McAlary intended to write about police concerns with the accuracy of the story.

The following day, after McAlary's first column appeared, Police Commissioner Bratton called a press conference and said that a lab report showed physical evidence of rape, and he offered an apology to Jane Doe. The principal evidence—a lab report indicating the presence of semen on the woman's body and running shorts—led to some confusion. The report did not actually say that semen had been found; it reported the presence of another substance, a P-30 antigen that is found in semen. Two days later, on May 1, the police issued a memo explaining that although P-30 is characteristic of semen, "it is found in other secretions produced both by males and females." McAlary read that report, but a subsequent police memo, correcting the first, escaped his notice. It said that "the protein known as P-30 antigen is exclusively produced in the prostate gland and only secreted by MALES." McAlary's third column, claiming that no semen had been found, appeared three days later.

Although Miller corroborated a small part of McAlary's story, he was directly at odds with most of its implications. McAlary had testified that he had spoken with about twelve people before writing his first column. But as he was questioned regarding his sources, it emerged that the dozen included his wife and several newspaper colleagues; only two of them were police sources. One, obviously, was Miller. The other was unnamed and perhaps, the suspicion grew, nonexistent. Miller was wary of being trapped into the position of standing alone as the source of McAlary's information. Asked to assess the validity of McAlary's columns, he replied: "Based on what I knew of the investigation, I could support informationally eight tenths of what he said, but not his conclusion that it was definitely a hoax or that she was going to be arrested."

A few weeks later Miller offered a more candid assessment of the columns in a telephone interview with *Newsday* reporter Gabriel Rotello. Unaware that their conversation was being tape-recorded, Miller commented in some detail on McAlary's reporting techniques and the manner in which he drew his conclusions:

". . . I mean, the next stop must be censorship, which in Mike's case might be a positive thing. I mean, what the hell do you do with him? He called me after the first column, you know, kind of saying, can you lock this thing down, can you bail me out, can you this, can you that? I'm like, Mike, what the fuck is the matter with you? First of all, if everything in that article were true, how the hell can you lead to the conclusion it was a hoax? I mean, who knows what happened there? Do you need to have semen or sperm to prove a sexual attack? No. Could he have stuck a kell light up her ass? I mean, he could have done that too. Is it possible that he could have not ejaculated? Yes. All of these things are possible. So where do you jump to this conclusion that a) it's a hoax or b) more outrageously, that she's about to be *arrested?* Excuse me: They didn't arrest *Tawana Brawley.* You think they're gonna lock up some woman in Prospect Park? I don't think so. I mean, I think he's made some giant leaps here. I think he's brought himself way out onto the end of a limb, and I think there's been, you know, a fairly regular attempt . . . to drag the police department out on that limb with him, and we ain't going."

The conversation had taken place on May 14, 1995, but I didn't learn of its content until early the following year when Rotello decided to make the tape available to me. It would be introduced into evidence in March when we were given the opportunity to depose McAlary again, specifically regarding his use of Miller as a source.

In the meantime, I was having troubles of my own. The case had been receiving fairly wide coverage, and I was beginning to hear murmurs of discontent from other First Amendment attorneys who were critical of my representing a plaintiff in a libel suit against a member of the press. They were concerned that a favorable decision might have the effect of punching holes in the shield that protects a reporter's privilege, making it more difficult to prevail in future libel actions. I had no such concerns. I had defended the shield law in thirty states and would continue to defend it. But the shield law was designed to protect a reporter's sources; it was not a license to play fast and loose with the truth while taking refuge behind a cloak of anonymous, perhaps nonexistent spokesmen.

The issue finally came to the attention of the Libel Defense Resource Center, and it was then that the trouble started. The LDRC, as it is known in the trade, consists of nearly two hundred law firms that represent defendants in libel cases. It is sponsored in large part by the First Amendment bar and the insurance companies that pick up the tab for the defense in many costly libel suits. It was the involvement of the insurance companies that was the sticking point. They generally withheld financial support when attorneys were not on the LDRC's approved list, and since few libel defendants had the means to pay for their own defense, loss of "accreditation" could effectively put a First Amendment attorney out of business.

I was not unaware of the problem when I took Jane Doe's case. But I felt the circumstances were extraordinary, and I had the conceit to believe that my handling of the case would be treated as an exception. My commitment to First Amendment issues was clearly beyond question. Few other attorneys in the field had, over the past three decades, been more outspoken in their defense. Few had put themselves at greater risk in the interest of those whom the system seemed to have abandoned. I had thought that my record would be taken into account. I was wrong. I received a call from a representative of the LDRC informing me that they had received a number of complaints and that if I continued to represent a plaintiff, my status in the organization would be in jeopardy.

I cannot deny having wavered a bit. Membership in the LDRC was by firm rather than individual, and so I was obliged to consider the effect my decision would have on dozens of other attorneys whose future might be compromised. I explained my situation to Jane Doe and told her I might not be able to continue with the case. She said she understood. She was aware, of course, that I was representing her without the expectation of a fee.

"Last spring, days after I was raped," she said, "when people were calling me a liar, you believed me. I was defenseless, helpless, and I felt that the world was closing in on me. You filed a lawsuit where we publicly said that this man was lying about me. You saved my life. Anything you want to do now I will go along with. I can't tell you how important you were to me then."

I had been practicing law for three decades, and I knew that the choice I made now would be in some way definitive; it would color the way I would think of myself in all the years ahead. The question I had to answer was the disquieting one often prompted by the grudging awareness that one's past is now longer than his future: Am I, in the essentials, the same man I chose to be all those years ago when the stakes, at every turn, were calculated on the moral high ground, when the prospect of loss seemed only to heighten the fervor of the chase? I told Jane Doe that yes, we would continue.

The task, however, was soon made more difficult. In response to a motion by the defense, state supreme court judge Charles E. Ramos ruled that Jane Doe was a public figure even though she had never been named in the press. The judge's decision meant that we would be obliged to meet a higher standard of proof. As a public figure, Jane Doe would have to prove that McAlary acted with actual malice or in reckless disregard of the truth; a private citizen would need to establish only negligence. In support of his decision, the judge reasoned that the woman had transformed herself into a public figure through her political activity with gay and lesbian organizations.

"It is uncontested," he wrote, "that the plaintiff has engaged in social activism, projecting herself into the public debate on issues she cares about. In essence, she has chosen, in exercising her right, beyond the level of private discourse, to cross over from being a private to a public figure."

The judge's ruling turned its back on fifty years of First Amendment law. Not only had Jane Doe's identity been withheld by the press, as was common practice in rape cases, it was safe to say that had it been published, it would have been recognized only by those who already knew her. Applied literally, the decision would have conferred "public figure" status on an otherwise anonymous array of social activists who at one time or another had addressed a public gathering.

Still, the judge's rulings that day were not entirely one-sided. Addressing another central issue in the case, Judge Ramos decreed that McAlary could shield his confidential sources only if he did not intend to use them at trial. Otherwise, the judge said, he must reveal the names of his sources and what they told him, and he must do so at least ten days before the trial begins. He should not, in the judge's words, "be permitted to shield this information while using it as a sword."

In effect, the ruling stripped the shield law from McAlary's arsenal of defense. Now he was confronted with a Hobson's choice: He must either name the sources who he said provided him with confidential information or shoulder the burden of his accusations with no outside support. He would have to choose between the shield and the sword.

The choice would soon be moot, however, for it was becoming evident that McAlary had only one source. John Miller was the fulcrum on which McAlary would have to build his case, and we had in our possession a taped conversation that indicated how insubstantial a support he would be. We wanted to depose McAlary again, to question him regarding his conversations with Miller and measure his testimony against Miller's version of the story. We made our request in Judge Ramos's courtroom during a heated, five-hour hearing on a defense motion asking that the case be dismissed on summary judgment. Judge Ramos reserved decision on the motion to dismiss but, over the protests of the defense, ordered McAlary to sit for another session of depositions and answer questions about what Miller had told him.

McAlary, of course, was unaware of the remarks Miller had made in the *Newsday* interview until we introduced them at the deposition. In any event, he had little choice but to try to pin the story on Miller. His second police source indeed proved to be nonexistent. The "big detective boss" he alluded to earlier but whose identity he kept confidential was revealed to be Joseph Borelli, the chief of detectives. But McAlary now conceded he had never spoken directly to Borelli. Borelli's contribution, he said, had been funneled through Miller, whom McAlary repeatedly described as a "catch basin" for all police-department information. Finally, McAlary was moved to state flatly that "John Miller gave me the story."

There was no other direction in which he might turn, but his naming of Miller put him in the uncomfortable position of trying to reconcile his version of events with Miller's, and they made a poor fit. Their testimony clashed often, and McAlary's notes on their conversations proved to be as ephemeral as his other sources; he was able to produce only two of the twelve to twenty-four pages of notes he said he had taken; he said he had lost the rest.

In an attempt to square their contradictory accounts, McAlary claimed that the police were telling the media and the public one story—that evidence confirmed the rape and a vigorous investigation was proceeding—while feeding McAlary, and only McAlary, an entirely different story—that a hoax had been perpetrated and no investigation was being pursued. "Miller told me," he testified, "that the case would remain open for all of time, but they would never pursue it to find a guy, a rapist, or pursue it to see if she lied. Short of a confession by your client [Jane Doe], there would be no arrest in this case, and even then they wouldn't arrest her."

Miller denied saying anything to that effect. "Precisely the opposite" was true, he said. "The police department was to conduct a thorough investigation. . . . I told him [McAlary] that

our public position was that a crime was being investigated vigorously and that if it was reported as a rape, we were accepting
it as a rape."

While McAlary conceded that Miller had never used the
word *hoax* in their conversations, he said Miller agreed with the
term when McAlary suggested it. Miller himself had used words
like *impossible, fabrication,* and *bullshit,* the witness said, to describe investigators' views of the woman's story.

Again, Miller's testimony contradicted McAlary's. "I told
him," Miller recalled, "that we could not support, in any way,
on the record, off the record, or through any caveat, you know,
in terms of dealing with the media, his assertion that there was a
possibility that [the woman] would be arrested or charged or
for that matter that we were certain that it was a hoax."

It was now clear that if McAlary was telling the truth, then
Miller had committed perjury at his deposition. In effect,
McAlary was saying that Miller lied, the police department lied,
and Jane Doe lied; that Bratton lied publicly, that the other police officials lied, and that the only person who was telling the
truth was McAlary.

Four months after the deposition was taken, in July 1996,
we documented our case in a reply memorandum opposing the
defendant's motion for summary judgment and then dug in to
await the court's decision. The LDRC, for its part, moved with
greater dispatch than the judge. With little fanfare and no attempt made to hear my side of the issue, I was notified by letter
that my firm had been suspended from membership. It would
remain suspended, I was informed, "until it has ceased representing any plaintiffs in a libel action against a media defendant
or journalist."

The committee's action came as something of a surprise, but
it was not entirely without warning. A week earlier I had received a call from a lawyer who told me a vote would be taken
the following week. Ironically, this same lawyer had considered

filing a libel suit against McAlary just about a year before the Jane Doe case commenced. His wife was a public official, and he felt that McAlary, in one of his columns, had defamed her and cost her an important government job. He and his wife ultimately concluded that such a suit would cost more in time and money than it was worth, but when he heard I was suing McAlary he called to congratulate me and said he would help in any way he could. I was encouraged, therefore, when he told me he was a member of the committee that would be voting on my suspension. "How will you vote?" I asked him. "Well," he said, "the bylaws are clear on the matter. You're violating them by representing a plaintiff. I'll have to vote to uphold the bylaws."

I was utterly astonished. It seemed that the First Amendment Club, as the LDRC was sometimes called, was perhaps more than a club. Although most of its members were fine, competent lawyers, it appeared there was an ideological nucleus that felt compelled to demonstrate to itself the purity and sanctity of its cause. Of course every member of the committee I spoke with, each of them a competitor of mine, was quick to describe the ambivalence with which they cast their votes. They were, after all, just performing their duty; they hoped I would reconsider and withdraw from the case. They assured me that the suspension would have little effect on my practice. But their expressions of sympathy were not convincing, and they were certainly wrong in their forecasts.

Word of the suspension spread quickly through the publishing industry. The first call came from a major media client who said he was sorry but under the circumstances he could no longer employ my firm. He had learned of the committee's action at a meeting of the lawyers group of the Association of American Publishers. The announcement had been made by an LDRC member who had voted against me. Similar calls followed. Other clients did not mention the suspension but simply dispensed with my services.

Soon the mood within my firm began to show signs of strain. Some of my partners were clearly uncomfortable with my decision. A number of the younger attorneys expressed their concerns and asked me to reconsider. They were at a different stage of life than I was; they had large mortgages and college tuitions to pay. Now, suddenly, the shape of their future seemed uncertain. I could not help but be sensitive to the prospect of economic hardship that my action engendered, but at the same time I knew I could not withdraw from the case. I met with my partners and offered to resign from the firm. After some discussion, at which a variety of views were expressed, the consensus was that we should stay the course. I explained my position, as best I could, to some of the younger lawyers. They had, presumably, derived some benefit from working with me, and now they would have to pay a part of the price or, if they chose, go elsewhere.

Theirs was a situation with which I could sympathize, drawing on a bitter experience of my own. Nearly twenty years earlier, when I was roughly at their stage of life, I had found my own career to be in even narrower straits: I was threatened with disbarment by the New York City Bar Association. The circumstances, however, were not identical, for in that instance I had placed myself in jeopardy without anyone else's help.

In the summer of 1977, with my law firm still in its first year, I accepted the invitation of the International Commission of Jurists, the International League for Human Rights, and the authors' organization PEN to attend and report on two potentially explosive treason trials in South Africa. Breyten Breytenbach, the white Afrikaner poet, and twelve members of the banned African National Congress (ANC) were facing death sentences on a variety of charges, most notably treason, for attempting to overthrow the South African government. I attended both trials and returned to the United States two weeks later to write my report. Copies were furnished to the organizations that had sent me, then forwarded to Kurt Waldheim, secretary-general of the United Nations, after which they were released to the press.

In the report, which received wide press coverage both in the United States and South Africa, I stated that the ANC and Breytenbach trials were politically manipulated and concluded that they were "elegant façades covering one of the most vicious political states in the world. The judges," I wrote, "do not mete out the justice their procedures permit. . . . In part, because of these judges and because of the legal system, future violence, more terrible than before, is inevitable."

The report was front-page news in South Africa, where it, and I, were roundly attacked. The South African government labeled it "ludicrous, unprofessional claptrap" and persuaded *The New York Times* to carry a rebuttal. The attacks continued unabated for several months, and I began to sense trouble on the way. It came on October 27, when a complaint was filed against me with the Committee on Grievances of the New York City Bar Association. The South African government had asked that "Martin Garbus be disbarred because he does not maintain the ethical standards of a lawyer admitted to the Bar of New York." The grievance committee makes policy regarding lawyers who are alleged to be dishonest, and it contended that it was just as reprehensible to lie about South African judges as to cheat widows and children over trust-fund monies.

The comparison was odious, and the charges were in every sense outrageous. Other lawyers had written books and articles criticizing foreign courts, but I had never heard of similar proceedings being brought against any of them. Nonetheless, the complaint had been filed, and I was obliged to mount a defense. I had represented other lawyers facing disbarment, and I knew the procedure would be long, painful, and expensive. I knew too that I needed a top attorney. After several prominent First Amendment lawyers turned me down, I phoned Leonard Boudin. He agreed to represent me free of charge.

We prepared a brief saying that, as lawyers, we "were deeply concerned both with the independence of the legal profession and freedom of speech" and that we believed the disbarment proceeding was not constitutionally permissible. We told the Bar Association that if the charges were not dismissed, we would file a lawsuit against it in federal court in Manhattan. Our brief was filed in December, and for months we received no word. Finally, in April 1978, Boudin was told that the Bar Association would not pursue the case if we agreed not to make the matter public. He was cautioned, however, not to tell me "because we still haven't decided what to do."

As a consequence, I continued to practice law beneath the shadow of a pending disbarment proceeding. Almost two years passed before I heard from the Bar Association. Then, on February 7, 1981, I received an envelope marked "Personal and Confidential." It was from the Bar Association, and it contained a copy of a letter addressed to Charles Friedman, the South African lawyer who had filed the original complaint against me. Dated January 27, 1981, it read:

"This is to advise you that following an investigation of your complaint against the above named attorney, the matter was submitted to the [Grievance] Committee for disposition.

"The Committee has determined that there is no basis for taking action and therefore the matter has been closed."

My initial feeling of relief soon turned to anger. Why had it taken three and a half years to make this determination? When had the committee met, and what information did they have before them?

I called the grievance committee but was told I could not look at my file or the minutes of the committee's deliberations. The documents, I was told, were to be forever confidential.

While no such shroud of secrecy covered the LDRC's proceedings against me, the incident was hardly front-page news. It was an industry story, covered by publications like the *New*

York Law Journal and *Media & the Law,* but a month or two after the suspension I received a call from Susie Linfield of *The New Yorker,* who wanted to interview me for the magazine's "Talk of the Town" section. She planned to speak with other interested parties as well. The article, which appeared on March 11 under the title "Exile on Centre Street," contained remarks both of criticism and support. It was interesting to note that the critical comments came from other First Amendment attorneys, while members of the press were unanimous in their support.

Robert Sack, a well-known libel-defense lawyer whose clients include *The Wall Street Journal,* likened First Amendment practice to a religion, saying that some clients might think "switching sides is close to apostasy." Floyd Abrams, one of the country's best-known First Amendment attorneys, was even more outspoken. He was quoted in the article as comparing my representation of a plaintiff to "people who leave their role as prosecutor and rather quickly become counsel for drug defendants." He later clarified his observation in a letter to the editor, noting that he meant it would be "a betrayal for me to represent a plaintiff—for *me,* but perhaps not for Garbus."

The negative reaction of some high-profile First Amendment attorneys was not altogether surprising. With few exceptions, lawyers who do that kind of work now are strikingly different from those who populated the field when I started practice. Then they were chiefly lawyers committed to championing unpopular causes, representing clients who bucked the tide and had little muscle of their own. With relatively small practices and clients whose bankrolls rarely equaled the resources of the interests they opposed, they worked for modest fees and settled for lifestyles far removed from the centers of political or social power. Today, the pivot of First Amendment practice has shifted to the large corporate law firms that represent media giants, their engines driven by attorneys who are all but indistinguishable from their corporate counterparts. Free-speech defense now pays very well indeed.

It was from the press, whose freedom of expression I was said to have placed in peril, that I received my staunchest support. Two writers from *The New York Times,* Anthony Lewis, who was quoted in the *New Yorker* piece, and Herb Mitgang, who was not, both backed my position. Lewis described McAlary's use of "unnamed sources" as a "blot on our profession." Mitgang, in a personal note, wrote, "I'm proud of what you're doing. . . . McAlary cheapens a once-respected profession. . . . You're on the right side of this case; to be on the other side is to be a hypocrite."

Critic, columnist, and author Nat Hentoff, ever quick into the breach on such issues, told Linfield, "It would ordinarily be extraordinary for Garbus to take a case against a reporter. But to pillory a woman with anonymous sources—it was so disgusting that I'm with Garbus all the way." Hentoff also wrote an op-ed piece for *The Washington Post,* which identified him quite properly as "a nationally renowned authority on the First Amendment and Bill of Rights." In his article, Hentoff quoted James Goodale, another First Amendment attorney, who said, "I don't think he should have done it, but suspending him is silly. What about the LDRC's respect for the right to speak out on such central issues as this case presents?" Hentoff then concluded: "But Garbus would not have been punished if he had just spoken out. He did something much worse. He actually followed his conscience to help someone he believed had been terribly wronged by a columnist and his newspaper.

"Let this be a lesson to law school students. An act of conscience may tarnish your professional status."

On February 6, 1997, nearly four years after I took the case and three since my firm was suspended, the court finally rendered its judgment. Judge Ramos granted the defense's motion for summary judgment. He ruled that McAlary's columns accurately reported statements from a high-ranking police source, and while the statements were wrong, McAlary was not at fault, since he reported them correctly. In his decision, Judge Ramos wrote that Jane Doe had not provided any evidence "that the defendant's reporting and commenting on the events surrounding the assault on her were grossly inaccurate or unreasonable."

The judge based his decision on two distinctly different aspects of libel law. In the first, he interpreted previous legal rulings to mean that the press cannot be sued for fair and accurate reports of official information, including statements by government representatives. That was straightforward enough; it was, in fact, an argument I had made in the Matthiessen case. The second part of the ruling, however, played havoc with thirty years of legal precedents in the field. Judge Ramos stated flatly that the United States Supreme Court had improperly eroded the Constitution's free-speech protections in a series of decisions dating back to *New York Times* v. *Sullivan* in 1964. It was a remarkable bit of judicial commentary. Never before had I seen a state court judge base a decision on the notion that the rulings of the Supreme Court have been in error for more than three decades. I discussed the issue with my client, and we decided to file an appeal.

Despite the adverse ruling, Jane Doe felt vindicated by the court's determination that she was telling the truth when she said she was raped; she was found not to be a hoaxer. My own position, however, did not improve at all. The LDRC chose to leave my suspension in force while the appeal was pending.

Six months later, however, Jane Doe came to me and said she wanted the case ended. She had had enough. While I would have preferred to proceed with the appeal, I certainly sympathized with her desire for closure. She had been through a lot and now wished to move on with her life and put McAlary and the *Daily News* behind her. We dropped the case. My firm is now, once again, a member of the LDRC.

PART VII

Reinventing the
First Amendment

Chapter 15

Now, ten years later, the city was far different from the one I remembered. It was breathtakingly beautiful even then, but in the late fall of 1989, Prague had taken on a new aspect, its Old World charm embellished by the open face of deliverance. An incipient student revolution, a bloodless coup of sorts, had begun to pry Czechoslovakia loose from the grip of communism, and its effects could be seen and felt in every quarter of the old city. A sense of liberation seemed to brighten the quaint, cobblestoned streets and cleanse the layers of grime from the façades of buildings that had stood in place for five centuries. Prague was, after all, the only European capital that had been left untouched by World War II, spared the destruction of other cities as it fell to the Nazis by annexation rather than conquest.

I had been touched by the fragile beauty of the city during my first visit, in 1979, but my mood at the time was dampened by the nature of my mission. I was there in a fruitless attempt to lighten the prison sentence of the man who, a decade later, would become Czechoslovakia's first elected president in more than half a century. Vaclav Havel, internationally acclaimed playwright, poet, and political dissident, had been convicted of subversion and was to be sentenced on November 13, 1979. I was part of a legal team assembled by Amnesty International to submit a brief in his behalf. We appeared with him in an old courtroom, where we spoke for the first time, but it was to no avail. Havel was sentenced to four and a half years at hard labor. It was not the first time he had been convicted of subversion. In 1977 a fourteen-month sentence had been suspended. This time, despite all protests and legal intervention, he was going to jail.

While the outcome came as no surprise, I left Czechoslovakia with a feeling of utter despair. One of the country's foremost writers, an heir to the legacy of Franz Kafka, was on his way to prison for having exercised his gift of expression. And Czechoslovakia, the only Eastern European country born to democracy, had become the very image of totalitarian repression. It was no small irony, then, that when I returned ten years later, almost to the day, it was to a nation that was trembling on the very edge of a rebirth of freedom. The Communist regime was rushing toward oblivion with little more than a whimper; Vaclav Havel was the popular choice for president of what would become a new democracy, and I would soon be discussing with him the need for a Czech constitution with a free-speech equivalent of our own First Amendment.

I was drawn back to Czechoslovakia for reasons I could not easily define. Its brief history struck chords that seemed to resonate from somewhere deep inside me: a nation of bright promise that had fallen too soon; a literary tradition that had endured the stifling oppression of successive tyrannies; a land that seemed determined to preserve the best of its past toward that day when it might finally resurrect its claim on the future.

Czechoslovakia was, by all measure, a young nation, barely grown beyond adolescence, whose years had been marked by trauma. The independent Czech Republic, as it was known, had been carved out of the Austro-Hungarian Empire shortly after World War I, a product of Woodrow Wilson's doctrine that a strong democratic state in the middle of Europe would serve as a bulwark against Germany's instincts for expansion. Its first president, Tomáš Masaryk, was a disciple of Wilson's, and the country's first constitution, drafted in the United States, was a model of parliamentary democracy and human rights. But its independence lasted just two decades. It was ceded to Germany in 1938 as part of the Munich Accords and occupied by the Soviets immediately after World War II. A new, high-sounding constitution was drafted but totally ignored, and Czechoslovakia soon became one of the most repressed states in Eastern Europe.

But the magnetic pull that drew me back to Czechoslovakia, to Prague in particular, was perhaps more personal than conjecture would allow. For I began my second visit exactly as I had begun and ended my first, with a trip to the Old Jewish Cemetery in the center of the town. It was an astonishing sight, old and cramped, whose power to move me grew with each succeeding visit. More than twelve thousand graves in a dozen layers are wedged into a tiny space, the headstones angling through the ground, leaning against and jostling one another. The oldest tombstone dates to 1439, the most recent 1789. But although no one has been buried there in more than two hundred years, it summons visions of the more recent past: Jews herded and crammed into ghettos, then into freight cars, then pushed and crowded and finally stacked as corpses in the concentration camps. Even today, scraps of paper bearing prayers and requests are found stuffed in the cracks of tombstones, along with valuables buried in the sliding soil, hidden there by Czech Jews before they were transported to the death camps. When I left the cemetery, I went to the Old-New Synagogue, an early Gothic structure built in 1270, and then to the Pinkas Synagogue, whose interior walls are inscribed with the names of 77,000 Jewish men, women, and children who were liquidated by the Nazis.

I carried these images with me as I ventured into the streets of Prague, cold and gray with the promise of winter but alive now with the sounds of protest. There was the full sense that something momentous was about to occur and that it would happen soon, but there was no way to know whether it would be the rattle of guns signaling a bloody massacre or the trumpet blast of voices sounding the call of freedom on the chill November wind.

The story of what was taking place in Prague was written on its walls, hanging from the windows and balconies along the city's streets, plastered on the sides of buses and pasted on automobile bumpers. Words were taken very seriously in Czechoslovakia. Under the Communist regime, typewriters were invested with the power of guns; they had to be registered. Possession of an unregistered typewriter or the use of an unauthorized printing machine were treated as criminal acts. So the word from the underground was sent out by any means available. Students typed their messages on home computers or school typewriters; hand-painted posters carried news of meetings and rallies; and the city seemed papered with a photo of a gagged Samuel Beckett, whose plays were banned in Czechoslovakia, with a legend reading, "If Samuel Beckett had been born in Czechoslovakia, we'd still be waiting for Godot." Jan Urban, a member of the Civic Forum, the opposition group led by Havel, called it "a war on walls. In a system where the state owns and controls the mass media," he said, "this is the only way to begin a campaign against the regime."

Gradually, day by day, I saw the war move from the walls to the streets. It began with the students; then the intellectuals, the artists and writers, joined in; and finally the workers swelled their numbers, from 50,000 to 200,000, then 600,000. They poured into Wenceslas Square, in the heart of Prague, and then spilled over into the streets where they were confronted by cordons of soldiers and police, fully armed, carrying shields and wearing face masks. The students, armed with nothing but flowers, began passing them out to the soldiers, and to everyone's amazement the soldiers accepted them graciously and simply stepped aside. The armed phalanx melted away, offering not even token resistance, and the demonstrators passed through without event, and you knew then that you were a witness to history. The Velvet Revolution, as it came to be called, had succeeded; an entirely new order was on its way in Czechoslovakia.

Even as the Communist leaders were preparing to resign, the idea of Vaclav Havel becoming president of the new Czech Republic stretched the imagination. Nothing in his past suggested the possibility of a political career. He was a writer of great repute, a social activist driven by ideology with no apparent appetite for public office. He had become a hero, particularly to the young, without really trying. One might as readily have envisioned Andrei Sakharov being tapped for high office by the Russian electorate.

When I first met with him, around the middle of November, the prospect of a Havel presidency never was raised. Our first meeting had as its subject a more personal matter. I was acting as emissary for Samuel Beckett, now near death in Paris, delivering to Havel a signed manuscript copy of Beckett's play *Catastrophe,* which in its brief three pages tells us as much about totalitarianism as any other piece of writing. Beckett had dedicated the play to him in 1982 when Havel was serving his prison term, but it was not until after his release from prison that Havel read it, and he immediately responded with a play of his own entitled *The Mistake.* Havel accepted the manuscript with pleasure, and we proceeded to discuss other issues concerning the future of Czechoslovakia. I found him to be a forceful, ingratiating personality, boyish-looking despite his fifty-three years, short, stocky, and direct in his manner. He came at you straight ahead, without pretense or evasion, his words bubbling forth with no attempt to disguise his tentative command of the English language. He did not choose to be a politician, he said, and was astounded that the chain of events was moving him in that direction.

We met several times over the next six weeks, and with each visit I found him drawing closer to the inevitable. Our conversations were interrupted by the persistent ringing of the telephone, by visitors entering and leaving his office in the Civic Forum. As a writer accustomed to spending his days in relative isolation, he was clearly unprepared for the turmoil that now engulfed him. The people who surrounded him were no better equipped to deal with the situation than he was. They were writers and artists, intellectuals and students, none of whom knew their way through the dips and turns of the machinery of government. Events unwound in a cheerful, lighthearted atmosphere suggesting that, indeed, the inmates had taken over the prison. There is, nonetheless, a vast gap between the guerrilla tactics of an opposition movement and the subtle strategies needed to guide one through the snake pit of political maneuvers. Yet it was clear that Havel was preparing himself to take the plunge.

At a press conference on December 7, he declared his readiness to serve as president of a Czech Republic. Two weeks later I again sat with him in his office, while outside a throng of students chanted, "Godot has arrived" (they had not yet learned that earlier that day Samuel Beckett had died). Vaclav Havel was elected president of Czechoslovakia a week later, on December 29. The day after New Year's, as I was preparing to return home, I met with Havel for the last time. We sat around a table with janitors, train conductors, and factory heads—some of them former prisoners—who would later become ambassadors and members of his cabinet, and discussed the prospects of a Czech democracy. Havel was familiar with my background as a constitutional lawyer, and he asked me if the American experience would be a good starting point for creating a new constitution.

"The Japanese make computer chips," I told him, "Americans write constitutions."

"Do it," he said.

It was, of course, not quite so simple a matter. It had taken more than a year for the United States to draft and ratify its own constitution, and our founding fathers had the advantage of starting from scratch. Czechoslovakia was encumbered with the baggage of many centuries—deep historical divisions between Czechs and Slovaks, an entrenched bureaucracy, and the stymied sense of possibilities that comes from having lived the past fifty years under totalitarian regimes. Still, it was an opportunity I could not let pass.

When I returned home I spoke with Herman Schwartz, a professor at the American University School of Law in Washington, D.C., who had represented Havel at his criminal trial. Schwartz had solid connections in both the legal and political arenas, and he was eager to get started. He immediately drew Lloyd Cutler, former counsel to President Jimmy Carter, into the fold. Cutler, an international presence, enlisted the aid of some of the best legal scholars from Western Europe. The idea of holding a full-scale constitutional conference came from Wendy Luers, wife of William Luers, former U.S. ambassador to Czechoslovakia. Luers knew something about fund-raising and promptly enticed a pledge of $200,000 from Texas billionaire Sid Bass.

Word of the ensuing conference spread quickly, and there was no shortage of volunteers. In the end the list included eight Western European and fifteen American statesmen and constitutional scholars. Numbered among them, in addition to Schwartz, Cutler, and myself, were former Canadian prime minister Pierre Elliott Trudeau; Harvard law professor Laurence Tribe, who had assisted in the drafting of the Marshall Islands' constitution in the early eighties; A. E. Dick Howard, professor of law and public affairs at the University of Virginia School of Law; and Harvard law professor Charles Fried, former U.S. solicitor general, who was born in Czechoslovakia and had left when he was three.

The conference was held in April 1990 at Dobris Castle, an eighteenth-century landmark just outside of Prague. It was an imposing structure and well suited to the occasion. The first of Prague's rococo châteaux, and by all accounts still the grandest, it was a monument to the baroque notion that nothing succeeds like excess. The room in which the conference was held was sprawling and so lavishly appointed that the eye could not quickly absorb it. Every inch of the walls was covered with magnificent paintings, banked against the deep red hues of the room's decor and refracted through the sparkle of crystal chandeliers. The doors leading into the room were ten feet high with the handles almost at eye level because, I was told, the original owner of the castle would often ride into the salon on horseback and open the doors from his saddle. Beyond its visual splendor, Dobris Castle was an ironically appropriate site for a discussion of freedom of speech. Prior to the revolution, it had served as headquarters for the anti-free-speech Writers Union.

I began my presentation by urging that the new Czech constitution take as broad a view of permissible speech as our own First Amendment. After all, I said, just a few months earlier the Red Army's tanks and troops had been routed by a piecemeal cadre of demonstrators whose only weapons were their voices and placards. Rarely before had speech alone toppled a dictatorship. My remarks were applauded as enthusiastically by Communist party members as by the non-Communist academics, justice-ministry officials, parliamentarians, and members of Havel's staff. But it was not long before I discovered how difficult our task would be. When the audience was invited to ask questions, one of the prime Czech architects of the new constitution rose and said, "Everything you said was perfect, but of course one can't be allowed to criticize public officials." A few minutes later, after one of my American colleagues had outlined the full First Amendment protections, including those related to libel and invasion of privacy, a leading official in

Havel's new government complained, "I feel as if I'm in an automobile showroom being shown a Mercedes-Benz when all I can afford is a Skoda."

Such observations suggested the dimensions of the gulf that would have to be breached to bring their vision in line with our own. I was reminded of an analogy offered by a black social activist in the sixties when he was asked why he distrusted the good intentions of white civil rights leaders. He said, "It's as if you had a big pie on the dining room table, and every time I reached for a slice you slapped my hand. Then you offer me a piece of the pie and you wonder why I expect to get my hand slapped." It would not be easy, I understood, to replace the conditioning of five decades of repression with a legal concept that had been evolving in the United States for two hundred years.

But the process, though disheartening on occasion, was also instructive. I had been given a seat at the same table as the founding fathers of the new Czech Republic. As I listened to Communists, Socialists, and Civic Forum Democrats debate which was better, a strong central government or a loose federation of states, I reflected that just such a debate had doubtless taken place in postcolonial Philadelphia. The arguments in favor of and against a central bank hovered across a distance of more than two centuries. The division between Czechs and Slovaks roused echoes of the distrust between Yankees and Southerners.

Our own founding fathers had initially papered over these conflicts by establishing a weak central government consisting of a one-chamber legislature in which each of the thirteen states had a single vote—a model favored by some Czech ethnic minorities. But the United States had the luxury of time. When our first political system failed to function as hoped, we were able to evolve constitutionally toward a stronger central government. It was not at all certain that Czechoslovakia, torn by an ethnic separatist movement, would have that chance.

The specter of these divisions colored the perceptions of Czech officials and shaped their response to our proposals. Our hosts often chided my colleagues and me for being too tolerant of free speech and for having a court system that is too accessible to ordinary citizens claiming violations of their rights. My response was that the First Amendment not only protected the right of the speaker to say anything, but also guaranteed the audience the right to hear everything. "If you can't say something," I argued, "then you can't think something, and if a society stops you from thinking anything, it ceases to be free."

Czech officials, however, had reason to be wary. Such logic, they thought, could allow the Communists to stage massive demonstrations and attempt to topple the Havel government. Consider the irony of those who had systematically denied dissidents the right to speak freely now being granted that right and using it to unseat those from whom it derived.

There were other issues that the new republic was obliged to confront that did not plague its constitutional ancestors in Philadelphia. The United States was structuring a system from a concept that had no precedent; the new Czech democracy was emerging from half a century of darkness that had left behind a legacy of suspicion and paranoia. The most contentious question to be resolved was whether the light of free speech and freedom of the press should be turned on to illuminate the secrets of the past. The closed archives of the Communist regime were crammed with files on hundreds of thousands of citizens, ranging from employees of the secret police to unwilling collaborators, including many who gave information without knowing they were speaking to a secret agent. Few doubted that much of the information contained in those files was totally false. Disclosing their contents to the public, in accordance with Western legal concepts, would therefore have the effect of ruining thousands of innocent lives.

Aware that calls for the release of the unexpurgated archives would be chiefly an attempt to settle old scores with the Communists, Havel was concerned, even before he became president, that if such a campaign of vengeance were carried out, there would be little opportunity to proceed with the political and economic reconstruction of the country. All the same, his efforts to prevent the press from disclosing the contents of the files resulted in accusations that he was acting as censor.

Michael Zantovsky, Havel's press secretary, responded to those charges. "There are journalists trying to get hold of the list in order to publish it," he said, "and, of course, it would be a major scoop. Well, we thought about it and decided that anyone who publishes this list will go to jail. Not because most of those people weren't guilty but because some of them were victims rather than perpetrators of wrongdoing."

And so the leaders of the young democracy, acting on the principle that the innocent must be protected even at the cost of freeing the guilty, felt compelled to abridge a degree of First Amendment liberty as they began to cobble from the past a canon of freedom sturdy and flexible enough to guide them through the unknown perils of the future.

The free-speech provision that would finally emerge drew its inspiration from both the U.S. Constitution and the European Convention on Human Rights. It contained four short paragraphs, the first three of which were perfect. They read:

> Freedom of expression and the right to information are guaranteed.
>
> Everybody has the right to express freely his or her opinion by word, in writing, in the press, in pictures, or in any other form, as well as freely to seek, receive, and disseminate ideas and information irrespective of the frontiers of the State.
>
> Censorship is not permitted.

The fourth paragraph, however, sagged beneath the weight
of the past and summoned the possibility of undoing the good
intentions of the first three:

> The freedom of expression and the right to seek and dis-
> seminate information may be limited by law in the case of
> measures essential in a democratic society for protecting the
> rights and freedoms of others, the security of the State, pub-
> lic security, public health, and morality.

It was a limitation that offered the potential of disaster, for
its language was broad enough to allow a totalitarian regime to
squash free speech and yet remain within the framework of the
constitution. Even in the United States, with its long history of
constitutional protection, "the security of the State" has often
been taken as license to suppress unpopular speech. In the context of Eastern European countries, such terms can be code
words for ceding unbridled power to the state. The language in
their "first amendments," therefore, should be more protective
of freedom, not less, than our own Constitution. If exceptions
to free speech must be written into a constitution, a premise I
do not accept, those exceptions should be spelled out in the
most specific terms possible.

Of course, the language of a constitution is little more than
a guide when it comes to defining human rights. It is an unfin-
ished map that points the way to one's destination but leaves
uncharted the twists and turns of the route to be taken. Charles
Evans Hughes, prior to his appointment as Chief Justice of the
United States, said, "We are under a Constitution, but the Constitution is what the Judges say it is." And that concept, plain
enough in a nation whose most cherished precepts were forever
being reshaped in the changing light of circumstance, was particularly troubling to these new founding fathers.

The Pentagon Papers case, with which most of them were

familiar, seemed to hold a special fascination. Many of Havel's colleagues could not come to terms with a privately owned newspaper's publishing a report that the government had declared secret and harmful to the national interest. The government, no matter how oppressive or corrupt, still represented parental authority, and the citizens of the state were subjects whose primary duty it was to serve the state's interests. What they found even more perplexing was the uncertainty that surrounded the outcome of the case and the differences of opinion among the judges. How, they wondered, could a legal system that has been in place more than two hundred years leave room for doubt regarding an issue so fundamental as the rights of the state in relation to the freedom of the press? How could judges on the same bench still differ with regard to the merits of such a case? They could not comprehend, finally, that the law is a pliable instrument, that although it transcends the whims of those who apply it, it nonetheless takes its shape from the mood and manner of each man's vision. They had lived for years under a system that offered certainty in place of nuance. Now they were being asked to wander into the wilderness of a legal structure that promised the unexpected at every turning.

As I listened to the framers of Czechoslovakia's new constitution puzzle over the issues and debate their merits, I could not help but consider the prospect of the country's constitutional scholars, two hundred years from now, speculating on the "original intent" of its framers. I, for one, was hard pressed to find one, and I was certain that the conservative justices on our own Supreme Court, forever busy trying to ascribe a unified "intent" to the diverse minds that fashioned our constitution, would have found it no easier. It seemed to me that over the years no one had come closer to the truth of the matter than Justice Louis Brandeis, who in the now famous Brandeis brief wrote that the intent of the framers of the Constitution was "to draft a living document, the meaning and application of which would evolve over changing times and circumstances, and which would be interpreted by an independent judiciary fully briefed on the contemporaneous social and economic impact of its decisions."

Czechoslovakia's new founding fathers would have done well to look to the future with Brandeis's vision, but his was the kind of wisdom that did not come easily. Still, given the hazards that confronted them, they had probably done as well as could be hoped. Laws cannot outpace political, social, and economic realities. Under circumstances that were often trying and at times fractious, the Czechs had managed to craft a constitution that allowed for flexible interpretation and the evolution of key legal concepts such as freedom of speech. It did not happen quickly. More than a year passed before the constitution was finally ratified, with new adaptations and revisions being faxed back and forth across the ocean, but by the time I left Prague it was with the conviction that much had been accomplished. The Civic Forum's newspaper had run an article calling me the Thomas Paine of Prague, and the term was picked up by several publications when I returned home. But in truth I felt less of a connection to Thomas Paine than to more immediate, personal roots.

Although I had never been much devoted to the practice of religion, I now felt the unmistakable tug of my Jewish heritage. I could not help but ponder the symmetry of events that drew me back to a section of Europe from which my father had been forced to flee the rising tide of persecution. True, it was in Poland that his back had been broken and his spirit crushed, but except for the brief period between the world wars, the area that is now Czechoslovakia had its own history of anti-Semitic oppression. At around the turn of the century, a pogrom had raged through Prague. Jewish-owned shops and businesses were looted, synagogues were desecrated, and anyone suspected of being Jewish was beaten or killed. Just a few years later, in the Jewish community of Polna, a shoemaker was accused of ritual murder and the entire town was ransacked. It was a story that varied by degree or intensity but that was written each time from the same script.

Throughout my adult life I had not identified closely with my Jewishness. I took a modest pride in the heritage of Judaism but was in the main committed to trying to purge our legal system of the constraints it placed on other minorities still struggling to climb the ladder one rung at a time. However, my visits to the Jewish Cemetery, the Pinkas Synagogue, the Terezin concentration camp outside of Prague, served to kindle a flame from the past. I still looked with disdain on the more hawkish elements of the Jewish community, which viewed the struggles of Israel in the most simplistic terms, and rejected the dictum of those who said, with Ariel Sharon, "If I am not for me, then who is?" but I remained, it seemed to me, without a viable structure of my own.

More than three decades as a trial lawyer had taught me to sift the truth from available evidence and present it in a courtroom. But that was always a tentative truth, shifting ground with each new case and the needs of my client. But where was my own truth? I was beginning to suspect now that, whatever it was, it could be found only by shuffling and scraping through the shards of the past, that it was somehow inseparable from the truth of my father and his father before him, and that even when found, one would not necessarily know it. For a truth so subtle and so enduring would not have the power to transform, but it would be potent enough to sustain and nourish a vision that I could call my own and that was itself immune to time.

Epilogue

On a soft spring afternoon, more by impulse than design, I found myself headed for my old neighborhood. I left my office in midtown Manhattan and walked the thirty-odd blocks to my apartment on the Upper East Side. Then, instead of entering the building, I got into my car and began driving north, along the FDR Drive, then onto the Major Deegan Expressway and up through the Bronx. I was not conscious of my destination until I saw the sign reading BEDFORD PARK BOULEVARD. I parked my car and gazed at a landscape I should have recognized immediately but now found just vaguely familiar. It was the campus of Hunter College, as it was known in the fifties when I was a student there, since rechristened Lehman College, and it had undergone a physical transformation that was no less dramatic.

What I remembered as an open, sprawling campus whose fields of green and flagstone walks seemed benignly incongruous amidst the gray concrete canyons of the Bronx had sprouted a myriad of new buildings whose architecture seemed to be competing for attention. The four quaintly engaging Gothic structures that had formed a quadrangle around a fifty-foot-high flagpole at the center of the campus now seemed lost in an ongoing frenzy of construction. Two new classroom buildings had been added, a concert hall and theater were squeezed into the mix, and on the expansive North Lawn that bordered

Bedford Park Boulevard, where I now stood, the skeleton of a massive gymnasium building was already several stories high.

I strolled onto the campus, tentatively at first, looking to stir some long-ago memories. I had not walked these paths in more than thirty years, and they seemed strange now. I felt like an alien in this place that had nurtured me in my youth. Had the Bronx campus not been opened to men in the fall of 1951, I might never have gone to college at all. Where would I be now, and what would I be doing? Would I really have spent my life in my father's candy store, which even in college I had believed to be my destiny, cramming ice cream into containers and jerking sodas from the fountain? I walked from one end of the campus to the other and then, to my consternation, had trouble finding my way out. When I finally exited, it was on the eastern end of the campus, where the elevated train rumbles above Jerome Avenue on its way south, past Yankee Stadium, and then ducks underground, into the maw of Manhattan, to Grand Central Station and points beyond.

Now I knew precisely where I was going. I walked east along Bedford Park Boulevard, then turned left onto the Grand Concourse. The Concourse, as we called it, was the Champs-Elysées of the Bronx in those years before and after World War II; from curb to curb the widest thoroughfare in all of New York City, with its two landscaped strips dividing four lanes of traffic in each direction and the elegant apartment buildings on either side now looking worn and haggard, like aging dowagers whose stately beauty had surrendered to the years. I turned right one block to Valentine Avenue, which, after nearly four decades, still looked more like home to me than any place I had ever lived. For here, along these friendly but undistinguished streets, were scattered the bits and pieces of my childhood and youth. Each step seemed to waken echoes from the past, to pry loose from the vaults of memory sounds and sights and smells that I thought had been swallowed by time but that I knew now

were never far beneath the surface. There are only two custodi-
ans of the past—time and place—and time has no memory.

If my old college campus had undergone a metamorphosis
that took it beyond recognition, the landmarks of my old neighborhood appeared much as I had left them. There on my right
was the vacant lot, still empty, where we played childhood
games like Johnny-on-a-pony and king of the hill. On the other
side of the street was Joe's Barbershop, where I had gotten my
hair cut every few weeks for the better part of twenty years. The
barber pole stood on the same cracked pavement, its red-and-
white stripes twirling upward in a magical twist of perpetual
motion. It was in this shop, waiting my turn, that I got my first
look, in magazines like *Beauty Parade* and the *Police Gazette,* of
a species of woman that would inhabit my fantasies for years to
come; long-legged women in sheer stockings and high heels;
women spilling out of swimsuits, smiling seductively right at
me, their heads cocked to the side, their long hair lightly embracing their shoulders. These pages held a wonder of riches
that I had yearned to one day make mine but that I realized
later belonged exclusively to the imagination of the young.

Joe, with the soft medleys of Italy still on his tongue, was
one of the first non-Jewish immigrants I had ever known and
the first adult, other than teachers, with whom I discussed
world politics. I recalled his trying to persuade me, when I was
about ten years old, that Mussolini was really a man of quality
and substance. "The common people like him," he told me.
"Don't believe the papers, Marty. Whatever he is doing, he is
being forced by Hitler. If Mussolini was free, he would be good
for everybody. He is not an anti-Semite."

Joe was a young man at the time, not much more than thirty,
I would guess, but he seemed old to me then, in the same way
my father always seemed old. I had always felt a certain close-
ness to Joe because, like my father, he came from another coun-

try and, also like my father, he spent all his working hours standing on his feet with no pause for rest during his day.

Now, as I peered through the window, I was more than surprised to find Joe still there, looking not much older than I remembered him, cutting the hair of a young boy who might have been me forty years earlier. Inside, it was as if the shop had been frozen in time. The big fish tank, Joe's enduring pride, was still there, the white enamel tiling sparkled, the wall-to-wall mirrors at either side bounced your image from front to back, and the shop emitted the same pungent aroma that all barbershops had back then—before the age of unisex hairstylists and female barbers—the sharp, welcoming scent of lilac vegetal shaving lotion, in the tall, thin-necked bottle, which stung the side of your face after the straight razor had been used on your sideburns. And there was Joe, now certainly in his seventies, looking as fit and dapper as ever, still crowned with a full head of hair, his mustache trimmed neatly, his hand manipulating the scissors the way a conductor wields his baton.

I took it all in in an instant, and then Joe noticed me standing there, turned his head slightly in my direction, smiled, and said simply, "Sol's son." We exchanged greetings, warmly but briefly, for Joe had customers waiting and what, after all, was there more to be said?

The building in which I had lived was just a block away, on the corner of 203rd Street and Valentine Avenue. It looked like every other building in the neighborhood—a red brick, five-story walkup with fire escapes out front and four steps at the entrance, which, to the dismay of the superintendent and the landlady, were used as launching pads for games of stoopball, played with the staple of our youth, a pink rubber Spaldeen. As I was about to pass the building I heard my name called. I looked around and then heard it again, "Martin," the voice said. It was Mrs. Gersten, the landlady, who, so far as I knew, had no first name, much as Joe seemed to have no surname. She was just Mrs. Gersten, and after all these years still landlady of the building and the occupant of Apartment 1A on the ground floor.

"You recognized me so quickly," I said to her.

"Why not? Why shouldn't I recognize you?" she said. "I see you on television, I see your name in the papers. You're a big-shot lawyer now, but I remember when you worked in your father's candy store, when I used to chase you and your friends from playing ball in front of the building. Even if I didn't want to, I would still remember you."

She brought me up to date on her daughter, who was a child when I last saw her, but who now apparently had a good job and lived in Manhattan.

"She's still single," Mrs. Gersten told me. "You should give her a call sometime."

"You know, I'm married," I said.

"I know you're married," she said. "But you can still call. What harm can it do? You might like to see her."

The candy store, my final destination, was still three blocks away, and as I began to step the distance I tried to calculate how many times through the seasons of my youth I had followed this route and in how many moods and circumstances, as I ground my way through the agonies of adolescence and the uncertainties of what might lie ahead. These three blocks, I was aware, had circumscribed my father's entire existence. He never crossed Bedford Park to the south and rarely ventured north beyond 203rd Street. He knew nothing of the larger world of Manhattan or the life that pulsed to its own beat all around him. And I remembered how I did not want it to be that way for me but felt resigned nonetheless to a compressed and solitary lifestyle from which I could see no exit. Now, having touched life in virtually every corner of the world, I could still sense that feeling of hopelessness as I walked these streets, and I understood that the past is not neutral and never really dies; it remains with you always, cruel and unforgiving, defining your sharpest perceptions and shaping the contours of your future.

I had always marked the halfway point of my trek to and from the store by glancing up at the window of Rosalie Rubin's apartment. Rosalie, the love of my life through grade school at P.S. 8, lived on the second floor, her room facing an alley, and I would look up on the way to work and again on the way home to see if her light was still on. Approaching the building, I glanced in that direction and wondered whose room it was that looked into that alley now and whether Rosalie Rubin had left behind any traces that might serve to connect the present with the past.

But as I neared my final destination, filled with thoughts of youth and images of landmarks transformed by time, I felt the pull of remembrance fade a bit. Suddenly, all that had gone before seemed to be no more than prologue to what followed, a prism through which the future gleamed as brightly as the past. I could sense my step growing lighter now, buoyed by the assurance that the challenges that lay ahead would be no less compelling than those of the decades past. The battle, long since joined, was not over but only just begun.

In the midst of such musings, I arrived at the candy store to find it still intact but not exactly as I remembered it. The wooden newspaper stand was no longer out front, and inside, the fountain with its four stools had been ripped out, giving it a more spacious, if somewhat forlorn aspect. It was now what was known in the trade as a dry store, which meant that soda was served only in bottles and the ice cream was prepackaged instead of being scooped and crammed into cardboard containers with a generous mound at the top, giving the buyer a bit more than he paid for. The store was crowded with customers when I entered, and I waited for it to clear out before introducing myself. The owner, a Korean immigrant, had bought the store from my father about ten years earlier. He looked as weary and worn as my father used to look late in the day, and I knew he still had a day's work ahead of him before closing.

When he heard my name, he smiled. "Oh, yes," he said, "you are the lawyer son of Mr. Garbus."

His wife appeared from the back of the store to extend her welcome. "We had heard," she said, "how hard the Jewish family worked here. This is a very hard store."

The couple's son, a slightly built boy of eleven or twelve, was working behind the front counter. His father called him out to introduce us.

"This man's father had the store before us," he said, "and he worked here, helping his father after school and on weekends, just as you do. Now, he is a very famous lawyer. And he once stood where you're standing now."

Acknowledgments

I owe a debt of gratitude to a large number of people who helped me in different ways. In particular, I want to thank my daughters, Cassandra and Elizabeth, whose ideas, values, and editing skills helped with the writing of this book; they always helped to keep me on a path they knew was important to me. My brother, Albert Garbus, and my sister, Robin Baker, have always been supportive of whatever I did.

I am grateful to those who fought what I think to be the good fight: judges, lawyers, my friends, and my clients (many of whom also became friends). It is often easier to fight for principles than to live by them. There are clients and friends, some mentioned in the book and others not, who did both. I specifically want to thank: "Jane Doe," Samuel Beckett, Emile Zola Berman, the Boudin family, the Cheever family, Daniel Ellsberg, Jules Feiffer, Michael Frankfurt, Allen Ginsburg, David Halberstam, Vaclav Havel, Alfred Kazin, Rita Klimova, Spike Lee, Ephraim London, Nelson Mandela, Peter Mayer, Herbert Mitgang, Gabriel Motola, Robert Redford, Barney Rosset, Andrei Sakharov, Leonard Weinglass, and Elie Weisel.

This book would not have been written without Stanley Cohen. It was his idea, his involvement and commitment, both to the book and to the values we share, that led to the beginning and finishing of this book. I cherish his friendship and talent.

Stan wishes to express his gratitude to his wife, Betty; his children, Linda and Eddie Diaz and Steve and Monique Cohen; and his grandchildren, Michael and Jessica, for their love and support throughout the course of this project.

The Random House people who had faith in the book and helped so much, Harry Evans and Luke Mitchell, also deserve mention, as does our agent, Clyde Taylor.

Index

289

ABOUT THE CO-AUTHOR

STANLEY COHEN was born and raised in the Bronx, New York, and educated in its schools and neighborhoods. He holds a BA in journalism from Hunter College and an MA in philosophy from New York University. He has worked as a reporter for an international news service and as editor and columnist for several newspapers and a national business magazine, earning numerous awards for journalistic excellence. He has taught journalism and philosophy at Hunter College and served as a member of the adjunct faculty in NYU's writing department. Mr. Cohen is the author of five previous books: *The Game They Played; The Man in the Crowd; A Magic Summer: The '69 Mets; Dodgers! The First 100 Years;* and *Willie's Game* (with Willie Mosconi). He also compiled and edited a book on the practice of engineering in the United States. Mr. Cohen resides in Tomkins Cove, New York, with his wife, Betty, to whom he dedicates this book with appreciation for her cheerful patience and support during the long, often arduous process of writing.